Slow Dancing in Fast Times

Independently published
ISBN: 9798681442417

Book layout and design by Michael Spillane

ACKNOWLEDGEMENTS

The shaping of this story was championed by two kings.

Since this was my first attempt at writing a novel, I began the project by reading Stephen King's publication: *On Writing: A Memoir of the Craft.* The book serves as both a biography and a master class. As a guidebook, it provided me with practical techniques for writing, editing, and editing again (and again). Upon finishing King's memoir, I could no longer claim ignorance about what tools to use and when to use them.

The second, and more personal influence, came through my conversations with a dear friend, Thomas H. King. As a successful First Nations writer, Tom would take a sip of espresso and dispense well-earned wisdom such as, *"Don't be kind to your darlings."* We probably talked more about cornet playing than novel writing but, in the end, I always walked away with a better understanding of what NOT to do.

When the writing was completed, the next task was to find the right individual who could help bring this project to fruition. I have known Michael Spillane for more than two decades. Michael is a true Renaissance man and brings together a number of interconnected practices: he's a composer, guitarist, writer, editor, book designer, visual artist and instructor. Since we both were involved in the music business around the same time, I knew he would not only get the time period but also spot any inaccuracies.

I deeply appreciate the proofreading efforts of Jane Lewis and Jackie Maric. Thanks for catching glitches, and missing commas.

Finally, thanks to my family who gave me the necessary space during the early months of a COVID-19 pandemic. I needed the luxury of time to complete this writing marathon.

With gratitude, Gary

Dedication

*I dedicate this publication to my fellow musicians,
manager, and road crew in*

Blues Train.

*Our wild ride together informed many
facets of this story.*

Slow Dancing in Fast Times

BY

GARY DIGGINS

PRELUDE

Several years ago, some friends and I took a leap of faith and bought a building located near downtown Guelph. We gutted the largest area, then renovated the entire building to serve as an artistic incubator (we liked that phrase). Today, the main space seats about seventy people. Almost every night since we opened, a steady offering of performances and workshops happened under the banner of "Guelph's portal for adventurous music." (We had a knack for slogans.)

My personal studio sits in a back area and is packed with instruments collected from around the world. This is where I see clients for an expressive arts practice called *Soundwork.* I combine counselling with contemplative soundscapes to support individuals going through difficulties.

After the COVID-19 pandemic hit in March of 2020, the building lived up to its name – *Silence.* Everything went quiet. In accordance with the self-isolation and physical distancing restrictions, *Silence* and my practice went from being hyperactive to comatose. After a week of adjusting, I set up a table in the empty performance area and began writing my novel, *Slow Dancing In Fast Times.*

As cliché as it may sound, I felt the story had been brewing in me for a long time. Each day, I devoted my artistic energies to the discipline of listening, crafting, re-writing, and editing. As strange and stressful as the pandemic was for my family, my vocation, and for my partners in *Silence,* the restrictions gifted me the equivalent of a writing retreat. I became curiously grateful that my usual regime and routine was disrupted for over four months. This story might not have emerged under normal conditions.

I do not wish to spoil your journey through *Slow Dancing In Fast Times* so I won't say too much about the storyline or the characters. Instead, let me draw attention to the backdrop for this novel. It is set against the social and musical experimentations of the late sixties. I am part of the baby boomer generation. Not only did I witness some of the major upheavals in the United States and Canada during that period, I was also ensconced in the counterculture scene.

From 1966 to 1970, I played in an eight-piece band that worked extensively in Detroit. My group – called Blues Train, after a John Coltrane song – shared the stage with Alice Cooper, Bob Seger, Ted Nugent, the MC5, Sly and the Family Stone, and many other artists. Being involved in the music business of that era brought me face to face with some fascinating individuals. In addition to 'far-out' hippies, I lived through tough encounters with bikers, cops, dealers, and druggies. Before I was twenty, I had faced guys armed with knives, guns, batons, and badges. Not all was peace, love, and grooviness back then. What enabled many of us to navigate the worst of the troubled waters was music. I was especially fortunate to play in a band that made experimental music together. In the end, we survived – except for my bandmates Gord, Andy, and my brother, Wayne. Casualties and tragedies happened which, decades later, informed this story.

Not unlike my own life, the central characters in this story are musicians. The circumstantial themes they wrestle with mirror some of the cultural shadows of that time: addiction, racism, homophobia, and even the infiltration of organized crime into the drug haze of the sixties. The story begins during the Summer of Love in 1967 when the counterculture was flowering with a psychedelic flare. It was a time of contrasts. For example, while hippies were dropping out and tripping out, a riot was boiling during the month of June in Tampa, Florida. Martin Chambers had been shot dead by the police after, allegedly, robbing a camera store. The unrest in the streets lasted several days.

It is my hope that, as you follow the main story, you will also feel a resonance with the backstory – the upheavals of the times and how these issues parallel our woes today. For instance, the late sixties witnessed a greater rise of the civil rights movement, a long struggle by African Americans to end legalized racial discrimination, disenfranchisement, and segregation in the United States. On the Canadian side, we saw other movements such as the decriminalization of homosexual acts between consenting adults.

The hippie mantra of "Make Love Not War" rang out in stark contrast to an explosion of violence in North America: the assassinations of John F. Kennedy, Malcolm X, Dr. Martin Luther King Jr. and Robert F. Kennedy; the US military aggressively entering the Vietnam War on March 8, 1965; the 1967 Detroit riot (better described as the Detroit Rebellion); the shootings of 13 unarmed Kent State University students by the Ohio National Guard, and more events that went undocumented.

Throughout all the turmoil, there was a definitive soundtrack to the times. I'm not referring to sugary pop songs that spewed a steady stream of disposable tunes out over Top 40 AM radios. Instead, I refer to the imaginative artists and sound engineers who were boldly summoning up revolutionary sounds, innovative recording techniques, and a poetic approach to writing lyrics. Certain types of music were medicine back then and, in different ways, some of the non-commercial music of today continues to deliver a medicinal charm as well as a call to social activism.

In this story, I highlight what happens when music is experienced as a live and communal event. While I got to witness Jimi Hendrix in concert, I also experienced fierce and wild improvisations in small clubs. In 1970, my band appeared at a Detroit venue called the Palladium. We opened for a band that was fresh from Miles Davis' recording of *Bitches Brew* – Tony Williams on drums, John McLaughlin on guitar, Larry Young on organ, and Jack Bruce (from Cream) on bass. At the time, that fusion band was channelling music from the future. You had to be there to be challenged and changed by that offering. Watching a video recording years later on a large screen with the best sound system available would only hint at what really went down. Long reign *live* music.

So, Dear Reader, thank you for purchasing *Slow Dancing In Fast Times*. Feel free to drop me a line and let me know where the story took you. Once you come to the end, I have included a Cadenza that might help you better understand the interaction between the life I lived and the story I wrote.

Blessings, Gary Diggins

CHAPTER 1

S cotty parked his Rambler outside the club. As he reached into his khaki knapsack, he flashed on a cartoon character from childhood – Felix the Cat. Felix dragged around a checkered bag. Anything he needed could be pulled out of his satchel – from an escalator to a telescope. Scotty's knapsack didn't look as magical. It was a ratty item bought from Windsor's Goodwill Thrift Store. Once upon a time, Scotty stashed a lot of psychedelic goodies in his bag of tricks. In this moment, though, what he really wanted wasn't going to magically appear – not even for Felix. Scotty had dutifully removed all drug paraphernalia. Even his joints were gone.

It was Father Jaggs who insisted that Scotty drop his rationalization about smoking pot to take the edge off. Getting buzzed was not part of any recovery strategy, especially for heroin users. Father Jaggs put it more succinctly. "You're an addict playing with a real possibility of relapsing. Miracles stopped in the Bible. On behalf of the divine, let me say this once: don't fuck up."

Scotty preferred to talk with Father Jaggs privately. When the clergyman was running a support group, he could get too churchy. The Father would come at the recovery group as if they were glued to the pews. A captured congregation. Phrases would drop like manna from heaven.

"This too shall pass."
"God will not let you be tempted beyond what you can bear."

Talking with Father Jaggs one-on-one was more direct. The minister would ream your ass out if he caught you drifting. He knew his stuff when it came to recovery. Sure, the Father was a man of the cloth. He had also been a man of the bottle. He knew the demons of addiction as intimately as the angels of redemption.

1

As Scotty fumbled around in his knapsack, he felt two pieces of paper. One was a pamphlet containing The Serenity Prayer. Father Jaggs faithfully launched his weekly support circle with this invocation. Only fragments were rolling through Scotty's memory banks now. The fog had drifted in.

"So that I may be reasonably happy in this life..."

In this moment, Scotty felt a long way from being reasonably happy. Father Jaggs had warned him that things could get rough. This phase of maintaining abstinence was on par with Job's accepting his boils, from head to toe. *"You might have difficulties making decisions. You might get overwhelmed with waves of anger and grief. You might drop into dark moods of hopelessness."*

Check. Check. Scotty ticked off each symptom.

"Look Scotty, staying clean is bloody hard. Each day you'll struggle. Each day you have to choose whether to focus on long-term wellness or immediate gratification. Some days your life will seem worse not better. You'll go through cycles of depression, agitation, and flashbacks."

More checks.

Scotty knew by heart what the second piece of paper contained. It was a Sanskrit chant passed on from his Hindu friend, Bishnu. He wasn't sure why or how the chant worked. He just knew that repeating those few lines sometimes did the trick. The troubled waters would settle enough for Scotty to get his bearings.

Sarveśām Svastir Bhavatu
Sarveśām Shāntir Bhavatu
Sarveśām Pūrnam Bhavatu
Sarveśām Mangalam Bhavatu

Scotty sang it softly. He felt a kind of droning sensation, as if his bones were humming. More than the religious intention, the resonating phenomenon caused Scotty to relax. Bishnu had written out the English translation for him.

May there be happiness in all
May there be peace in all
May there be completeness in all
May there be success in all

Feeling a tad calmer, Scotty got out of the car and reached into his jeans. "Shit." The relaxation dissipated. He came up empty. No key for the front door. His hands snaked through a jungle of hair cascading down his head.

Being the first to arrive at band rehearsal meant two things: Remember to bring a key and a flashlight. The club was pitch black until you turned on the electrical panel. You needed an industrial source of illumination to get to the switch. A lighter wouldn't cut it. He reached into his knapsack and found what his Scottish father called a torch.

Flashlight Flashback: Scotty once learned another use for a flashlight through a rough encounter. A Windsor cop pulled him over one night. Scotty was wasted. When the officer shone a beam in Scotty's face, the musician reached down and retrieved his own flashlight. He shone it back, through the driver's window, into the cop's eyes. The interrogation escalated to another level. That's when Scotty discovered another use for a flashlight... from beacon to weapon.

Hoping for a miracle, Scotty banged on the locked door. No response. The electrician who wired this cinderblock building had placed the electrical panel behind the bar area, on the right wall. All the stage lights, dance floor lights, washroom lights, and even the lights in the hallway to the second floor were controlled by a master switch. Once you flipped it on, the space transformed from a dingy dive to an illuminated club. In a second, you went from Neanderthal cave to neon club.

Coyote, who managed the space, insisted that the last person out had to shut off all electricity. *"When you leave, pull the plug on everything,"* Coyote said. *"That includes the beer fridge. If some joker breaks in, I want that motherfucker to face the toughest break and enter in Windsor's history."* The truth was, Coyote didn't like paying additional costs on a hydro bill. Fans, lights, and a running beer fridge all added up.

Exiting required thief-like skills. If successful, you slipped meticulously out the back door in total darkness and emerged onto an unlit parking lot. Option B was to pick your way through chairs, steps, and maybe a stretched extension cord to exit onto one of Windsor's busiest streets. In either case, it helped to remember that boy scout adage: Be prepared and bring a flashlight.

Scotty never participated in cubs. His preparedness in certain areas was hit and miss. As a last-ditch effort, Scotty reached into the outside pocket of his trumpet case. Maybe he left a key mixed in with a half-filled bottle of valve oil, a well-used roach clip, a mouthpiece cleaner, and a condom. To his relief, Scotty fished out a bronze key, unlocked the heavy door, and slammed it shut. Immediately, he was enveloped in darkness and stagnant air. With the ceiling fans turned off, the space smelled like a mausoleum discovered in an archeological site. The musty air matched his mood.

Some cat-like sensibility kicked in after a few moments of adjustment. Scotty turned on the flashlight, negotiated a couple of tricky steps down to the dance floor, and glided toward the bar. He hoped no one had left a Fender amp along his route. This wasn't the first time Scotty had pulled off a sleuth entrance. More than once, he had escorted a young woman through the darkness. Why draw the attention of a passing cop car who might investigate what was going on in the space at 2 a.m. Consequently, Scotty usually kept a flashlight in his knapsack.

With the aid of a yellow beam, Scotty could hold the hand of a potential lover and guide her to the upstairs lounge. Under the big couch that consumed much of the green room, he kept another bag. This one contained beeswax candles, a box of Redbird matches, and Nag Champa incense. In prior days, the bag held Zig Zag papers and weed. In some areas he was more boy scout than others. *Click.* The panel leapt from OFF to ON. The space lit up.

Coyote dubbed the facility Club Sotto Voce. He wasn't a musician but he did possess a canine ear for phrases that could stop you in your tracks. Scotty suspected that Coyote overheard the phrase *sotto voce* used in a musical context. He probably liked the sound of it. Later, he figured out what the words meant and claimed the phrase as if he had invented it.

Scotty remembered the meeting when Coyote sat the band down and presented the Sotto Voce concept. "Here's the deal," Coyote said, pacing the floor like a restless cur. "Imagine a space so underground, the only way you find out about it is through word of mouth."

"Not exactly a great business model," someone scoffed.

Not missing a beat, Coyote continued to deliver his pitch. "What happens if you open a new venue in Windsor? The first week is slow, then it starts: the dealers show up, the bikers hang out, the cops squeeze you, and the brawlers bust it up. After a year of headaches, you close down."

Scotty challenged the broad generalizations. "Not all spaces end up that way. Look at the Seminole House or the Dominion House."

Coyote shot Scotty a look and went on. "You know damn well that the DH is a university pub. It's a watering hole for students. You'll find more undergrads at the DH than in any classroom. My idea is similar – create a space that only appeals to a select tribe. We don't serve drinks. We don't serve food."

Sal laughed. "Do you serve Latinos?"

"We serve music, period! The audience comes because, once a week, we offer a serving of live music they can't find anywhere else."

Scotty was feeling cocky. "Let me guess, Polish polka music… all you can eat."

"OK smart ass, listen up. You're all musical geeks. Some of you are classical nerds. For two bucks, who can tell me what the term sotto voce means?" Sal shot up his hand like an eager student. Sal (shortened from Salvador) came to Canada from Venezuela on a music scholarship. He was a hardworking musician immersed in compositional studies and performance at the U. of W. Within months of arriving, Sal had landed steady work as a mallet player and percussionist with the Windsor Symphony as well as the Windsor Light Opera Company. Scotty never pried into Sal's exit from Venezuela, but he detected a plotline more twisted than the scholarship description.

Sal spoke up, as if he had memorized page 103 in The Royal Conservatory music theory handbook. "Sotto voce, in notated music, indicates that a singer or instrumentalist should dramatically lower their volume."

Coyote smirked. He continued pacing. "That's a partial answer. Not worth two bucks. It means 'under the breath. Something said softly.' Back in the day, if you were laying out a truth that could shock or offend, you would communicate that sotto voce."

Hoping to win a little more prize money, Sal chirped in. "When Galileo recanted his theory that the earth pivots around the sun, he muttered the phrase *eppur si muove* – and still it moves. That's a non-musical example of sotto voce."

"I'll add fifty cents to your winnings," said Coyote.

After coming up with the name and concept, it took Coyote weeks to find the right space. He wanted something innocuous, situated on a bland stretch of Tecumseh Road. East. The neighbourhood, where Sotto Voce eventually landed, supported a Chinese restaurant, a pizza joint, a shoe repair shop, a barber, and two convenience stores. From the street level, this two-story building mumbled understated. The bland box sat in a dull landscape. There was no indication that it housed anything vibrant or artistic. The club didn't display a sign. There wasn't even a symbol attached to the façade. Only a street address was stencilled onto the mailbox.

Despite the banal look, a group of phantom figures would appear at Sotto Voce every Saturday night. They slipped into the space between 8 and 9 p.m. Patrons paid a $2.00 admission fee. A little after 9 p.m. the band casually walked on stage. True to Coyote's vision, their niche music appealed to a select audience. Similar to the building, the band's sound was difficult to pigeonhole. Descriptive words such as free-form improvisation, acid rock, or psychedelic music were loosely applied. Not one of these labels stuck.

Although Sotto Voce existed on a small scale, Coyote paid the rent, organized the shows, managed the band, and kept the scene hushed – under the breath. Scotty once estimated that on a packed night, the door take could be upwards of $250, a decent earning for a place that didn't supply food or drinks. Each band member was paid $25 cash, regardless of attendance.

Scotty wondered how Coyote could float all the financial obligations. A sketchy character once told Scotty about scoring some amazing blotter acid at the club and boasted that a regular supply of chemicals or weed was always available. Scotty suspected that the club housed not just an underground scene but a subterranean level, one that didn't involve the band. Alongside of managing, Coyote was likely dealing.

The band didn't keep a close eye on Coyote. They did look out for Scotty. Each player had witnessed Scotty graduate from LSD, mescaline, opium, and into harder drugs. Heroin was the bottom. The group subsequently supported Scotty through a residential recovery program at Crossroads, a rehab facility outside of Windsor. When Scotty got out, everyone had attended a least a couple of support meetings with his counsellors.

Although Scotty was clean these days, his mind wasn't. In AA, the phrase "stinking thinking" refers to an alcoholic's reversion to old thought patterns and attitudes. Scotty's rendition of stinking thinking was tied to a belief that psychotropic plant medicines could help him gain spiritual insights. He was currently reading *The Teachings of Don Juan* by Carlos Castaneda and was fascinated with the use of mind-altering substances in shamanism. His plan was to get through the abstinence phase and withdraw from heroin. Once he was stable, Scotty was convinced that he could safely experiment with peyote and magic mushrooms to advance his quest for understanding. If Father Jaggs got a whiff of that bullshit, he would have surely clocked Scotty out cold.

Scotty and Coyote grew up in the tough east end of Windsor. It was easy to score dope or harder drugs in that environment. The Ford and Chrysler automotive plants existed within walking distance of that 'hood. Everyone had a brother, uncle, father, or neighbour employed in the car industry. The running gag in high school was that you hoped to attend the University of Chrysler upon graduating. Factory work could be mind-numbing, hence the popularity of mind-stimulating substances.

East end residences looked like they were punched out of a factory. Both during and after the Second World War, the government provided floor plans to builders. Cookie-cutter homes were constructed like assembly line cars. They housed people who worked in war-related industries. As the war wound down, more pre-fab homes emerged for returning vets and their growing families. Typically, these structures were one-and-a-half storeys with steeply pitched roofs, clapboard walls, small sash windows, and metal chimney stacks. The main floor usually had a living room, a kitchen, a bathroom, and at least one bedroom. The upstairs had two more bedrooms. A lot of drama, from traumatized servicemen, happened in these small spaces. The description "a tough neighbourhood" aptly applied.

Scotty still lived in his parents' home. Coyote, being several years older, had moved out of Windsor for a stretch. He later returned to the downtown area. Everyone you talked to seemed to know Coyote. As they said on the streets, he was *well-connected.* For all his popularity, Coyote's backstory remained vague. One unlikely telling saw him studying in Detroit, at Wayne State University on Warren Avenue. Another version (which Scotty thought was more plausible) placed Coyote working for Bernie Finkelstein in Toronto. Bernie managed The Paupers and Kensington Market. Coyote would have received a good street education from Professor Finkelstein, training as a talent scout and booking agent. Another rumour portrayed Coyote as the renegade farmer. It was said that he tended to marijuana-growing sites scattered throughout Essex County. That story seemed highly credible to Scotty.

Most individuals assumed that Coyote's nickname came from the popular cartoon figure, Wile E. Coyote. Every Saturday morning on the TV, the cunning canine would attempt to catch his nemesis, the Road Runner. Scotty never bought into that cartoon association. In his readings of shamanic cultures, Scotty knew coyote to be a totem animal. In the legend and myths of indigenous cultures, Coyote personified the paradoxical – a trickster figure. He held wisdom but practiced craftiness. The message was: don't get fooled by appearances.

Coyote possessed an entrepreneurial genius. He could make wild dreams happen on practical levels. Just how Coyote did that, and how much was legal, was really not Scotty's concern. Music was his priority. When Scotty wasn't focused on music, he was trying to follow his interpretation of sobriety.

So it was that, week by week, Coyote drew a disparate group to a nondescript space with the goal of hearing a quirky quartet. Everything about the band was odd. They didn't play songs. They definitely didn't entertain. Other than a projected light show on the wall behind them, the band didn't have what music critics called a visual stage presence. They simply walked out, started with a drone note, and dropped into a kaleidoscope of shifting sounds that went on for upwards of ninety minutes. The audience responded to their experimental jams by dancing, free-form style, or by sitting with eyes closed, tripping out.

Although Coyote didn't interfere with the band's musical direction, he shaped how they were presented. In fact, it was Coyote who gave the group its name: NADI. The band loved it. NADI derived from the Sanskrit word for river. The image embodied their wandering excursions with sound. NADI, like a river, was constantly changing yet always remained a river.

The notions of permanence and impermanence guided their improvisations. To emphasize a constant element in their music, they incorporated droning sounds. Usually the first sustained sound came from holding down one or two bass pedals on a Hammond B3 organ. In Western music, combining a root note with a second sound, five consecutive notes up, generates a perfect fifth. The anchoring sound proved perfect for hippies who were so spaced out that they needed to orient to something consistent.

NADI, if pushed to describe their music, called it modal. While they steered clear of formulaic structures, they did organize their signature sound around four main ingredients: pad, pulse, pattern, and poetics. The pad element was covered by droning sounds – a departure from chord changes used in popular music.

The pulse element was largely initiated by Sal, their main drummer and percussionist. Unlike rock drummers, Sal's kit setup looked like an explosion from an ethnomusicologist's studio. Bells from India hung next to gongs from Indonesia. His bass drum was actually a Japanese taiko drum turned on its side. As well, everyone in the band could play straightforward rhythms on instruments ranging from djembes to congas.

Pattern, the shape-shifting qualities within NADI, came from intersecting melodic lines on tuned instruments: keyboards, guitar, plus Scotty's trumpet. A Fender Rhodes electric piano was always positioned near the organ and could be played by anyone in the band during the set. Scotty played keys most of the time, but others would take over when he switched to horn. The only rule was that anyone using the Rhodes had to think like a thread in the overall tapestry. The notion of grandstanding, or endlessly soloing, wasn't part of NADI's ethic.

The poetic voice referred to anything spoken or sung. The band preferred to think of this ingredient as vocalizing, rather than singing. Scotty had sung in choirs as a kid and carried the lion's share of vocalizing. Along the way, he had developed a style that used an imitative language called vocables. The term referred to sounds the human voice could make without referencing any cultural tradition. Scotty would sound like a primitive tribe one moment and monk-like the next. It helped to be high to fully appreciate Scotty's vocables.

The band differed from other groups in the Windsor-Detroit area. NADI rarely played anywhere but Sotto Voce. Partly this was due to the complexity of hauling gear. Their equipment, in addition to a cumbersome sound and lighting system, ranged from a Hammond B3 organ with a Leslie speaker cabinet to a three-octave Musser vibraphone.

The vibraphone belonged to Sal. He was reluctant to move it anywhere. Each of the silver finished bars had been hand-tuned and their matching resonators remained in impeccable condition. Sal bought the instrument from the Windsor Symphony. He kept it covered between rehearsals and performances. Two Shure microphones were positioned on boom stands over the upper and lower registers. Whenever the band's volume increased, the sound guys could jack up the two mics, ensuring that the Musser's resonant tones wouldn't get lost.

After Scotty's arrival at rehearsal, Sal was the next to arrive. He shouted from the front entrance. "Hey amigo, you messing with my vibraphone?"

Scotty shot back. "I like you as a person, Sal, but I rarely fantasize about touching your vibraphone."

"You're strange, Scotty. Did anyone ever tell you that?"

"I'll take it as a compliment, Sal."

Not far behind Sal was the next member to arrive. The organist in the band was known as UB. His full name was Eubie Wilson, a name that earned him the school taunt of UB Strange. His parents, with the best of intentions, had named their son after the great American composer of ragtime jazz – Eubie Blake. While it pointed UB toward a joyful style of music, it did nothing to erode his introvert leanings.

UB came from an African-Canadian background. He sported an Afro hairstyle on top of a tall, skinny frame. At seventeen years of age, he was immersed in music, both as a passion and as a means of hiding out from life's complexities. At his parents' urging, UB began piano lessons around four years of age. His first teacher was a strict, intimidating nun from the Ursulines Catholic religious order. She used a conductor's baton across his knuckles if UB's posture slouched. If his fingers slowed down during a difficult passage, another *whack* would be delivered.

When UB's parents heard of the Sister's teaching methodology, they went ballistic. Concerned with their son's wellbeing, as well as other young students, they threatened to write an exposé letter in the *Windsor Star*. The nun was transferred elsewhere, quickly and quietly.

Despite a rough start, UB was at home in the community of nuns. For over a decade, he grew up with them. He studied and eventually taught in their aging facility on Riverside Drive. He watched how social changes in the '60s affected the Ursulines. After a steady exodus of younger members, the remaining nuns had to adapt to more contemporary times.

UB saw firsthand the abandonment of strict religious habits, literally. He watched the Ursulines take on a larger profile in teaching The Royal Conservatory methodology, especially to young pianists and vocalists. UB earned a decent wage accompanying vocalists who were preparing for their Conservatory examinations. He also mentored individual students on subjects such as music theory and history.

Outside of his classical duties and studies, UB had access to a church hall near his downtown neighbourhood. The organist at that church suffered from severe arthritis. When her condition flared up, she would call UB's parents to see if their son could substitute for a Sunday service. Having entry to the church was really about having access to their Hammond organ. Sure, accompanying the choir was meaningful, but what really lit up UB was improvising on the organ when nobody was around. In the mid-sixties, he was enamoured with Larry Young, an American jazz organist who was pioneering a more experimental approach to playing. The empty church was his laboratory and UB was the mad scientist in residence.

Scotty waved, "UB, my man. You still backing up the singing nuns?"

UB just flashed a peace sign to Scotty but continued to walk over to the organ. Next on the scene was Nardello.

Bruno Nardello hailed from a hardworking family on Erie Street. They ran a modest grocery store in Little Italy. He had two sisters who practically lived in the store. Little Bruno figured out early on that he had better cultivate a skill that would free him from stocking shelves for the rest of his days. Fortunately, Bruno had a talent for playing the guitar. That musical key opened the prison gates. He made a break for it.

A year ago, Scotty had dubbed the guitarist Nutella Nardello. When the Italian company Ferrero first introduced their sweetened hazelnut spread to Canada, one of the few places you could find it was in NARDELLO'S. It was a big seller. Scotty was picking up Bruno for a practice one afternoon when he spotted the sweet treat. It wasn't long before the name Nutella Nardello got tossed into the air. Fortunately, for Bruno, the rest of the band politely called him by his last name: Nardello. "Comrades!" Nardello announced. "You're looking at the proud owner of a new Fender Telecaster guitar with a maplewood fretboard and Humbucker pickups."

"Holy Mother of God," Scotty exclaimed. "You gotta sell a lot of olive oil to pay for that blonde baby. How did you score?"

"The bigger question is where did I find it?" said Nardello. "Let's just say, I had help from Mr. Domenic Troiano." The room went silent as if the name of a saint had just been uttered. Domenic Troiano, the Toronto-based guitarist, was the musical heart and soul of a Canadian band called Mandala. When that band played at a Windsor high school, the previous year, every musician in town had walked away stunned by the level of artistry that exploded from their performance. Nardello, in particular, studied all the licks and solos masterfully crafted by Troiano on their Atlantic recording, *Soul Crusade.*

Nardello placed the case on the stage and reverently took out the holy grail of guitars. An uncharacteristically candid question came from UB. "Is this new instrument going to change our sound?"

Not missing a beat, Nardello swung around and shouted. "Fucking right it will."

The message was clear. This Telecaster was about to shoot forward like a Cuban missile onto the airwaves. It was primed to detonate old versions of the NADI sound. As if to let the guitar speak for itself, Nardello plugged Blondie into his pedals. In under a minute, Nardello's 1964 Fender Twin Reverb amp was weeping and wailing like a dark angel. Nardello laughed. "I guess that answers it. Any further questions about influencing our sound?"

The band, inspired by Blondie's fresh swagger, flipped switches, adjusted mic stands, and turned on the sound board. In this midst of setting up, three large figures strolled off Tecumseh Road and stood near the entrance – Bikers!

Guys who liked riding motorcycles and guys who hung with other riders were more into clubs than gangs. In Windsor, the small percentage of motorcyclists involved in criminal activities were called Satan's Choice. Scotty recognized two of the guys from the Choice gang. They broadcasted Choice colours – the insignia patch of a smiling devil. Choice members wore their colours on cut-off vests. The attire identified their membership and, equally as important, their territory.

One biker shouted from the doorway. "Where's Coyote?"

"Not here," shot back Scotty.

Biker number two was less amiable. "Tell him we need to talk."

"Who shall I say called?" Scotty said.

"Don't play dumb, dickhead. Coyote knows how to find us. Just pass along the message."

Scotty spoke up with less attitude this time. "You got it."

The trio turned and headed out to their bikes on Tecumseh Road. Within seconds, their choppers roared to life, howling like prehistoric beasts. Breaking an awkward silence, Sal spoke up: "Woah! That felt heavy."

"Yup, you don't wanna mess with those boys."

"You think Coyote's in trouble?" asked Sal.

"Satan's Choice are trouble," Scotty said.

Nardello broke the tension by blasting out the guitar riff from "Born To Be Wild" by Steppenwolf. It was a biker anthem. UB, who rarely quoted popular music, instantly chimed in with the organ part. Although the band specialized in improvised music, they were not immune to the music of the day. If the moment was right, they could imitate Hendrix or Cream. Soon the entire band was jamming away on a Steppenwolf vibe.

Scotty was still figuring out how to boost the vocals on the sound board when Coyote walked in with the roadies and overall crew for NADI. The duo of Brian and Ron set up gear, tweaked the sound, operated the light show, and hauled off gear for repairs. Coyote was smiling and moving as the band was jamming away. When he spotted the new guitar in Nardello's hands he shouted, "Whoa. Whoa. What's this?"

The band screeched to a halt. "This, my man," cooed Nardello, "is my new Fender Telecaster. Blondie meet Coyote. There's a long story as to how she came into my hands but let's say I am grateful that I got connected to Domenic."

"Seriously?" said Coyote.

"Just one Italian helping another," sang Nardello.

Scotty laughed. "Wasn't that Al Capone's explanation?"

Coyote approached the stage. "OK wise guys. We gotta talk. I need you all to huddle. I've got some big news to share."

"You've fallen in love with a Satan's Choice biker named Billie?" scoffed Scotty.

"What?" Coyote was not smiling now and was staring, eyes narrowed, at Scotty.

"Just joking," softened Scotty. "We had some visitors earlier who are keen to share an intimate tête-à-tête with you. I wouldn't delay if I were you."

"Thanks for handling that," said Coyote. "Those boys appreciate being treated with respect. Meanwhile, I need you all to circle up for an in-house conversation." Brian and Ron grabbed some chairs from the side walls and pulled them into a circle on the dance floor. The musicians turned off amps, put down instruments, and completed the circle. From time to time, Coyote used circles to work out band details, such as investing in a better sound system. Scotty always thought these meetings were better dubbed listening circles. Coyote usually did most of the explaining and then left space for everyone to agree.

Once the group was somewhat focused, Coyote began with a question. "OK, Sal. For two dollars, who is Al Linnell and what is your relationship to him?"

Sal turned red but managed to blurt out, "There's no relationship with Al."

"Ahh! A partial answer once more. No money for you," said Coyote. "Al Linnell, as Sal well knows, is the principal percussionist for the Windsor Symphony Orchestra."

"And," added Scotty, "the drummer of choice for jazzers around town."

"Yes, but we digress," said Coyote. "Al is a union rep in the WSO. He's pitched an idea to boost attendance in the symphony's next season. The WSO have regular subscribers but they aren't attracting younger audiences."

"Damn right," contributed Sal. "They just keep serving up the same menu from dead, white composers – predictable music for predictable patrons."

Coyote grabbed back the focus. "Precisely. So Al, and a few more progressive members of the symphony have proposed an unusual concert. It would be free to high school and university students. The show's going to be co-funded by the city council, the WSO, and a few heavy donors."

Sal spoke up. "It would take more than free tickets to attract kids listening to Ted Nugent and the Amboy Dukes."

"Bingo," said Coyote. "That's why Al and his posse want to promote a concert that blends classical and contemporary music."

Nardello chirped up. "You mean like jamming with the WSO. Anybody wanna play a sixteen-bar blues with a medieval swing?"

"Alright, you pricks," said Coyote, feeling impatient. "Here's what the board of the WSO and the city council agreed to support. They want to put together a Saturday night concert held in three months. That gives enough time to prepare and get the word out. I've been hired as the main promoter. The concert title they settled on is 'From Bartók to Hard Rock.'"

"A comment and a question if I might," chimed in Scotty.

"Yes?"

"That is the lamest title in the history of concerts. I can't imagine anyone in our circle wanting to check it out."

"Well at least with Béla Bartók they moved up a few centuries from Bach," added Sal.

"Look," sighed Coyote. "I didn't have any say in the title. I don't have any say in what the symphony plays that night."

"Absolved," continued Scotty. "Now for my question: What the hell does any of this have to do with us? Please don't say you want us to help promote this half-assed idea to our friends."

Coyote paused, as if to intentionally create a dramatic effect. "Better than that, my man. Our band has been invited to play the second half of the concert."

"The *Hard Rock* bit?" asked Sal.

"You got it."

"A small, but significant point," said Nardello. "The MC5 or the Stooges rock and they rock hard. We don't play that kind of music. You can't invite fans of that genre to a concert where the music is anything but that. The first riot in WSO history could go down."

"That's why we sell the idea to our crowd. They get a change up from coming to Sotto Voce. Plus, they get in for free."

"And what?" Scotty said. "They dance wildly in their cushioned seats."

"Why all the negativity?" said Coyote. "This could be a big deal for NADI. Here's the added perk. We get a featured article in the *Windsor Star*."

Sal groaned. "Oh no, they'll send that Martin guy. He's a snob, a classical music critic who doesn't even play an instrument."

"No," said Coyote, "they have agreed to let John Laycock cover our concert. They've promised to publish a build-up piece prior to the event."

Ron and Brian had remained quiet during the discussion. It was Ron who spoke up. "Here's my confession. The only time I attended a WSO concert was as a kid in public school. We heard *Peter and the Wolf* performed at the old Tivoli Theatre. The orchestra took up the entire stage. NADI may be a small band but we take up a lot of space. Do you have any idea how many stagehands it would take to dismantle an entire orchestra while we set up? Not only that, we rely on a decent sound system that can project. Are we hauling all our gear, plus our light show, just to deliver a short set?"

"We get forty-five minutes," said Coyote. "As for gear, the WSO has mallet instruments, which Sal plays all the time."

"Yeah," confirmed Sal. "I don't have to move my Musser and I can add a concert marimba if needed. As for other gear... UB, you should know that the WSO has a real symphonic organ. We're talking a serious pipe organ, not a church organ."

"I'm in," said UB. "I've always wanted to pull out all the stops, E. Power Biggs' style. Let's shake the rafters with Bach's Toccata & Fugue."

"There are no rafters to shake," pointed out Sal, "plus the organ sits at the back of the space where we wouldn't see you."

"Oh, you'd hear me," said UB. "No sound system needed."

Coyote spoke up: "Alright, we clearly have a lot of detail to work out. I want you guys to sound amazing."

"And look good," joked Nardello. "Tuxes and tails."

"Just be yourselves," said Coyote. "And, the pay will include rehearsal time."

"Why rehearsal time?" asked Scotty. "Don't tell me you agreed for us to do a collaboration with the WSO. The Moody Blues took care of that idea with *Days of Future Passed.*"

"No," said Coyote. "We aren't playing with the symphony. We're including a musical guest who will play the first and second half of the program."

"You mean someone other than Sal?" asked Nardello.

Coyote pulled out a piece of paper from his jeans to make sure he got the information correct. "There will be a guest violinist in the first half, featured on Béla Bartók's Violin Concerto No.1."

"And we get to play No. 2 in our set?" quipped Scotty.

"Sure, wise guy," shot back Coyote. "Look, it's dead simple. This guest violinist will come to a couple of our rehearsals, jam with us, and play the second set at the concert."

"How do we know this guy can jam?" asked Nardello.

"Not a guy," corrected Coyote. "A woman, a violinist not from around these parts."

"Listen Coyote," Scotty spoke up. "I respect what you're trying to pull off. But I gotta tell you, there are only a handful of decent, free-style improvisors on the violin. You've got Jerry Goodman out of Chicago and Jean-Luc Ponty out of Paris."

"And John Unger out of Leamington," interjected Nardello.

"All I know is that this chick is apparently a killer classical player and she improvises too."

"I'm not sure the term killer and classical player go together," said Sal. "What's her name?"

"Tamara Chandra. She's moving from India to North America. She landed a teaching position at the Interlochen Arts Academy."

"Classical credentials aside," said Sal, "can she improvise?"

Coyote took his time tucking the paper back into his jeans. "Let me level with you. Tamara has a sponsor, a relative with deep pockets. This family member is paying for her trip over and will help her get settled in Canada. You should know that he's also chipping in a big chunk of change to make this event happen. We either snag this opportunity or some other band will gladly step up."

Coyote was not sitting in his chair now but moving quickly, like a boxer in the ring. His eyes darted from player to player as if to challenge them to go one round with him.

"OK," said Scotty. "When do we get to meet her? I mean, we gotta try it out. See whether she's actually going to fit in or just stand on stage looking like somebody's idea of inclusivity."

Coyote spoke with a slightly softened tone. "She arrives in two weeks. We'll let her get settled and then invite her down to jam. Meanwhile, I need Ron and Brian to provide a wish list. Tell me what you need in terms of sound gear, a truck rental, and tech requirements for the WSO."

"Meeting adjourned?" asked Nardello. "I have a date with Blondie. She wants to jam with the band."

"Fire it up boys," laughed Coyote. "We're about to take NADI to the next level."

CHAPTER 2

It was Scotty's idea for the band and Tamara Chandra to meet at The Himalayan Restaurant on Ouellette Avenue. It boasted authentic dishes from North India. Over many years, Scotty and his family had regularly celebrated birthdays and special occasions at the restaurant. Scotty was just a child when he first met Bishnu, the owner and head chef.

A series of memorable events led up to the connection with Bishnu. It began with Scotty's father not being truthful about his age when he enlisted in the British Army. Toward the end of WWII, Jake McPherson signed on and ended up in the Southeast Asian nation of Burma. One year later, Jake and his small battalion of British soldiers were transferred to Delhi. The end of Britain's rule in India had been dramatically playing out over the last decade. As fate would have it, Scotty's father was present in 1947, along with over a million others, when Lord Mountbatten handed over the Declaration of Independence. He heard Jawaharlal Nehru address the nation as he became the first prime minister of India.

A few years later, after Sara and Jake McPherson had immigrated to Windsor, Scotty's father was driving along the King's Highway – the 401. Jake was heading home on a night drenched in rain. He had just reached an area outside of London, Ontario, when he spotted a hitchhiker. The man was taking shelter from the downpour, waiting underneath an overpass. Jake pulled over. Although he had been stationed as a British soldier in an occupied country, Jake had experienced countless acts of kindness from Indian civilians. Here was a chance to return a favour.

The traveller was Bishnu. The man had just arrived from India and was hitchhiking his way from Toronto to Windsor. The kinship between Jake and Bishnu was instantaneous. That night, Jake not only helped Bishnu settle into Windsor's YMCA but also connected the new immigrant with a friend who owned a small import company. The enterprise brought in fabrics and other goods from India. Bishnu was hired on the spot.

The next time Jake and Bishnu saw each other was at the opening of The Himalayan Restaurant. When Jake heard about a new Indian restaurant opening in Windsor, he hauled the family down to the Ouellette Avenue facility. Jake and Bishnu instantly recognized one another, embraced, and the McPherson family was treated to a sumptuous meal. Bishnu refused to accept payment from Jake.

Over the years, Scotty took his friends to the Himalayan and so the band was quite at home in the space. Bishnu's wife, Gurbeen, was fussing over the young men like an auntie, treating them to copious amounts of green tea plus the odd mango lassi. They were seated at a large lunch table waiting for Tamara to arrive.

"I hope your guest will like this new statue of Saraswati," said Gurbeen. She gestured toward a wooden carving of the Hindu deity playing a stringed instrument. "She is our goddess of wisdom, music, art, and learning."

Looking at his watch, Nardello asked, "Does she preside over punctuality?"

Gurbeen smiled back. "Not to worry, my friend. Women are cyclical beings with a rounder sense of time."

"That may be a problem when it comes to starting the symphony concert on time," Nardello said. A tinkling bell over the front door announced the guest of honour.

The Tamara who entered did not match the image Scotty had envisioned. His version of the musician was more severe, studious, and older. This Tamara was akin to a dancer – lithe, light, and close in age to everyone in NADI. She wore white linen pants with a traditional sari that flowed below her knees. Draped over her left shoulder was a yellow shawl that shone like a dandelion in spring. Tamara's long, dark hair hung wildly over her right shoulder. She wore no jewelry and no makeup.

Gurbeen floated across the floor to welcome Tamara. The two women mirrored each other with their hands pressed together, palms touching and fingers pointing upwards. Each woman held her thumbs close to the chest and gave a slight bow. The phrase Namaste was softly spoken. Scotty was familiar with this gesture and understood the phrase to mean "I bow to the divine in you."

As Gurbeen ushered the guest over to the band's table, the musicians each rose from their chairs. Coyote was the first to reach out his hand. "Welcome, Tamara. It's great to finally meet you. These guys may look dangerous but they're harmless. This is UB, our keyboard player."

Despite his shyness, UB confidently reached out his hand and looked straight into Tamara's eyes. "Thanks for joining us. I'm looking forward to playing with you and especially hearing you tackle the Béla Bartók concerto."

"Sweet," Tamara replied. "I brought a gift for you by the way. Unfortunately, I left it at my uncle's place. It's called a shruti box. It works on a system of bellows, similar to a harmonium. In our classical Indian music, the shruti provides a constant drone."

"So kind of you," said UB.

"And this is Bruno Nardello, our guitarist," said Coyote. "We caught him listening to some sitar music the other night. Maybe he wants to impress you."

"Ah," laughed Tamara. "I've heard enough sitar masters to last this incarnation. What I haven't heard is enough Hendrix, Clapton, or Beck."

Nardello blushed. "Those guys set the bar pretty high for us hacks. Anyway, great to meet you."

"And our man on percussion, from kit to cowbell. This is Sal," said Coyote.

"Hello Sal." Tamara reached over toward Sal. Just before they clasped hands and shook, Tamara seemed to lightly touch her fingers on Sal's palm and whispered, "Tha Ki Ta Tha Ka Dhi Mi."

"A seven beat tala," Sal smiled. "I've been studying a bit with Gurpreet Chana in Toronto. He's been introducing me to Indian rhythms."

Tamara grinned back. "Good catch. That one's called Misra."

"And finally, our vocalist, pianist, and trumpetist all rolled into one messy guy named Scotty."

Scotty instinctively put his hands into a prayer position, ready to give a traditional namaste greeting. Before he could complete the gesture, Tamara put on a Scottish accent and blurted out, "Fit like?"

"What?" said Scotty. He was taken aback.

"Well," continued Tamara. "You were about to give a traditional Hindu greeting and so I thought to send you a bit of slang from the quines and loons of old Aberdeen. As a Scot, I assumed you would know that *fit like* means how are you?"

Scotty laughed and gave back the traditional response.

"Nae bad."

"I did some time at the Royal Academy of Music in London," said Tamara. "Whenever we had a break, my mates and I would take the train to Aberdeen. I learned more about the communal nature of music in the pubs, listening to fiddle players."

Strangely enough, Scotty didn't have a snappy comeback. Instead, he gave a goofy shrug and smiled. Tamara was shown a seat in between Coyote and Scotty. Gurbeen handed out menus to everyone. "Thanks auntie," Tamara spoke up. "Assuming the boys don't want burgers, what would you recommend?"

"We have a tandoori clay oven so certainly the lamb tandoori to share among those who eat meat. I can also bring an array of our specialities: tofu matar, aloo gobi, bhindi do pyaza, eggplant bharta, chana masala, palak paneer, and veg korma. How about I start you off with some samosa chaat and pakoras?"

"Lovely," smiled Tamara. "My comfort food. Do you make a decent dal too?"

"Indeed," said Gurbeen. "I'll bring it with some naan and rice."

Scotty surveyed the table and flashed upon his high school chemistry teacher. It was Mr. Blake who introduced the definition of a catalyst: a substance that increases the rate of a chemical reaction without itself undergoing any permanent chemical change.

Tamara's presence and energy were having a catalytic influence on each member of NADI, himself included. True to the definition, she was not undergoing any noticeable change.

The lunch conversation began with questions directed to Tamara about how she was able to straddle classical and popular music. She spoke about getting conversant in the playing styles needed for any musical context. Eventually, their talk drifted more toward the gear required to play with amplified instruments. This topic seemed to draw everyone in. The band was enamored with how developments in technology were expanding the palate of sonic textures for musicians. Better amps, effects pedals and pickups were constantly being introduced.

Tamara was particularly passionate about innovative advances being made by luthiers, especially relative to new designs for electric violins. She told a funny anecdote about one of the first attempts in the 1930s to amplify stringed instruments. The early pioneers attached a megaphone device to the violin's body with the primary intent of boosting volumes.

Later a jazz violinist in the '40s and '50s, named Joe Venuti, used a type of microphone secured to his acoustic instrument. It was called a DeArmond and was the most commonly used electric technology at that time. Since violins weren't a solid body instrument, they suffered from the same unwieldy feedback and inferior tone that plagued hollow body guitars back then.

Because of their love of jazz and improvised music, the musicians around the table were familiar with violinists such as Stuff Smith and Don "Sugarcane" Harris. Tamara talked ardently about these masters and how they were pushing the envelope in terms of fusing styles. Gear wise, she lamented, nothing had seriously developed. The actual instruments these artists played were mainly acoustic violins painted a different color with a pickup added.

Since she had the rapt attention of the musicians, Tamara laid out how, in 1958, Fender manufactured Leo Fender's first design for a solid body, electric violin. It came in a snazzy, sunburst finish. "Those early attempts at a solid body violin didn't catch on," Tamara said. "Advances and upgraded designs, in my opinion, came from one particular luthier, Mark Woods. As a violinist, he was playing regularly with rock bands in the Port Washington area of New York State. He would build a new solid body instrument in his father's woodworking shop and then take it out at night onto the stage."

Tamara explained how Mark, while he was jamming, would be analyzing what needed to be cut off, sanded away, or where the pickups needed to be repositioned. The instruments, consequently, reflected the way Mark heard sound. He wasn't distracted by an aesthetic goal of making his instrument look like a wood sculpture. Tamara shared that her electric violin was inspired by Wood's prototypes as well as the original Fender design. She proudly announced that her current instrument was made in India. It came with a twist: an additional fifth string.

Nardello was hanging on every word of this tech talk, especially when Tamara dropped into her pedal set up. Inspired by Jimi Hendrix's guitar effects, Tamara put her electric violin through a series of effects. Her choices included a Vox wah pedal, a Dallas-Arbiter Fuzz Face, a Uni-Vibe expression pedal, and an Octavio made by the sound technician, Roger Mayer.

When Gurbeen brought out the sharing dishes, she coaxed her husband, Bishnu, to come out of the kitchen. Everyone at the table, except Tamara, had dined at the restaurant before. Bishnu subsequently gave a general welcome to everyone but paid special attention to the guest of honour. Within a few exchanges, Tamara and Bishnu had narrowed down their histories in the vast subcontinent of India. They realized both had family in Simla, the capital and largest city in the state of Himachal Pradesh. Scotty knew of this region. It once was the summer capital of British India, due to its cooler temperatures.

After Bishnu and Gurbeen left, the passing and sampling of food occupied a good deal of the ensuing conversation. Later, Tamara veered the small talk into social matters troubling North America in that year of 1968. With television sets becoming prevalent in homes outside of America, Tamara was like millions of others watching tumultuous events shaking up and breaking up the U.S.

Tamara was especially curious about the rise of the Vietnam War and whether the musicians had helped any draft dodgers find sanctuary in Windsor. As a border city, with only the mile-wide Detroit River separating Canada from the U.S., war resistors frequently crossed over via the Ambassador Bridge or the Detroit-Windsor Tunnel. Only a few risked night crossings in a boat.

Coyote seemed to have the most experience helping draft dodgers. He shared how, in the spring of '68, there was a larger surge of young men crossing into Canada; especially after footage surfaced of U.S. ground troops killing more than 500 Vietnamese civilians in the My

Lai massacre in South Vietnam.

"I've been booking some bands with Jeep Holland, out of Ann Arbor," said Coyote. "Jeep founded A-Square Records and then got involved with managing bands. The guy has a lot of artists in his stable. None of them want to end up in a body bag. He's developed a technique for trying to get guys out of the draft. About a month before someone has to show up for an armed forces medical exam, Jeep puts the dude on a brown rice diet. He keeps the guy sleep deprived, maybe a little drugged. When the musician reports to an army doctor, he's a basket case. It's hit and miss but sometimes someone gets lucky. He might be disqualified for mental health issues. Everyone prays for a 4-F classification. It indicates that a person is not acceptable for service in the armed forces."

"And if that procedure doesn't work?" asked Tamara. "What if a 4-F isn't issued?"

"I have a 2-F option. My Ford Fairlane," said Coyote. "The latest passenger I brought into Canada was an American bass player named Mike Tilka. I have a feeling that more runs are on the horizon. There was an anti-war protest at Columbia University recently. The New York cops came down heavy on the students. I tell 'ya, something big is brewing in the States. It feels like a rebellion could happen."

UB spoke up. "It's not just the Vietnam war that's troubling. As a black man, I don't feel safe going into Detroit these days. The cops are trying to reassert their control. There are places in Detroit that feel like a war zone. The whole city was just beginning to recover from the '67 riots and then Dr. King was assassinated this past April."

"Followed by Robert Kennedy going down in June," added Nardello.

"Not to scare you, but there's a violent energy in the air," said UB. "Some people are organizing to resist the power brokers. Have you heard of the Black Panthers and the SDS?"

"Yes," Tamara said. "I was in Paris recently. They have their own version of Students for a Democratic Society. Nothing like the Black Panthers though."

"People think the Black Panthers are all about violence," said UB. "I would say they're more about watching the cops than organizing for a revolution. Huey Newton and Bobby Seale stood up in Oakland. They helped people challenge the police brutality against the black community. Just like people in the Detroit ghetto, the citizens had enough of cops coming down on them. They coordinated a vigil system called cop watching. The Panthers also started a lot of social and educational programs for the black community."

"Well," said Tamara, "it sounds as if you're all informed and concerned. Having lived in London and Europe, I can tell you there's a global movement growing there. The question is, and maybe this can be a topic for another dinner, what can we do to be engaged as artists and activists?"

Scotty, who had been fairly quiet during the conversation, spoke up. "I'm not convinced that all artists need to become activists. I'm not personally drawn to writing protest music for the masses." It was a personal statement and he wasn't expecting it to be challenged.

"Then what, if any, responsibility do you think artists have?" asked Tamara.

Scotty seemed stymied at first but then spoke up. "Different forms of music can inspire cultural change. Not all music, mind you, stimulates new values. Some music exists solely to entertain. But take jazz, for instance. Hard core jazz has a long history of upsetting the status quo. At one point, it integrated the people that the southern states kept separated. Maybe some types of music can sound out a revolution without anyone getting shot."

"Are you saying artists don't have to risk anything?" said Tamara. "What about Billie Holiday singing 'Strange Fruit' or Nina Simone putting out 'Mississippi Goddam'?"

"I'm not against some artists becoming activists," said Scotty. "There's a place for songs that name what's going down or songs that rally us. Last year we had that anthem, 'For What It's Worth.' People think it was an anti-war song by Buffalo Springfield, but Stephen Stills wrote it because of the Sunset Strip curfew riots that happened in Hollywood. Audiences just wanted to go hear music at places like the Whisky a Go Go. But the cops, who were backed by business owners, the city, and local residents, enforced these bogus laws about loitering. The riots happened, people got hurt, and a lot of venues got shut down."

"Are you saying that artists should just keep quiet?" asked Tamara. "Should we merely entertain?"

Scotty let out an exasperated sigh. "Come on. Look at us. We're clearly involved in a movement. We're trying to birth a new culture out of the old establishment. In the process, we just don't want what is emerging to get crushed by the old order. You probably heard that we run a club. It provides a gathering place under the radar. In Sotto Voce we can build a counterculture environment without getting our heads bashed in."

"At the risk of sounding rude," said Tamara looking directly at Scotty, "maybe it's not only about creating a safe space but also knowing when to stop playing it safe. Imagine America if Dr. King had only delivered his sermons in churches to black congregations. Imagine India if Mahatma Gandhi had not challenged the British-imposed salt tax with his 24-day protest march to Dandi. Imagine the southern states if Rosa Parks had passively relinquished her seat in the coloured section of the bus and given it up to some white passenger."

It was Coyote who broke the tension by reaching onto his lap and lifting a crisp, white napkin. He waved it in circles above his head. Everyone immediately understood the gesture. This was the international sign for truce, ceasefire, or negotiation. "Not to break up this enlightening conversation," said Coyote. "It's just that we have to get down to some matters of business. There are rehearsals to schedule. There are technical needs to discuss. Even promotional materials have to be generated."

Sal groaned. "Really? No photographs please. Can't I just wear a bandito mask? There are some individuals in Venezuela who don't need to know that I'm here in Canada."

"Sure," said Coyote. "We'll make you look like a musical version of Zorro... with cap, cape and claves."

To emphasize that all debates were done, Coyote reached into his satchel and pulled out his daily planner notebook and pen. Suddenly Gurbeen, as if she had been listening from the kitchen, appeared with a small mountain of gulab jamun. It was Scotty's favourite dessert after an Indian meal (made with khoya, fried golden and finally dipped in saffron-infused sugar syrup). Despite the excess sweetness of this tasty dessert, Scotty's mood had soured.

27

CHAPTER 3

After lunch at the Himalayan, Scotty wrestled for a few days as to whether he might call Tamara. Midweek he stopped waffling, picked up the phone, and dialed a number he got from Coyote. A soft-spoken Indian man answered. Scotty explained who he was and why he was calling. Scotty wanted to invite Tamara out on a road trip to the Leamington area. The man listened without interruption and then explained that Tamara was out. He would pass along the message. Scotty provided his home phone number to Tamara's uncle.

The morning was already warm and the sky was sunny when Scotty drove his 1964 Rambler station wagon up to the address on Riverside Drive East. Tamara's uncle came out to greet Scotty. He could feel that both the car and driver were getting a thorough inspection. After a few moments of small talk, the uncle wanted to know specifics: what route Scotty had planned to drive and when he might expect Tamara back home.

Tamara emerged from the house looking more like she hailed from London's Carnaby Street. She wore a sleeveless yellow cotton dress that stopped above her knees. Her hair was pulled off her shoulders and somewhat tucked into a wide-brimmed tan hat. The hat item seemed part cowgirl and part San Francisco hippie. Her feet appeared ready for the outing; she sported a pair of yellow Puma training sneakers with flowers embroidered on the outside. A cloth handbag was slung over her shoulder. Tamara said a brief goodbye to her uncle and climbed into the front seat.

"A perfect day for an outing," she sang.

"It's roughly an hour's drive to Point Pelee National Park," said Scotty. "We're going to make one short stop en route. It shouldn't be too crowded at the Point today. Weekends get crazier with tourists, families, and beach parties with students."

Scotty swung the car out onto Riverside Drive and, after two blocks,

Tamara asked him to pull over. "Are you OK?" Scotty asked. He pulled into a convenience store parking lot. Tamara swivelled in her seat to face Scotty directly. "I'm fine. I just need to be clear about a few things with you. First off, as a driver, are you high?" The question came out of the blue but Scotty figured that Tamara may have been briefed by Coyote or one of the guys.

"Clean as a lab coat," Scotty replied.

Tamara was quiet for a moment and then spoke thoughtfully. "Thanks for being straight up Scotty, and thanks for being honest. I really do appreciate you taking me out on such a glorious day. Do you mind sharing exactly why you invited me on this little excursion?"

Scotty let the question hang for a moment and answered slowly. "After our first encounter at the restaurant, I felt weird. Maybe it was just me but... some of our interactions felt more like a debate. I know you're smart, well-informed, and have opinions. But, if we're going to play music together, it's important for me to have the right chemistry with a person."

"Maybe chemistry doesn't always have to feel comfortable," responded Tamara. "I don't want to presume too much but you strike me as someone who has a charming way with the opposite sex. To be clear, I prefer authenticity over charm."

"Ouch!"

"I didn't mean to prick your male ego," Tamara laughed. "I just needed to get clear about a few things and set some boundaries. With that settled how about we dive into a beautiful day and agree to be ourselves."

"Cool with me," said Scotty. "I promise not to play Prince Charming. Besides, you don't strike me as someone who needs rescuing."

"You got that right."

They drove without putting the radio on. Soon the city landscape was replaced by rural scenery: fields of corn, wheat, tomatoes, and other cash crops. Tamara was beguiled by the flat Ontario landscape and the great expanses of space. Out of the blue, Tamara raised another prickly point. "Not to be a pain in the ass, but my uncle made me promise that I wouldn't go into the water. He said the park boasts the longest natural beach in Essex County but that even strong swimmers have to contend with undertows and rip currents."

"That's a fact, Jack. Huge waves too," added Scotty. "How about this, we can walk along the beach. I definitely want to show you the Point. The park comes with a lot of history and natural beauty." Scotty almost said *like you...* he stopped that thought before it tumbled out.

"The Point Pelee we're gonna see is not like the one 6,000 years ago, when the original people lived in the forests and fields. That area of Southern Ontario was once covered in vast white pine forests. Then, in the late 1700s, the British logged the area for shipbuilding."

"It takes a lot of resources to expand the empire," said Tamara.

"Don't we know it," said Scotty. "Along come the Brits and the Chippewa were forced off their land. The government gave some bogus excuse, like they wanted it preserved as a national park. It was supposed to be a dedicated conservation area. Man, some things never change."

"Don't forget," said Tamara, "I'm from India. Not that long ago we were part of the British Empire. We know how Indians can be treated."

"Yeah, my father told me stories from when he was stationed with the British forces in the New Delhi area."

They drove on further, enjoying the rural scenery, and hearing stories about Scotty's father. "You mentioned that we were going to stop somewhere en route," said Tamara. "Is that still happening?"

"Yeah," said Scotty. "We're almost there. Up ahead is a little farming town called Cottam. When we drive through it, there's a small market garden on your right side. The family owns about 13 acres. It's a small-scale operation, mainly fruits and vegetables. Look for a light blue building set back from the road. They have a display area stocked with fruits and vegetables. The owners make home-made breads too. They operate a small bakery offering baked goods and bread. When tourists head out to Jack Miner's Bird Sanctuary or Point Pelee Park, the cars and buses like to pull over. They stock up on picnic supplies."

"Sounds yummy."

"You can probably pick up some homemade jams for your uncle there. The family makes preserves and other canned goods from their own produce."

30

They passed through the town of Cottam quickly. It consisted of a hardware store, a park, a gas station, a grocery store, and a small church. Just outside of town, Highway #3 took a sharp left. At that juncture, the Green Acres sign and a bright blue building came up quickly on the right. Scotty slowed the station wagon down and veered into the gravel parking area, near the produce stand. Without saying a word, Scotty sat with his hands still on the steering wheel. Tamara sensed something emotional had been stirred up.

"Everything alright?" asked Tamara.

"Not yet."

Still holding the steering wheel, Scotty's story trickled out. "Do you smell the bread?" he asked. Tamara nodded. "Most of the bus drivers, who take tourists out to Kingsville or Leamington know about this place. The drivers like to stop here for their passengers. Kristóf, who owns Green Acres, appreciates the business. He might give a loaf of bread or a jar of jam to the driver for bringing in customers. About three years ago, a rookie bus driver was coming around this bend. He smelled the aroma of fresh bread, attempted to gear down and skidded on the gravel stirring up a cloud of rock and dust."

"Was he able to stop the bus?" asked Tamara, sensing that something happened.

"The bus fishtailed but finally stopped. It was the car behind them that got into trouble. The driver tried to swerve. He slid into the opposite lane. The rear of the bus clipped the vehicle. Within seconds, the driver and his passenger went spinning into that tree."

Scotty pointed to a sturdy black oak tree on the opposite side of the highway. Tamara instantly spotted two white crosses at the base of the tree, just past the irrigation ditch. Scotty exhaled and continued. "My father was driving the car. My mother was in the passenger seat. She died upon impact. He held on, pinned by the steering wheel. When help arrived, my father kept saying my name over and over... until his last breath."

Tamara reached her hands over to Scotty's arm. "Oh Scotty, I'm so sorry."

"I lost both my parents that morning. I lost my way too. After that accident, I spun off on my own rough ride. The loss was so painful that I got into heavy drugs. I was addicted to heroin. People tried to help but I was pretty shut down. My mother's sister became my appointed guardian. She came to live with me in our family house. She tried to be as kind as possible but we were both hurting. Those were crazy years."

Scotty took his hands off the steering wheel and wiped his wet eyes. They both looked up to see Kristóf coming out of the front field, walking toward the car. Tamara and Scotty opened their car doors. Despite the dust and dirt caking Kristóf's overalls, Scotty gave the older man a full-bodied hug. The farmer spoke with a noticeable Hungarian accent. "You haven't been out here since last fall. I was worried."

"Things are good now, Kristóf. The music scene keeps me focused. I want you to meet a friend of mine. She's visiting her uncle in Canada. This is Tamara."

Kristóf, extended his hand, "welcome to Green Acres. As my guest, I will get you a jar of strawberry jam. We have acres of strawberries in the back, way too many to harvest. When we can't get to the berries, we put out a *Pick Your Own* sign. Families come with quart baskets and screaming kids."

"That's very generous," said Tamara. "We don't grow strawberries where I come from. I did live in England, though, and developed a fondness for this particular strawberry jam made by Wilkin and Sons. It was sanctioned by the Royal Family."

"I can only give you my Kristóf seal of approval," the farmer laughed.

"Look around while I get Scotty to help me find the jam." Tamara watched as the old man put an arm around Scotty's shoulder and led him towards the back of the produce stand. It was obvious to Tamara that Kristóf cared kindly for Scotty. Several minutes later the two men emerged with a loaf of bread, a bag of field tomatoes, and the promised jar of strawberry jam. Tamara paid for some fresh flowers. They said their goodbyes and were soon back on Highway 3.

"Kristóf was the first person to help my father before the firefighters arrived. They had to cut open the driver's door. My father was in shock from the accident but aware that he was dying. Kristóf knew it too. He said little prayers in Hungarian to my parents. That man has a golden heart."

More of Scotty's teen struggles came out during the drive to Point Pelee. Tamara learned about Scotty's dark period of drug abuse. He got in trouble with the law and risked being expelled from high school. It was UB's parents that got Scotty enrolled in a rehabilitation program. Scotty recounted his high school years and talked about three good people who influenced his life during his struggles.

The first person was Mr. Dresser, who led the music program at W.F. Herman Secondary School. Scotty had already been studying and playing trumpet when he entered high school. After the traumatic accident, Mr. Dresser took a keen interest in Scotty. He made sure that the young student remained passionate about his musical studies. Alongside of playing in the concert band and smaller ensembles, Mr. Dresser helped Scotty hone his skills in composing and arranging. He and Scotty started the school's first jazz ensemble.

The second teacher who helped Scotty was Mr. Creed. He taught English Literature at W.F. Herman. Mr. Creed, outside of the required reading assignments, steadily fed Scotty books ranging from Herman Hesse novels to Walt Whitman poetry. He encouraged Scotty to write song lyrics, open verse poetry, and maintain a daily practice of journaling. It was Mr. Creed who showed Scotty how to channel his forces of rage and sorrow. Instead of conflict ricocheting inside his heart, Scotty got those energies out and onto the page. "Poetry is the antidote to running away," said Mr. Creed. "Whether you are writing or reading it, you can't dash about on surfaces."

The third influence brought controversy as Scotty explained it to Tamara. A woman named Anita had already graduated from high school when Scotty met her. He was finishing up Grade 13 while Anita was completing her studies at the Ontario College of Teachers. In the mid-sixties, individuals who aspired to be educators could graduate from high school and directly enter teachers college. Anita was a few years older than Scotty when she came to W.F. Herman to complete an internship in the music department. Outside of the classroom Scotty and Anita became romantically and sexually involved for several months.

"I know this may sound strange," explained Scotty, "but she helped me with my broken heart. Back in those days, I could be emotionally shut down or all over the map. Anita brought a healing energy into my life – something I desperately needed. My aunt was less around those days and I was on my own a lot. I craved to be touched, to be held, to lie in the dark in someone's arms. Anita came along at the right time. She knew some things about the Kama Sutras and taught me different forms of intimacy. We loved each other deeply but I couldn't shake my drug habit and she left."

"Hold on," said Tamara. "I can appreciate how those male teachers helped you. But I have a real problem with the third person. How can a teacher cross such an entrusted border with a student? I don't care how you frame it, Scotty. That's just unethical. How do you know she didn't carry on that behaviour with other students after you?"

"I know it sounds weird but…"

"Weird?" said Tamara. "How about unscrupulous! And, what's with all this ripping off my culture? The Kama Sutra is a sacred practice, a 5000-year-old discipline. It has more to do with self-awareness than two North Americans exploring how they want to fuck!"

Something had set Tamara off. Scotty understood her rage but didn't know what had triggered it. He decided to let their differences hang for a while. This was his default. As one of Scotty's counsellors had stated, whenever disagreements arose, he would play out his habit of going silent. Interchanges that produced emotional distress and internal noise would cause Scotty to lose his voice. He would avoid the process of slogging through conflict to get to resolution, or at least a respect of differences. In this exchange with Tamara, he couldn't find the words to advance any understanding of why he and Anita became lovers. Underlining the silence was also the fact that Scotty didn't want his precious memories to be picked apart.

When it felt right, Scotty came at their conversation from a less loaded angle. He stepped into storyteller mode and wrapped up tid-bits from what happened when his parents died. He mainly stuck to factual matters and talked about how the bus company settled financially out of court. A trust fund was established. Scotty subsequently owned his parents' house and his aunt moved out. He left out large chunks of more personal matters, such as the excessive ways he tried to subdue the grief that couldn't be numbed.

Further down the road, well past the town of Leamington, the emotional clouds felt like they had passed. Scotty pulled the car over. They stretched their legs and, at Scotty's invitation, they read a plaque outside of the Point Pelee National Park gate. The information described how Point Pelee consists of a peninsula of land, mainly of marsh and woodland habitats. It tapers to a sharp point extending into Lake Erie. The Point is the southernmost extension of mainland Canada, on the same parallel with the northern border of California.

Tamara read that birders, during the spring migration, can spot between 75 and 150 species in one day. She learned that during late summer and early fall, monarch butterflies migrate to central Mexico from the Point. Thousands of monarchs can be seen on the trees and north shores of Lake Erie.

They got back in the car and Scotty pulled up to the park entrance. He rolled down the window and handed over cash for a day pass. The park employee reminded Scotty of Ranger Smith from the Yogi Bear cartoon show. "What are you hoping to see today?" asked the Parks Canada worker.

"We might do a little hike from the White Pine picnic area," said Scotty. "I was hoping to show my friend the tip as well."

"Good thing you mentioned the Point. We got a message this morning that the beach is closed up that way. It has to do with the E. coli bacteria count. Once it exceeds 100, swimming is not recommended. This morning the E. coli count was super high and so the beach over there has been officially shut down."

"That's a drag," said Scotty.

"Still, lots to see in the park. It's a great day to check out the marsh. You could rent a canoe. Two-thirds of the park is wetland. There's a ton of people over at Lake Pond. I'd recommend heading to some smaller marsh areas, maybe West Cranberry Pond or Redhead Pond. You might catch some turtles basking and the carp are particularly plentiful this year. A good day for watching nature."

"Very helpful," Scotty acknowledged. "Thanks for the input."

As they drove past the entrance, Tamara expected Scotty to be disappointed that the E. coli count had spoiled his plans. He wouldn't be able to show her the famous tip of Point Pelee. She was a bit surprised to see a grin on Scotty's face. "You don't seem too bothered about what we just heard," she said.

"On the contrary, the beach being closed at the tip means we'll have it to ourselves. The tourists will be off paddling their rented canoes and the party campers will probably go to the Sandbanks area."

"I don't understand," said Tamara, "If the tip is closed, won't it be closed to us? Or do you have special dispensation?"

"Let's just say that I know a way to get past where the rangers will have blocked traffic. We'll go by foot along a narrow trail and then walk more in the open, following the right shoreline. It'll be a bit of a hike to get to the tip and you might get your spiffy sneakers scuffed. Is that OK?"

"I'm up for an adventure," said Tamara. "You don't happen to be related to Captain Robert Falcon Scott by any chance?"

"Funny you should mention Scott. I did a history paper on the guy. Imagine tramping 850 miles over glaciers and ice fields so that you could become the first explorer to reach the South Pole. Imagine arriving there only to find that you had been beaten by Roald Amundsen, a Norwegian!"

"The male ego," teased Tamara, "crushed again."

"No such defeat today," said Scotty, "only victory!"

Scotty rolled down the driver's window as they drove slowly towards the point. He knew a fair bit about the park and told some funny camping stories. Tamara was slightly concerned to hear how Scotty and his childhood friend used to run behind a DDT spray machine. The truck rolled through the campgrounds every night. The foggy substance was used as a pesticide to kill off mosquitoes. Each night Scotty and his buddy would trail behind the fog, pretending to be ghosts.

A couple of miles from the point, Scotty pulled into a secluded spot where the car could be camouflaged by bushes and trees. He had stored a Mexican beach blanket in the trunk along with his knapsack and some picnic goodies. Tamara heard glass bottles tinkle and wondered if he had stored away some beer as well. She didn't drink and was hoping her driver was off alcohol.

"Let the expedition begin," said Scotty.

"Do you think we might see some monarchs today?"

"It's possible," said Scotty. "They won't be too sexy though."

"What do you mean?"

"Well, the ones that emerge in late August don't have the urge to reproduce. After all, they have to migrate. All their energy is dedicated to creating fat stores. Those reserves allow monarchs to make their journey across Lake Erie, down through the States, ending up somewhere in central Mexico. No energy for mating with that journey ahead."

"And how far is our journey?" laughed Tamara.

"We'll burn off some fat but it's a manageable hike. Every once in a while look up near the tree tops. Monarchs! When they close their wings they look a lot like dead leaves."

"Mr. Naturalist," said Tamara, "I'm impressed."

"This might impress you a little more," said Scotty reaching into his knapsack and pulling out a cream coloured, cotton kurta from India. He handed it to Tamara. "The bugs and branches can get nasty," said Scotty. "You may want to protect your delicate skin."

"Ha," Tamara said. "Just where does a red-headed Scot come up with a traditional kurta?"

Scotty looked at her for a moment and decided not to give a flippant answer. "Truth is," he said softly, "when my father died, I just wanted to smell him, as if he were still a presence with me. I went through his closet and picked out all his white, yellow, or cream coloured shirts. He used to wear this cologne called Aramis and his shirts had that lingering aroma. I took a pair of scissors and carefully cut the collars off each shirt. I never washed those shirts in case I would lose that scent."

"Didn't the aroma eventually evaporate?"

"I just wore a different one until all the shirts were all gone. It was Bishnu, over at the Himalayan, who picked up on what was happening. One day, when I went to the restaurant, he handed me a brown paper package tied with string. He told me not to open it until I got home. Later that evening, I opened the gift and found several neatly pressed, cotton kurta shirts. He included some small bottles of patchouli oil too. I had never encountered that scent before and quickly learned that, even when diluted, a little patchouli oil goes a long way."

"I know that scent very well," said Tamara. "I remember it as a slightly sweet, intoxicating aroma – very strong. At home it reminded me of wet soil, kind of like a musky-earthy smell."

Scotty nodded, strapped on the knapsack, and slung the blanket over his shoulder. He pointed the way forward. Tamara was grateful for the kurta shirt, which she slipped over her sleeveless dress. The day was getting humid and the mosquitoes were out. At one point, Scotty veered them off the trail and down to a sandy beach to their right.

Wooden picnic tables were spread out intermittently along the beach. Tamara was intrigued by the metal barbeque stations, used for burning charcoal and cooking outdoors. Large pieces of driftwood, like wooden sculptures, were strewn along the beach. The sand was warm and not too coarse. They removed their shoes and walked closer to where the waves met the beach.

The sounds of water and gulls mixed with fishy smells on a gentle breeze. Hardly anyone was around. The closer they got to the point, greenery faded away and Tamara took in an expanse of water that seemed ocean sized. She looked around, half expecting a park employee to stop them, or for signs posted about the swimming conditions that day. Nothing!

Scotty, who had been playing a combination of guide and raconteur, became noticeably quiet again. His eyes were fixed on a distant point where the two bodies of water converged. Tamara wasn't sure what urge she was feeling but, without giving it too much thought, she stepped beside Scotty and interlaced the fingers of her left hand with his right hand.

He didn't flinch. He didn't speak. They both kept walking in sync toward the tip. Tamara was well aware from her uncle's warnings that, as spectacular as the waters of Point Pelee could appear, they contained hidden dangers. She was told that the undertows and rip currents regularly swallowed family dogs eager to explore the waves. As she held tight to Scotty's hand, Tamara put her faith in this man's knowledge of what was and wasn't safe. He seemed calm enough but slightly entranced as if he was tracking something invisible to the eye.

When they neared the converging waters, Scotty's pace slowed down to a dreamlike cadence. Tamara flashed on those classic dreams where someone is being chased yet can only run in slow motion. Unspoken, they let their shoes drop onto the sand. Scotty slipped the knapsack off his shoulders and placed the beach blanket gently down. Walking several feet more, Tamara felt the cool waters envelop her ankles. They both stood on the edge of a special place and paused to take it all in.

Instantly, Tamara was transported back to the first time she visited Varanasi, in India. Before she entered adolescence, she and her parents made a sojourn to this sacred site. Varanasi holds great significance in the lives of India's 820-million-strong Hindu population. Located on the River Ganges in northeast India, this spiritual centre brings together history, religion, mythology and tradition. It is said that to die upon the banks of the Ganges is to be finally set free from the cycle of life, death and rebirth.

Tamara was caught up by the glittering environment of Varanasi. Vendors provided a staggering range of trinkets and offerings. These items were purchased by mourners as they headed toward the cremation sites on the shores of the river. Chains of flowers in vibrant reds, bright oranges, yellows and black hung from the stalls. Piles of incense sticks sat alongside mounds of candles. These candles would later float down Mother Ganga as friends and relatives bid farewell to a departed soul.

When Tamara arrived at Varanasi, it appeared to be a marketplace as much as a sacred site. The air was filled with jingling rhythms and mixed odours. It was densely populated by humans, cattle, and food. "Mother Ganga," whispered Tamara's father in quiet reverence as he guided his daughter toward the great waterway below. "She awaits."

Each evening the Ganga Aarti ceremony would be performed through prayers, offerings of fire and dance, and a ceremonial worship to the river. As a living being, Mother Ganga was praised for the life she sustains. The ceremony was a hypnotic display of synchronised, graceful movements. Despite its size and spectacle, the Ganga Aarti ceremony imparted a mood of intimacy to a young Tamara.

Only later, as she furthered her education, did Tamara appreciate how the Ganges River embodied a conundrum. On one hand, this 1,500-mile stretch of water was known to be one of the most polluted rivers in the entire world. Each day the river consumed billions of untreated sewage from the towns along its banks. At the same time, the river was believed to be sacred and was revered as a divine body of water. Despite the monumental health hazards that come with wading into infested waters, millions of individuals continued to practice the centuries-old rituals that honor Mother Ganga.

Tamara held these contradictions of science and the sacred as she stood with her feet in Lake Erie's waters. She recalled warnings about what happens if you swim in contaminated water. She knew polluted waters can cause gastrointestinal illness, skin, ear, respiratory, eye, neurologic, and wound infections. She also remembered how her world felt scintillatingly alive after her own immersion in the Ganges.

Whatever Scotty was feeling or thinking remained unspoken. He continued to gaze ahead at some point past the tip of the peninsula. He allowed the shallow water to lap around his feet. Then, without warning, Scotty reached his right arm out and wrapped it around Tamara's waist. She allowed herself to be drawn in closer. With her warm, pulsing body next to him, Scotty made some audible sighs that evolved into small sobs. His chest spasmed and tears ran down his cheek to the ebb and flow of watery sounds mixed with his own waves of emotion.

Pulling Tamara even closer, Scotty took one step and then another into the water. Tamara could feel the sandy foundation beneath her feet and the tugs and pulls of two different water bodies converging. She extended her left arm around Scotty's waist as they walked further into the rippling water.

When they waded up to their knees, Scotty released a mournful wail, like an injured animal. The sound bounced off the water and filled the air. She held him steady as he pulsed and convulsed. It was now her inclination to lead. Tamara guided Scotty even deeper into the surrounding waters until they were waist deep. The currents rocked them as if they were babies in a cradle. Scotty continued his heartbreaking lament. She had never heard a man heave and cry so deeply. The more he wailed, the more Tamara felt rooted and grounded in an unshakeable stance.

With her childhood steeped in Hinduism, Tamara was well acquainted with the belief that divinity is not limited to revered deities. The Great Mystery, however named, is present in all places and persons. The pulsing body of water and the sobbing body next to her were manifestations of a connected universe. Scotty was the murky swamp and the lotus flower opening. She remembered the Sanskrit phrase Nada Brahma. Her father explained that Nada Brahma meant the world is composed of vibration. Her responsibility was to stay fully present in the moment to the vibrational mix before her: waters, wounds, and wonderments.

There was no need to take away Scotty's pain or guide him onto safer ground. Instead, she began to hum. It wasn't a known mantra or a traditional puja to an entity. She hummed gently and, while doing so, placed one hand over Scotty's sobbing chest and the other hand on his spine. While Tamara hummed, she ushered Scotty even deeper into the waters until they were standing chest deep. The currents around them felt alive and protective rather than threatening. Scotty continued to mourn from deep inside his body. The sounds gradually took on more lyrical lines and shapes.

Tamara had spent time in Ireland and Scotland. To her musical ear, Scotty's vocalization reminded her of a ritual practice sometimes performed at a wake or graveside while kith and kin mourned the dead. She knew that the word keening came from the Gaelic word *caoineadh* meaning crying. On a few occasions, Tamara had heard the keening women (mnàthan-tuirim) pay their respects to the deceased and express grief on behalf of a bereaved family.

While Scotty keened, she hummed. After a while, Tamara took her right hand off his chest area and formed a cup with her palm. She reached down into the water. Like a priestess offering a holy rite, she poured water over Scotty's mangled red hair. It trickled down over his face, mingling with tears. Over and over again, she scooped water in her hand and let it tumble down over his hair, head, and chest.

Scotty rocked more gently now and his vocalizations shifted into longer, tender melodies – like someone playing legato phrases on a cello. She continued to hum with him. Their voices blended in the same organic way that the lake bodies intersected. They stayed in that space for an endless amount of time. The sun, now high in the sky, shone down upon them. Warm air enfolded them. Without a word spoken, they sensed when it was time to turn around and walk back to land. Unhurriedly, they waded away from the converging waters.

As they transitioned from lapping waves to sandy beach, something above caught their attention. Two monarch butterflies zigzagged in the air and headed out over Lake Erie – the migration of souls.

Scotty moved the blanket, knapsack, and shoes to a higher, drier area. Their clothes were soaking wet but the August heat began to promptly evaporate their soggy clothing. Exhausted, they lay on their backs, stretched out, faces to the sun. At some point, Scotty turned on his left side and Tamara cuddled him from behind. They drifted off to sleep like this.

When Tamara woke up, Scotty had already laid out some food on the blanket. The lids were removed from stainless steel containers to reveal dal makhani, chana masala, and kulcha, a type of mildly leavened flatbread. The clinking bottles came from one of her favorite drinks during childhood – nimbu pani, a lemonade beverage. Tamara momentarily wondered if Scotty had apprenticed at the Himalayan Restaurant or whether he simply pre-ordered the dishes.

They ate quietly, listening to the gulls, wind, and waves. Then, without hesitation, Tamara spoke. "In India, when a collective Sadhana is performed, a group of people sit together and pray for the sake of the departed souls. It brings peace not only to those who have departed but to all people and all things."

Scotty responded. "That's a beautiful practice. I certainly feel peaceful now, being here with you."

Tamara and Scotty stood up together. They could have held each other close, perhaps even kissed. Spontaneously, they touched forehead to forehead and closed their eyes for a few minutes. It felt as if the energies in and beyond their bodies were merging. The walk back to the car went faster. Scotty directed them along the park's main road. The Rambler, though parked in the shade, felt like a hot bakery inside. Thankfully, the heat dried up any last remnants of moisture in their clothes.

As they passed out of the park gates, heading back to Windsor, Tamara reached into her purse. Without a word of explanation, she pulled out a well-worn copy of the Bhagavad Gita. This 700-verse scripture is part of the epic Mahabharata. It is set in the literary style of a dialogue between Prince Arjuna and his charioteer, Krishna.

Tamara, without asking whether Scotty would like to hear a portion of the Gita, opened the book. She chose a section where Prince Arjuna is wrestling with despair. He knows that a battle against his own people will cause violence and death. Filled with this moral dilemma, the prince seeks Krishna's counsel. The discourse that ensues between Krishna and Arjuna constitutes the substance of the Bhagavad Gita. The guidance touches on matters far beyond war. Scotty revelled in the content as well as Tamara's poetic voice reading page after page. As they neared her uncle's home on Riverside Drive, Tamara concluded with this final passage:

"Show good will to all.
Be fearless and pure;
never waiver in your determination or
your dedication to the spiritual life.
Give freely. Be self-controlled,
sincere, truthful, loving,
and full of the desire to serve.

Realize the truth of the scriptures;
learn to be detached and to
take joy in renunciation.
Do not get angry or
harm any living creature,
but be compassionate and gentle;
show good will to all.

Cultivate vigor, patience, will and purity;
avoid malice and pride.
Then, Arjuna, you will achieve
your divine destiny."

CHAPTER 4

When UB turned sixteen years of age, the only gift he wanted was a private dinner with his parents. No presents. UB's father and mother sensed that their son wanted to share something highly personal. A good deal of care went into preparing the birthday meal and the setting.

Their family dinner table had always represented a place where UB's trials and tribulations could land safely. Here, his perspectives on people or events could be shared without hesitation. His opinions, however naïve or still forming, were respected. Since he was a child, UB's parents had always invited his say in family matters. He was intelligent and learned quickly to speak with the tone and vocabulary of an adult.

UB's parents, Will and Joan, loved their child. At the same time, they possessed an unlimited energy for their first passion – social change. UB knew he would always be cared for. At the same time, he also understood that the family's priority was what his parents called the *struggle*. They were dedicated to transforming cultural prejudices and narrow-mindedness. If he was bullied at school, those incidents became raw material for meetings with parents, teachers, and administrators. UB's skirmishes became less about one child and more about the wellbeing of all children.

UB's home life was not like other kids growing up. He didn't play sports, the family didn't go camping, and the television was only turned on for newsworthy events. Will and Joan were intensely focused on their roles and responsibilities within Windsor's Addiction Research Foundation. Both had graduated from the University of Windsor's Social Work Department and met at ARF. They fell in love, got married, and together tackled the ongoing bigotry, chauvinism, and injustices of the 1950s.

UB sensed that for all their hardships, his parents preferred their struggles over a more comfortable existence. Each night, they would fall asleep exhausted from the day's caseloads coupled with the many volunteer hours they offered to local causes. UB didn't ask for much as a child. He was happy to be loved and content to be respected.

Will prepared the main meal – a chicken breast wrapped in bacon complemented by a fresh salad, sautéed spinach, and a rice dish with vegetables. Joan concentrated her culinary skills on a triple layered chocolate cake. Before the sweet dessert was served, UB put down his utensils and asked his parents for their undivided attention. Each of them stopped eating and leaned forward to listen."I've given this matter a lot of thought. First, I want to give you some context. Do you remember Sister Sophia?"

"Yes," replied Joan. "She taught history and theory at the music school. We weren't surprised when she left the order. Sophia struck us as being more liberal than her peers."

"That's her," UB said. "I studied music history with her. I still use her material with students preparing for their conservatory exams. She had a big influence on me."

"How so?" asked Will.

"When I was getting into the history of composers, Sister Sophia shared facts about European or American composers that you wouldn't come across in standard textbooks. One day, when we were looking into the life of Händel, she told me that he socialized in circles in which homosexuality was practiced, secretively. Händel moved discreetly within the Italian and German courts, as well as among his peers in London. This wasn't stuff she dreamed up. She lent me this book called *Handel as Orpheus: Voice and Desire in the Chamber Cantatas.*"

"Händel never married, right?" asked UB's father.

"Never," said UB. "But Händel wasn't alone. Sister Sophia told me about Tchaikovsky. He wrote at length to his brother about his homosexuality. Tchaikovsky was afraid of challenging the conventions of his time. He could never live openly with a male partner. The closest Tchaikovsky came to revealing his sexual orientation was when he dedicated his Symphony No. 6, *the Pathétique,* to his lover Vladimir Davydov. Even to this day, a different biography is told in Tchaikovsky's homeland of Russia."

"I'm not surprised," said Joan.

"Sister Sophia never held back with me. She told me about Samuel Barber's relationship to his fellow composer, Gian Carlo Menotti. She pulled back the curtain on Benjamin Britten and his partnership with the tenor Peter Pears. One day the Sister talked about Leonard Bernstein. Apparently, Bernstein knew that orchestra boards wouldn't tolerate an openly gay music director. That's why he married Felicia Montealegre."

Will reached over and put his hand on UB's shoulder. He spoke kindly. "Hey son. If you look back, why do you think Sister Sophia shared these anecdotes with you?"

UB paused. He thoughtfully weighed what he was about to say next. "Sister Sophia was a lesbian. She left the convent because of that reason. And she could read people. I think she saw more than the student in me. She knew something back then that I hadn't admitted to myself."

"Which was?" asked his mother.

"That I'm gay. That I'm attracted to men."

UB's father and mother let the words register and were careful not to interject. Finally, Joan spoke. "Honey, you likely have figured out by now that we respect you as a person, first and foremost. What you may not have figured out is that your sexual orientation is something only you can work out. Our job is to act as a sounding board, a listening space, and a resource if that's what you need."

UB's father slipped away for a moment, went into their bedroom, and reappeared shortly with a binder. Will handed it over to UB without a word of explanation. Inside the binder were articles clipped from various newspapers, periodicals, and magazines. Each piece related to the emerging gay rights movement in North America.

"Your mother and I started collecting these articles when you were around twelve," explained Will. "Like the Sister, we had a sense of what might be in your stars and the battles that might come with that path."

Joan leaned over and turned to a page near the front, dated April 25, 1965. "This news story is about a group of 150 people who gathered at Dewey's restaurant in Philadelphia – a city that is supposed to be the city of brotherly love. The group participated in a sit-in because the manager of Dewey's refused to serve several individuals who he thought looked gay. The police showed up. Four people were arrested and convicted of disorderly conduct."

UB turned a few pages and scanned a clipping from the *New York Times*. It reported on gay activists staging a sip-in at a bar in New York City called Julius. The group was challenging a state liquor authority regulation prohibiting the serving of alcohol to homosexuals on the basis that they were known to be disorderly. The complaint to the liquor authority resulted in no action but New York's Human Rights Commission declared that such discrimination could not continue.

Clearly UB's parents had kept a watchful eye on debates, reactions, news articles, and stories related to gay rights. Long before their son talked openly to them, they had prepared for the combat ahead.

"Last year," said Will, "Pierre Trudeau was Minister of Justice. He introduced an Omnibus Bill to overhaul Canada's criminal laws. This Bill included the decriminalizing of homosexual acts. Trudeau told reporters that there's no place for the state in the bedrooms of the nation. He made it clear that what's done in private between two consenting adults doesn't concern the Criminal Code."

"That's when we did some volunteer work for the Liberal Party," added Joan.

"What we're trying to say," said Will, "is that our concern is not with who you choose to love or how you express your sexuality. Our concern is for the ways you will have to negotiate your personal choices within the narrow norms of society."

"I have been discreet," offered UB.

"That has its place," replied UB's mother. "As well, changing beliefs sometimes means challenging prejudices openly. We've been following this man, Frank Kameny. He was fired from his job as an astronomer for the Army Map Services. His dismissal had to do with homosexual behaviour. Kameny refused to go quietly. He openly fought his case, appealing it all the way to the U.S. Supreme Court. He's been a vocal leader of a growing movement. He and others are calling for a gay liberation movement, a united front to counter homophobia."

UB could feel where this conversation might head, especially with parents so deeply involved in what was called consciousness raising. To bring it down to something more personal than social, UB spoke up. "I've met someone. He's a few years older. He moved here from Venezuela. His name is Salvador. I call him Sal. He's studying composition at the university. We met at the WSO's summer camp for young musicians."

UB went on to describe how Sal won a scholarship to study in Canada. Complicating the story was the fact that Sal had to get out of Venezuela to save his life. Sal had become involved with the son of an army colonel. The Military Justice Code banned same-sex sexual activity. They came down heavy on those who knew of such relationships and did not report them. You could be imprisoned for one to three years. The army colonel, well aware of harassment and violence toward gay men, made it possible for Sal to leave Caracas.

Joan and Will suggested that UB invite Sal for dinner. That dinner happened, as did many subsequent meals. One of those gatherings included a fifth person, a young musician they were guiding through rehab. His name was Scotty.

By the time NADI formed as a band, the committed relationship between UB and Sal was obvious to everyone. No one ever uttered a derogatory term, such as fag or homo. If anything the circle grew tighter, maybe even protective of UB and Sal's partnership. On a few occasions, Nardello sensed some strain between his two bandmates and would speak up. "You two alright... you seem a little sensitive today? My folks love each other to bits but fight like crazy. Maybe, as a couple, you should do the same thing?"

When Tamara first met UB at the restaurant, she picked up on his orientation. What she didn't discern was the fact that Sal was UB's lover. Tamara didn't have an issue with same-sex partnerships. Homosexuality had been prevalent across the Indian subcontinent throughout history. It was only during the 18th century, when British colonial rule came to India, that homosexuals were considered inferior.

CHAPTER 5

When the band arrived for their first rehearsal with Tamara, several chairs had been set in a circle. A meeting was about to be called. Sure enough, before Nardello could tune his Telecaster, Coyote requested that they circle up. Coyote's agitated energy got everyone's attention. The circle formed without hesitation. "We need to figure something out. There's a big beef about our concert with the WSO."

"Does it concern me?" asked Tamara.

"Nope. More complicated. One of the symphony's sources of funding comes from a Christian congregation called The New Evangelical Church of Canada. The pastor's daughter plays oboe in the symphony."

Sal shook his head as if he could anticipate the troubles ahead.

"For the past several years, the pastor has leaned on his parishioners to become subscribers to the symphony. As well, the congregation holds fundraisers. That's all cool but, as the saying goes, money talks. This pastor has a lot of pull and, apparently, he has a problem with a concert that promotes rock music. He equates rock music with a moral corruption."

Nardello laughed. "He's got that right."

"Well," continued Coyote, "he's petitioning the symphony's board to yank the concert."

"And if they don't?" asked Sal.

"He's threatened to organize a protest, probably drawing on the flock from his church. They'd gather outside the Cleary Auditorium on the night of our event. They'd boycott the performance."

Nardello cut to the quick. "If an audience doesn't show, do we still get paid?"

"Yes," said Coyote. "But the point of the collaboration was to draw an audience of regulars mixed in with a younger crowd. If it's half full, that doesn't look good in terms of the press coverage we want."

"Windsor Rock Band Drives Away Classical Audience," said Nardello. "Not a bad headline for the *Star*."

"There's another matter in this scenario." Coyote looked directly at Sal and UB. "I'm not sure how the pastor got wind of your relationship. Maybe his snooping daughter was watching more than the music in front of her. Anyway, the pastor is raving on about homosexuality in our band. He's saying that the symphony, by hosting this concert, is condoning homosexuality – an aberration of God's natural laws."

Scotty spoke up. "Man, I don't care how much we're getting paid or how much press this gig generates. We've always stood by UB and Sal. They don't need more trouble. They don't need to put their relationship front and center. They don't need some fire and brimstone minister whipping up more homophobia. Let's just pull the plug and…"

"Play it safe?" Tamara finished Scotty's sentence. "What then? Nothing changes. The status quo remains the same."

At first Scotty went silent, but then found his voice. "Things aren't staying the same. The gay rights movement is getting stronger. The old guard feels it. That's why there's this controversy. The *Establishment* is pushing back. Sal and UB can tell you how, every day, they have to endure hassles from assholes living in the Dark Ages. That stuff can be draining."

Some in the circle could feel another debate surfacing, especially between Scotty and Tamara. As Scotty and Tamara got into it, no one really noticed that UB and Sal turned their heads, had a quick exchange, and voiced their perspective. "We're in," announced UB. "Sal and I are willing to play the gig, take the heat, and stand up for our rights."

"You realize this could get ugly," said Coyote.

"Ugly compared to what?" said UB. "My parents were part of the second march from Selma to Montgomery in '65. That was ugliness unleashed."

"Ay caramba!" shouted Sal. "Don't even get me started on crackdowns in Venezuela. This is Windsor. We're talking about a protest with a small group of church folk outside of the Cleary Auditorium. What could happen?"

"Don't underestimate what could come of this in a positive way too," said Tamara. "Gandhi taught us that you can profoundly shake the world in a gentle way."

"I know we could discuss this all night," broke in Coyote. "But we have a rehearsal to tackle. Let's get down to it. Does everybody agree to perform and roll with the consequences? Scotty... are you in?"

"As long as UB and Sal are up for it, I'm in all the way."

With that business settled, the band focused on their rehearsal. Initially, NADI's stage set up required adjustments. The Rhodes had to be moved over to make room for Tamara. Ron and Brian figured her electric violin sounded better plugged directly from the pedal board into the sound system. It took time to work out levels.

Undergirding all the logistical matters was the fact that a new player was coming aboard. She might disrupt the band's pre-existing mindset, how they intuited musical possibilities as a group. They were either going to include her influence or merely tolerate her as a tag on. She could become like a miniature hula dancer on a car's dashboard... pretty to look at but not essential to the journey.

Scotty appeared more agitated than anyone. He wanted this to work with Tamara. He also didn't want to sacrifice what NADI had developed as a band. He was not feeling neutral about including her. Once they were ready to go, Tamara didn't take a passive approach. She turned to the four musicians and confidently addressed them.

"I have a suggestion about how we might start. Since this is the first time we've played together, I can show you a technique for getting focused and relaxed at the same time."

Nardello teased her. "Does it involve inhaling?"

"It does indeed involve inhaling but exhaling too. It's the basis of Pranayama Yoga. Just think of it as a meditation practice."

Tamara read the band's mood. They seemed curious but also eager to get down to playing. Consequently, she gave them a simplified instruction. "Close your eyes or soften your gaze. We'll start by being silent.... Listen to each inhale and exhale. Anytime a distracting thought

51

pops up, observe it with no judgment. Just return to the breath. If your mind generates mental chatter, keep breathing and observing your thoughts... with detachment. You don't need to label thoughts as good or bad, just let them go. Relax, yet remain attentive. Keep breathing in an audible way, like the sound of waves lapping upon the shore."

Tamara was careful not to let her breathing meditation go on too long. After several minutes, she quietly drew her bow over the violin and produced a sustained droning sound. It was evocative, drenched in harmonics. She pressed her wah pedal down slightly. She added treatment to the overtones. The other players let her sound occupy center stage, without interference.

As Tamara shaped the drone, she flashed back to London and her first session with Dr. Nachmanovitch. When the dean at the Royal Academy of Music, heard about Tamara's trauma the appointment with Dr. Nachmanovitch was immediately booked. She was given an address in central London and told to bring her violin.

As both a psychologist and music therapist, Dr. Nachmanovitch specialized in working with orchestral musicians and opera singers. She saw individuals who suffered from anxiety, depression, mood swings, phonophobia, and more. Her Ph.D. thesis explored four main areas of the human brain affected by trauma: the hippocampus, the amygdala, the prefrontal cortex, and the brain stem.

During her decades of working with patients in private practice, Dr. Nachmanovitch developed a range of treatments for addressing post-traumatic stress disorder (PTSD). She recognized how a traumatized individual, when feeling threatened again, releases stress hormones such as cortisol and adrenalin. The body's muscles would tense up and the individual would go back into a fight, flight, or freeze response.

Dr. Nachmanovitch's relaxation response techniques were proven to help address the physiological manifestations of prolonged stress. *The British Medical Journal* had published her findings related to the health benefits of guided relaxation: lowering heart rates, affecting blood pressure, and reducing muscle tension as well as chronic pain.

Tamara's reason for seeing Dr. Nachmanovitch began during her first year at the prestigious Royal Academy of Music. When Tamara auditioned for entrance into the Academy, she performed several prepared pieces before a panel of adjudicators. She also had to sight read sections from various orchestral and ensemble compositions. The Academy was especially tough on international students. The institutional standards were rigorous, the musical competition was fierce, and the cultural makeup of the school was not diverse.

Despite an inbuilt bias toward British students, Tamara received candid and constructive feedback from almost all the adjudicators. The exception was Professor Simon Bell. While it was never said out loud, every panelist knew that Tamara would be an exceptional asset to the Academy. She already possessed an ability to concertize as a young soloist and not merely occupy a chair in an orchestra's string section. The panel head, therefore, was surprised when Simon spoke up with a critical tone.

"Past all your flourish and flare, I'm not convinced that your technique is embedded in the type of sound most European orchestras want. From where I sit, you would require additional mentoring above and beyond the school's workload. As head of the Academy's String Program, I recommend that Miss Chandra be accepted only on a probationary basis. I am willing to take on the additional tutoring, assess her development, and report back to this grouping."

From those unchallenged words, the premise was established for Simon Bell to enter Tamara's life. Little did anyone on the panel know that he was scheming to be more predator than mentor. Simon's methodology, which he had refined from stalking previous students, began by breaking down Tamara's confidence in her musicianship. Behind closed doors, Simon was highly attentive but emotionally distant in his initial sessions. He would require Tamara to perform pieces that would emphasize emotional expression over violin technique.

In one early session, Simon handed her the second movement from Tchaikovsky's Violin Concerto. This concerto was completed in 1878 when the composer was recovering from a broken marriage and another bout of depression. The Andante movement fluctuates from light passages to darkness. It eventually emphasizes hope. Simon asked Tamara to play it with meaning and feeling. Tamara knew this movement well and didn't need to struggle with phrasing and technical issues. She poured her heart into a rendition beyond her tender years.

Simon didn't say anything when she was finished. After a prolonged silence, he spoke gently. "I was not moved by your interpretation. You played it correctly. I grant you that. However, music must be comprised of more than notes played in tune or phrases performed accurately. We must examine why you were unable to bring sentiment and subjectivity into your interpretation."

Tamara listened respectfully as she knew her continued studies at the Academy rested in the hands of Professor Bell. "I want to be careful with my words," he continued. "You have come to this school as a young person. I want to take into account that, perhaps, you are yet tender in life experience. Imagine this... Tchaikovsky wrote this movement from a place of suffering. His heart had been broken. The music, thorough and well-crafted, confesses a series of emotions. How are you able to lift those feelings off the page and onto the air?"

Tamara, usually assertive and confident in her exchanges with men, chose not to reply in that moment. Simon rose out of his chair and placed a warm hand on Tamara's shoulder. He continued. "Trust me. Over time, as you mature, your sensual nature will awaken. If you are so lucky, romantic energies may flood your body and probably confuse your mind. If it is meant to be, you may encounter the wild passions that caused great composers to channel erotic sensations into sublime works of art."

Simon ended the session by taking the violin concerto off the music stand and putting it into his leather satchel. "When I was around your age, I came to understand the depth of this work through suffering. My one and only fiancée left me for another man. I was crushed. I was unable to perform this piece for years. When I finally performed the concerto for the first time in public, I could feel the audience welling up. They were weeping with me as I shared my suffering."

Tamara left that first session feeling flat. As a child, her family constantly teased her for being such an emotional creature. In a single hour, she could pass through extreme sentiments, temperaments, and excitements. Her father constantly repeated a phrase from the Gita: *In joys not overjoyed and in sorrows not dejected.*

Subsequent coaching sessions with Simon continued to be less about her violin technique. Tamara was puzzled by this departure since his initial observation, and objection to her Academy entrance, had to do with her technique not being firmly rooted in the type of sound most European orchestras wanted.

In the next session with Simon, he stated that they would concentrate on a body-centered technique of playing. "If you observe great conductors or gifted soloists," said Simon, "you might note that the artistic beauty they produce is always intertwined with their body. At the risk of sounding prejudicial, I have noted how Asian violinists stand rigidly while performing the most ardent music. I don't know much about Indian performers in general but I have observed you. It's as if you have disconnected your musical self from your physical nature. If the muscles of your body are taut and tense, how can you release the sensual qualities of sound?"

Simon asked Tamara to put down her instrument and stand in the center of the practice room. Pulling an LP from his satchel, Simon walked over to the record player that sat in one corner of the space. He explained that he was about to play a recording of Richard Strauss's *Salomé – Dance of The Seven Veils.* Simon asked Tamara to close her eyes.

"I want you to imagine that you are a not a violinist but a dancer. This composition contains an eroticism of music that arouses the body. As you lose yourself in the piece, you will feel the rise and fall of distinct elements. I want you to embody the embellishments of melody, the quickening of pace, and Strauss's growing excitement through his compositional techniques. He gives us a timed crescendo."

Tamara, in privacy, had regularly moved to music. She freely improvised twists, turns, dips, and dives according to the fantasies the music inspired. Dancing for another person, and a professor at that, was strange. Nonetheless, when the needle hissed and dropped into *Salomé,* her body brought forth all the movement vocabulary she had absorbed from years of participating in the Kathak form of classical dance.

Tamara forgot about Simon being in the room and allowed herself to move without inhibition. When the piece finished, she surfaced from some entranced place. Her heart was beating and her body was sweating with energy. It took her a moment to get her bearings. When she came into focus, Tamara was shocked to find that Simon was no longer in the room. She did not hear him leave. Bewildered, she packed up her instrument and left.

A week later, Simon's bizarre methods of breaking her down came to a peak. Simon listened to Tamara play a few warm-up scales and then asked her to put down the violin. Under the pretense that the tension in Tamara's bowing wrist originated elsewhere, he commanded her to face away from him and play an invisible violin.

Within seconds of her complying, Simon forced her up against the practice room wall. She felt him fondle her breasts while he dropped his pants. He was masturbating while trying to lift her skirt. Tamara's momentary confusion quickly dissipated. From deep within her body she discharged a series of primal screams. Despite absorbing tiles and baffles in the practice room, Tamara's shrieks were well heard throughout the adjacent hallway. Several teachers and students rushed to help her. They arrived in time to see Simon Bell trying to get his pants on with one hand while simultaneously attempting to smother Tamara's mouth. The bite she delivered to Simon's hand took several stitches to close.

During the subsequent investigation and trial, Simon's lawyer asked about intimate touching and at what point did they initiate petting. Tamara was repulsed by the term petting and made it known. The verb framed her as an animal and minimalized the severity of Simon's actions. She didn't hold back either in letting the lawyer know that touch was never reciprocal. Tamara never engaged in any form of mutual caressing. It was always a one-way activity on Simon's part. He had tried several times to induce sexual responses from her by inappropriate comments and physical touches. These gestures were consistently presented as ways to awaken her maturity as a woman.

Simon was found guilty of sexual assault. The sentence he received did not decrease Tamara's level of trauma. Once an outgoing person and passionate student, Tamara now felt numb. She grew detached from her peers. With male teachers, she could get overwhelmed with feelings of distress. Sometimes she would suffer from nausea, sweating, and a pounding heart. Nightmares invaded her sleep cycle. Her interest in daily activities and studies got to a point where she considered leaving the school. When the dean of the academy heard of the potential loss of a star student, coupled with the scandalous press around Simon's trial, she intervened. Tamara, like it or not, was sent to Dr. Nachmanovitch. By that time she could barely hold a violin bow without shaking.

After an introductory consultation, Dr. Nachmanovitch asked if Tamara would try a relaxation technique. It was the first in a series of trust building exchanges between the two women. The exercise was straightforward enough. Tamara lay on her back and let the carpeted floor take all her weight. Her tight leg muscles, through a series of visualizations and guided instructions, eventually felt longer, softer, and more flexible.

The next visualization entailed Tamara being able to pan in and pan out from her traumatic memories. The goal was to help her become more of an observer and less drawn into the flashbacks. As a visual aid, to help her shift from the general to the specific, Tamara tried to imagine the EQ knob on her electric violin pedal. By turning that knob, she could boost the highs or mids in her sound as well as make the EQ flat. As the doctor facilitated visualization, Tamara used her right hand in the air. She envisioned being able to dial up or down distinct EQ features – intensity, contrast, tone, colour, or compression. Next, relative to her memories, she could return to the scene of the crime, or not. Tamara could increase or decrease the range of sensitivity to her recollections. As needed, she could access a fine focus or broad view of her traumatic experiences.

In her next session with the therapist, Tamara was asked to hold her instrument while Dr. Nachmanovitch observed her. She could feel flashes of Simon's technique, when he would lay his eyes all over her. As if to bring her back into the room and into her body, Dr. Nachmanovitch asked Tamara to slowly bow a single string. As a proficient musician, this seemed strange and elementary. The only instruction was to select one of the four strings and maintain a continuous sound. Tamara chose the lowest string, the open G.

As Tamara held the single note, Dr. Nachmanovitch asked the violinist to synchronize her breathing with holding the long note.

Tamara closed her eyes. She paid attention to her belly region. With each inhalation and exhalation, she watched her diaphragmatic muscles expand and contract. "In your mind's eye," said Dr. Nachmanovitch, "see if you can envision a duet between muscles and music. As your sound becomes more relaxed, allow any tension to soften. Feel a kind of melting in the shoulders, arm, wrist, or even the back of your legs. As tension diminishes, it is replaced by an abiding strength."

Tamara could feel herself inhabiting her body again. It was as if she had been living outside of herself. The quiet sound was coaxing her down back into her body. Her skin, breath, blood, and total being, became coordinated once more.

Twice a week, for four months, Tamara faithfully took the London Underground to Dr. Nachmanovitch's office. The sessions blended talk therapy, body-centered movement, visualizations, music therapy, and a practice called Mindfulness for Stress Reduction that was being developed at the University of Massachusetts.

At times the process spun Tamara into dark moods, but the tools of self-awareness – such as noticing clouds rolling in and out – enabled her to stay present. Oddly enough, her musical technique returned faster than her emotional resilience. After her second month of working with the therapist, Tamara was playing advanced pieces again.

In addition to her classical studies, Tamara met up with some London art students who jammed regularly at a Covent Garden pub. They invited her to play anytime she wanted. Although the players brought more exploration than expertise on their instruments, she loved their freedom. As one of the guitarists was fond of saying, "One chord is fine. Two chords and you're pushing it. Three chords and you're into jazz."

Dr. Nachmanovitch always spoke frankly with Tamara. She encouraged Tamara to drop the idea of getting over this traumatizing incident. "You will carry a scar with you for all your days. Over time, it will be less of a gaping wound. Rawness will be replaced by an abiding sensitivity – tender to the touch. It's probably best to not think of healing as banishing the pain, but rather working toward gaining abilities that will help you hold your suffering skillfully."

Silence
Breathing
Bowing
Listening
Noticing
Suspending judgment

How long had Tamara traveled back in time? Could all those memories be condensed into a few seconds? Tamara opened her eyes and returned to Sotto Voce where she was still shaping one long note with her wah pedal. Tamara had no sense as to how much time had passed.

Sal was the first to respond to Tamara's drone. Sal owned different types of tambourines and was currently studying a South Indian type of tambourine called a kanjira. The instrument consisted of a circular frame made from the jackfruit tree. The frame had a single slit which held two small metal discs that had been fashioned from old coins. His teacher, Natarajan Kumar, owned several kanjiras that used lizard skin as the drumhead. Currently, lizard skin had been prohibited worldwide in order to protect the species. Sal's instrument used goat skin as an alternative.

Although Sal's ability on the kanjira was still evolving, he possessed a wide range of rhythmical possibilities from his studies of world percussion. In the free-form context of NADI, Sal wasn't hemmed in by classical or folkloric traditions. For this reason, he could reference sounds and rhythms that Tamara recognized from Indian styles of playing. Sal was capable of delivering these patterns with more of an experimental energy than a faithfulness to tradition. As he listened to Tamara, his intention was to put into practice a principle he heard from Miles Davis: When the band goes fast, I go slow. When they go slow, I play fast.

Since Tamara was playing one note, suspended and sustained in the air, Sal opted to percolate underneath. He wanted to imply forward motion. It worked well and, for a number of minutes, the rest of NADI sat out, allowing the duet to hold contrasts between a calming drone and the kanjira's excitement.

Scotty eventually added harmonic qualities on the Fender Rhodes. He was careful not to hem in the emerging soundscape. He stayed clear of familiar chord progressions. Instead he dropped in clustered notes that sometimes rang out and other times jabbed like Muhammad Ali in the ring. Tamara continued her fidelity to one note but incorporated a few rhythmical elements, acknowledging the movement underneath her sound.

UB was at an advantage. The Hammond organ was no longer needed as a drone instrument and so he brought his volume down to a barely audible level and approached the keyboard like a watercolour artist. His hands stayed away from scales and opted for swells that rose higher and lower, sometimes highlighted by increased or decreased volume.

Nardello had been holding back, laying out. He anticipated that his guitar input could inspire Tamara to shift from drone to direction. Nardello entered with a lyrical line that slithered down from a higher register, rose slightly, and then rested on Tamara's fundamental note. He repeated the phrase several times.

Tamara absorbed the shape of Nardello's riff. As the guitarist was about to repeat the line for the ninth time, Tamara joined him in perfect unison. They played together flawlessly until Tamara suddenly rose a third interval above Nardello's melodic line. From time to time she would introduce a variation. This caused Nardello to answer in response with a departure from the original phrase.

As the complexity developed, Sal switched from his singular kanjira and entered with new rhythmical material exploding from his hybrid drum kit. The band cooked.

UB, who often took a supportive part in NADI, made an uncharacteristic shift. As if he were a gospel singer suddenly touched by the spirit, he took off and soared with a virtuosic sermon. Using the full range of his keyboard he cajoled, preached, screamed. He held a series of notes and let the Leslie speaker whirl like a Sufi dancer. Never one to solo in the usual sense of the term, UB seized the moment.

The band growled and grooved. Intersecting patterns shifted, settled, disappeared, and emerged with fresh ideas. When UB was clearly finished, Sal cracked a rimshot on his snare and the band's dynamics instantly went from ecstatic to nuanced.

Scotty felt summoned by this transition. Leaving the Rhodes, he picked up his trumpet and stepped up to the nearby microphone. Scotty had always preferred a mid-range style of playing and avoided screaming or screeching textures on the horn. In the more hushed space the band was generating, Scotty took his horn way down into the darker, lower register.

Deliberately restraining his choices, Scotty limited his melodic options to four notes. He played them in different combinations, incorporating plenty of spaces. Risking the possibility of sounding monotonous, he didn't branch out beyond the four notes. Instead, he sought endless ways of working within limits. The band got even quieter. Out of the more spare and softer improvisation, the band heard an unusual sound. At first it wasn't clear as to what instrument was producing it. All ears turned to Scotty who, it seemed, was producing chords on his horn.

Most of the musicians in NADI were familiar with the American jazz improvisor, Rahsaan Roland Kirk. On stage, as a multi-instrumentalist, Rahsaan could play two and sometimes three instruments simultaneously. One of his techniques was to hum or sing into a woodwind instrument, such as a flute or sax, and thereby produce multiphonics.

No one in the band had ever heard a trumpet player tackle this sound. Scotty had never experimented with multiphonics in rehearsals or performances. Here he was, actually singing a note at a different frequency than the note he was playing on the horn. Several new notes emerged from this interaction. Scotty produced guttural growls and chordal clusters.

The band's reaction was to bring their volume down even more, as if they were playing without amplification. Scotty took advantage of this Zen space. He shaped tonal textures that were half breath combined with valves only partially pushed down. They watched as Scotty moved the Shure microphone right into the trumpet's bell. Pursing his lips in a more exaggerated way, like someone sucking on a lemon, Scotty produced notes so high that they resembled someone whistling softly.

When Scotty put down his horn, Sal cracked his rimshot again and NADI telepathically shifted to a dynamic that had no guitar, no horn, and no piano in the mix. UB held a droning texture that he would alter with the draw bars on his Hammond. Sal put down his drumsticks and used his hands to sketch out rhythmical patterns on anything with a drumhead. His fingers moved in a childlike manner – skipping, pausing, and scampering.

While Sal was well into his rhythmical exploration, Tamara put down her electric violin. She walked off the stage and over to the case where she kept her acoustic instrument. Gracefully, she took out the bow and her beloved violin. As Tamara walked back to the stage with her instrument, she swooped down and picked up a cushion from a nearby chair. Sal was still percolating away when she placed the cushion on the floor. She brought the violin not to her neck – the classical way of holding the instrument – but placed the violin against her shoulder. The neck dipped down toward the earth.

Ron, the sound man, grabbed one of the microphones on a boom stand and moved it closer to Tamara, being careful not to interfere with her playing space. Without drawing attention to herself, she brought the violin into tune and waited for an entry point. Sal's eyes were half-closed but he sensed that Tamara was wanting to engage with his rhythmical phrases. Without a word spoken or a gesture indicated, Sal cut his time in half giving room for Tamara to find a way in.

While the band had heard several jazz and rock violinists on re-cordings, no one in the group had ever heard the instrument played in a classical Indian style – in this case evoking melodies based in Raga Bihag. The initial aesthetics seemed like a woman singing but then took on the qualities of a sitarist, gliding from note to note. Graceful embellishments emerged. The ornamentations never detracted from a vocal quality.

Scotty and Nardello stayed out of the way. They let the trio of drone, rhythm, and soloist remain up front. Sal had not studied the talas of India but used his rhythmical sensibilities to match moods and modes pouring out of Tamara. Sometimes she would swing the tempo or her attacks would become more staccato. They performed as if they had played together for years.

At a certain point, Nardello picked up on a rhythmical phrase that Sal was repeating. Using one string, Nardello created a little riff that periodically drifted to a semi-tone above or below the drone, enough to add a little tension. Hearing what was emerging, Tamara joined in on violin and began to switch out of her classical style.

Nardello suddenly reached into his pocket and pulled out a small, metal tube. Slide guitarists used this version, or a bottle neck design, to produce an evocative singing quality. Nardello glided up and down the Telecaster fretboard as if he was a blues guitarist figuring out how to play a sitar for the first time. Tamara gradually faded out to give Nardello a wider field to explore.

The more they played the more everyone realized that the old NADI mold had been shattered. As a group, they had followed an unchallenged allegiance to playing layered sounds. Improvising as a unit was their ethic. Soloing didn't happen much. As a result, NADI developed a collective sound that rarely featured how an individual could wander within the whole or forget about the whole entirely.

When Nardello practised at home, he didn't have a group to vibe off. Instead, he would put on recordings of anything handy. Rock, jazz, blues, world music; it didn't matter. Whatever came through his inexpensive record player became a setting for untamed explorations. As a result, Nardello developed a private style of storytelling on his guitar that the rest of the band rarely heard... until now.

Nardello didn't socialize a lot. He didn't date anyone. He liked getting high from time to time. Music was his outlet for feelings that he couldn't put into words. His capacity for creativity was well exercised from practising at home. He had, as it's said in musical circles, CHOPS.

Now, having the space and permission to solo, Nardello transformed from a wise-cracking and laid-back individual to someone leading the charge into battle. He was Krishna with Arjuna. Out from his modest Fender amp, Nardello summoned gritty lines, scorching feedback, dissonant chords, and blazing guitar licks. He became a shapeshifter, changing from one genre to another as if to say... I can't be pinned down.

The band dropped out completely and gave Nardello room to swoop, soar, crash, burn, and rise again. Finally, they couldn't stay neutral. Rooted by Sal, the ensemble dug into a groove that didn't waver. Parts combined, like something from Sly and the Family Stone. Even Tamara's violin contribution came across as if she had been schooled by George Clinton's Funkadelic.

Who knows why? Maybe he was obsessive. Maybe he liked picking things apart. Maybe he hated stocking those goddamn shelves. For whatever reason, Nardello had done the grunt work. Behind his bedroom door, he had studied scales, chords, intervals, rhythms, and riffs. While the family was taking care of business, Nardello was screeching, wanking, and sometimes exploding one note like a punk who didn't know the first thing about music. He got the nouns and verbs down well. He also figured out gerunds, predicates, participles, appositives, modifying phrases, and non-restrictive clauses. Nardello knew his shit.

Up until that moment of glory, Nardello would have been described as a team player guitarist. He could support; he could complement; he could contrast and he could contribute. What the band had not heard was the undeniable fact that Nardello could kick ass. The bedroom door was flung open and Nardello was exposing what he had been doing during all those hours of dive bombing over tracks of southern blues, African drums, Gregorian chants, and psychedelic noise. He had been crafting a way of making his guitar speak pure Nardello. Blondie could be sexy, sleazy, slinky, or scary. She could be anything Nardello wanted because he had meticulously stacked the jars, cans, and containers in his exotic shop of musical delights.

With no audience witnessing, NADI became a new band that night.

CHAPTER 6

G rowing up next to the Motor City, Scotty followed the Detroit Tigers. From Windsor, you could pull in ball games on your transistor radio, broadcasted live from WJR. Scotty liked Ray Lane delivering his play-by-play broadcasts. The announcer could put you to sleep with a matter-of-fact, monotone commentary but then set your heart racing when something dramatic happened. Usually those adrenaline moments involved the Tigers' heavy-hitting-number-six-right fielder, Al Kaline.

Scotty adored Al Kaline's myth. It wasn't just a story of someone growing up poor and becoming a baseball legend. It was a tale of someone overcoming obstacles. When Al was eight years old, he developed an infection in the bone of his left foot called osteomyelitis. The subsequent surgery, which entailed removing a segment of bone, resulted in a permanent deformity. Undeterred, Al Kaline developed the ability to pitch a mean fastball, changeup, and curveball – all by the age of nine. As an 18-year-old, he bypassed the minor league system and joined the Tigers directly out of high school.

At the age of 20, Al Kaline held a .340 batting average, becoming the youngest player ever to win the American League batting title – a record previously held by Ty Cobb in 1907. In his 1955 season, Al Kaline hit two home runs in the same inning, hit three home runs in one game, and finished the year with 27 home runs. In 1955 he was selected to the Major League Baseball All-Star Game, the first in a string of consecutive All-Star selections that lasted through 1967. He missed 1968.

Al Kaline was consistently cool under pressure but, in the summer of 1967, Number Six lost it. In a moment of rage, the normally calm player broke a bone in his hand when he smashed a baseball bat against the bat rack. That act caused Al to miss a month of play. Then, in the 1968 season, Al Kaline missed two months of the season due to another injury, a broken arm.

When Al returned to the lineup, the Tigers manager benched the shortstop and sent their center fielder in to substitute as a shortstop. This shuffle made room for Al Kaline to get in the game as an outfielder. The Tigers were down against the St. Louis Cardinals. It was the 1968 World Series. The Cardinals had won three of the first four games against the Tigers. When Game 5 rolled around, the Tigers trailed the Cardinals by a score of 3–2 in the seventh inning. In that moment, with his deformed foot and broken bones, Al Kaline stepped to the plate. He hit a bases-loaded single to drive in two game-changing runs. The Tigers won that game, and the following two, to take their first world championship since 1945.

Everyone needs a hero. For Scotty, and millions of other kids in the Windsor-Detroit area, Al Kaline proved that miracles could happen when the chips were down.

On that August afternoon in 1968, the chips were down for NADI. They needed a miracle, badly. The equivalent, in baseball, is called a hotbox. It occurs when a baserunner is stranded between two bases. A classic scene happens when the runner is trying to make it to home plate but is caught between the catcher and the third baseman. In this trap, the runner may attempt to return to his previous base or home plate. The opposing team players, the catcher and third baseman, keep tossing the ball past the runner, forcing him to reverse directions again and again. This gets repeated until the runner is tagged out or reaches a base safely.

Coyote had been caught in a hotbox.

The bikers and dealers in Windsor didn't hassle small-time guys who scored some extra dope and sold it for a slight markup to their friends. Coyote wasn't even considered a pusher, more of a distributor of weed and some acid. He occupied a small sliver within a large pie. What changed the game was a sting. Bones, a known doper, asked Coyote to supply a larger than normal amount of weed.

"It's for a big party, dude."

Coyote pulled the order together but, when he showed up to deliver, found himself caught between a third baseman and a catcher, both playing for team Satan's Choice. The bikers could have tagged Coyote hard but made a deal instead. They allowed Coyote to get off with a warning and an agreement to get out of the growing-har-vesting-selling side of the dope business. In exchange they wanted something.

A moratorium – or possibly a recruitment campaign – was shaping up between Windsor's bike clubs: The Choice, The Vagabonds, The Lobos, The Nomads, The Queensmen, and The Outlaws. Knowing Coyote's ability to make things happen, the bikers wanted him to organize all the details of a bikers gathering. They wanted him to do the impossible – to bring individual bikers and clubs together, most of whom were staking out turf, not seeking truce.

With the "Choice," there was no choice.

"You got me guys. I'm cool with winding down and closing up shop. The other matter of calling the troops together is not easy. How many people are we talking about?"

"A couple of hundred," said Billie. "How many can your space hold?"

"Half that amount," said Coyote. "My club won't work. Besides, we're right on Tecumseh Road. The cops would spot all those choppers lined up and would be all over you like flies on shit. You need a place far away from the fuzz. I might have the perfect spot for you. It's near Kingsville. There's a barn where you could have the meeting and there's a farmer's field where you can party."

"At no cost, right?"

"Complements of Coyote, at your service. We have to do it soon, though; I've got some big things in the works for the band."

"Oh yeah," one biker said. "We want music at the gathering and we want your band... also for free."

"No way man," said Coyote. "Those guys don't travel light and, besides, there's no power in a farmer's field."

"Get a generator or two," said the second biker. "Make it happen and make it happen soon."

As abruptly as the conversation started, it ended. The bikers were not interested in small talk.

Coyote was well-connected in the biking community – if you could call it a community. He rode an overhauled 4-stroke Norton bike that he personally maintained. Coyote wore a patch on his jacket that declared he was a 99%er, the opposite of a 1%er. He had no affiliation with a club. That solo choice was respected at certain times. It could also be considered antagonistic, depending on the mood of the moment.

Within two weeks, Coyote had organized the biker meet as if he was orchestrating a performance. A partner in Coyote's grass-growing operation provided the barn to be used for all the club presidents and their crew. No one really knew whether the clubs were negotiating, settling scores, drawing territorial lines, or sharing assets. To accommodate all possibilities, Coyote put banquet tables in the middle of the barn, along with folding chairs.

Two pig troughs were set outside of the barn. On the party night they would be filled with ice and beer. The generators were noisy and so Coyote ran long extension cords to the makeshift stage to designate where the band would set up.

As for the band, they did not openly embrace the invitation to play outside, especially for a mob of bikers. In the end, it was more of an insistence than an invitation. Coyote had to come clean with everyone about his sideline business of selling weed. Coyote's distribution business was not the problem. The guys just couldn't understand why NADI had to get involved. There were plenty of rock bands, blues bands, and even freak music bands who would gig for free. Biker parties meant free booze or anything else you desired.

"They want you guys," said Coyote. "My ass is on the line and the music bit is non-negotiable."

Rather than lug around a Hammond organ and Leslie speaker cabinet, the roadies rented a Farfisa organ for UB. The Italian manufacturer began making electric organs in 1964. Distribution in the U.S. was handled by the Chicago Musical Instrument Company, which also owned Gibson. In terms of transportation, the Compact series came with integrated legs, which could be folded up and stored inside its base. UB already knew that Farfisa sound from listening to Spooner Oldham, the house organist at the Muscle Shoals Sound Studio. He heard Spooner on southern soul hits, notably "When a Man Loves a Woman," by Percy Sledge. When Sly Stone switched over to a Farfisa organ, UB was convinced.

Sal was fine with using a standard drum kit but skittish about playing the gig. Scotty was the least resistant about playing for bikers, he knew a number of them. His bigger concern had more to do with lapsing back into his addiction. In all fairness to the group, he promised to do the gig if Father Jaggs gave him the green light.

The exception in the group was Nardello. He was like a horse in a paddock, pawing the ground and wanting to get out into that farmer's field to rock it. Some fierceness had burst forth from the NADI rehearsal. Nardello wanted to get more of that wildness out.

The band did agree on one matter. Tamara was NOT invited to this party.

With the logistics worked out, Ron and Brian arranged a transport van to haul a smaller sound system, some general lights, another backup generator, and the rest of the gear. Scotty decided to leave his trumpet at home as just the appearance of a brass instrument in a bikers' meet would put the group at a disadvantage before a note was struck.

Two days before the gathering, Scotty received an afternoon call from Coyote. "Bad news buddy," said Coyote.

"You're becoming proficient in delivering bad news my man."

"Nardello's gone missing."

"As in disappeared?"

"For five days," said Coyote. "Remember the first time this happened? His folks phoned everyone Nardello knew looking for him."

"The guy hardly goes anywhere," said Scotty. "He bounces between his bedroom and the club. I hate to say it but... does this involve any of the biker clubs?"

"I had the same question," said Coyote. "I checked with all the players in that scene. Hardly anyone knows who Nardello is. I had to explain that he's a guitar player in our band."

"Did he hang out with anyone... have a secret girlfriend?"

"Nah," said Coyote. "The guy loved his guitar more than anything or anyone."

"Alright," said Scotty, "let's assume that Nardello is temporarily out of commission, for whatever reason... what then? I can't imagine you telling the bikers that we can't play."

"Oh, we gotta play. No doubt about it," said Coyote. "I had to find a replacement quick so I checked with Shapiro to see if he would sub in."

"Good choice," agreed Scotty. "He can cut all that psychedelic guitar but that means we better play some songs... Cream, Hendrix, Traffic, and definitely Steppenwolf."

"Brush up on your lyrics," said Coyote. "Once the party gets jumping, no one is going to be too picky about tunes. Choose some good ones for the first set and then some that are good for jamming. Shapiro said he'll bring a bass player too."

"Like who?"

"Gilmour," said Coyote. "Gordy's great for stretching out."

"The best... want me to prep Sal and UB?"

"Yeah," said Coyote. "That would be good. I'm going to shake some trees to try and find Nardello. And these aren't the most friendly trees in a rainbow forest, either! So, if you don't hear from me by tomorrow, better send out a search party."

"You move in territory far from my little world. There's underground and then there's *underworld,*" said Scotty. "I only know the top layer. Be safe."

Coyote survived the ordeal and in the late afternoon of the gig, everyone showed up at Sotto Voce to consolidate gear, grab some pizza, and head out to Kingsville. The band stressed about Nardello while chowing down the pizza. On the ride out to the site, talk turned more to possible songs for the night. Shapiro and Gilmour were working musicians and knew a ton of material. Chord changes were sketched out, lyrics were recalled, and three set lists were drawn up.

During sound check, the Farfisa sounded like shit. The generator's current was uneven. The fluctuations weren't so noticeable in the amps or the sound system but, as the power waned and waxed, the organ's notes would go flat or sharp. The wavy sound creating an illusion of being at sea. Ron and Brian had the foresight to pack the Rhodes and so UB had a backup keyboard that wasn't affected. He prayed that the Farfisa would kick in and hold steady for those Stevie Winwood tunes. And, UB couldn't imagine "Magic Carpet Ride" without the organ.

In between the barn and an outhouse sat an abandoned yellow

school bus. Coyote set the band up in the back with some kerosene lanterns, snacks and a cooler of beer. The bikers left them alone for the most part. A few biker chicks snuck in the front, lit a joint, got high, and left.

The first set sounded decent enough for playing outside. Unlike the club crowd, the bikers and their babes didn't dance and didn't seem all that interested in a 32-bar guitar solo over a blues shuffle in E minor. They drank, smoked, talked, showed each other their choppers, laughed, and threw anything wooden onto a bonfire. They pissed on the fire too.

During the second set, the drugs kicked in and the bikers got into the music the way crowds at the Midway love garish colours and background noises. When all the senses blended together, the band's meticulous crafting was just a big cotton candy treat to the stoned-out bikers. The odd person would shout out a request to play a Rolling Stones song and the band would respond each time with "Satisfaction."

The third and final set was about to begin when the president of the Satan's Choice Club wandered over to where Coyote was talking with the band about what songs they were going to play next. The club leader had about a dozen guys with him and each one was wasted.

"Heeeyy Coyote," said the Prez, "Fucking great party man."

"No problem," said Coyote, "just helping some friends have a good time."

"Yeaaahhh, we wanna show our appreciation."

With that, the Prez and his posse picked Coyote up by his arms and legs. He looked like a lamb about to be put on the spit. They carried him a short distance away. The band followed, fearing for what might happen next. When the crew reached an irrigation ditch, the Prez – who was a Goliath sized-dude – took over. He grabbed Coyote by his collar and pants, as if he were a rag doll, and tossed him face down into a steep ditch. It smelled as if it were connected to the barn's outhouse. A big crowd had gathered now. They hooped and hollered at Coyote's messy baptism – as if they were a congregation watching the conversion of a sinner.

Coyote didn't move for the longest time. He did lift his head to breathe. The members of NADI knew that, for all his cool, Coyote

71

was an east-ender and could explode before you knew what hit you. The bikers knew Coyote's reputation too and were equally curious as to how he might respond. Coyote took his time getting up on his hands and knees. He looked like a bad dog who jumped in the swamp. He smelled like one too.

The band was relieved when Coyote stood up, caked in crap, with a grin breaking through. "Good one, my man. That's a hell of a way to say thank you. I probably had that coming." Coyote extended his right hand for some assistance to get up the banks of the ditch. To his credit, the Prez bent over and reached down with his massive arm. Coyote latched onto it and with lighting speed, instead of being pulled up, he yanked the unsuspecting biker off balance. He dove head first into the awaiting abyss.

Scotty's mind flashed on a couple of speculative scenarios. The band would be tossed onto the funeral pyre as sacrificial symbols. The band's gear would be added to the bonfire. The band, as penance, would have to play "Born To Be Wild" until everyone went home.

What happened next was in the hands – the godawful-crap-caked-hands – of the Prez. The rest of the baked bikers went quiet. They waited for the Emperor to give either the thumbs up or thumbs down signal. The Prez, struggling to his feet, his colours layered in mud, looked directly at Coyote who had traded places with him and was now standing on the bank of the ditch.

"You motherfucker! You little cocksucker!" he yelled.

The Prez struggled up the embankment. He grabbed Coyote in a huge bearhug. Scotty stopped breathing and only let out a breath when he heard the Prez declare: "You've got balls my man!"

The embrace said it all. The pack of bikers yelped like wolves on a full moon night. They delivered a message of massive respect for Coyote. The band took this as a cue and dashed to their instruments to begin an epically long version of "Born To Be Wild." The rest of the night was a blur for one and all. Someone, probably at dawn, was able to drive the gear back to Sotto Voce.

Two days after the bikers' meet, the band found out that Nardello was resting safely at home.

CHAPTER 7

Tamara was disappointed that she missed the biker gig and Coyote's muddy immersion. As Scotty pointed out during a phone call, a woman in a sari, playing violin among two hundred stoned motorcyclists, could have ignited hundreds of reactions – including a high probability of her violin being tossed onto the bonfire.

On impulse, Scotty asked whether she might want a break from being a guest at her uncle's place. "Let me guess," said Tamara, "You want to take me fishing on the Detroit river?"

"Actually, I used to do that as a kid. My father and I got lucky one time and brought home twenty-two perch. I put them in my bathtub and my mother freaked out."

"Did you want to keep them as pets?"

"We should have just thrown them back in the river and kept count of how many we hooked that day. Perch can be filled with nasty chemicals such as PCBs and high levels of mercury. I buried them in the backyard because a neighbour said that fish make good fertilizer."

"Even with the mercury?"

"Never thought of that. Some local raccoons found them. They enjoyed a fish dinner orgy. Speaking of which…"

"The orgy or the fish?" said Tamara, teasing him.

"Dinner. I wondered if you might like to come to my place for some homecooked Indian food."

"Wait a second: a white guy asking a brown girl from India if she wants to sample his south Asian cuisine? That's as weird as me inviting you to my place for haggis."

"Do you want burgers instead?"

"No way. I am curious to see what a guy named Scotty would do with a dish like mutter paneer."

"As in peas and cottage cheese?"

"Oh man. I have to say this, and I mean no harm, but having studied in London, I used to go out to this pub where drunk Brits would get up and try to sing with an all-black backup band. The musicians were amazing and could play anything from funk to Motown. The real entertainment, though, was watching white guys trying so hard to sound black. They would murder an Otis Redding song but assume they had nailed it with soul."

"Ahhh…I fail to see the point you're making."

"Okay," said Tamara, "I'll try to be less obtuse. You seem fascinated with all things Indian. It's endearing up to a point. Maybe it's part of your yearning for a type of philosophy not found in the West. But, come on Scotty, there are plenty of cool things to be found in your own hereditary roots."

"Like bagpipe music?"

"Well don't slag that sound. I love it, alongside of Robert Louis Stevenson and Arthur Conan Doyle."

"Not to mention Robbie Burns."

"Yes, and yes," said Tamara.

"Meaning?"

"Yes, to dinner. Yes, to your version of Indian vegetarian. Just remember that there are other spices to add other than curry."

They finalized a night that week. Scotty agreed to pick her up at 6 p.m.

As Scotty drove Tamara into his neighbourhood, she was impressed by how every house had been cut by the same design – known as Strawberry Box Houses. Despite a common look, each owner had individualized the prefabricated homes by adding a porch, landscaping the lawn, or painting the clapboard siding. When they pulled up in front of Scotty's place, she noticed the addition of white aluminium siding and a well-kept flower garden out front. The small hedge around the perimeter was trimmed. The lawn had been recently clipped.

"You didn't have to spruce everything up just for me," said Tamara.

"You're special but not that special. My parents took a lot of pride in what they called the grounds. When they died, I tried to maintain that look, although there were a few years when things got as shoddy as my state of mind."

"Show me the backyard."

Even though it was small in size, Scotty had tended to a vegetable garden, pruned the apple tree, erected a wooden fence, and installed a birdfeeder. "My grandfather fought in World War 1," said Scotty. "After being discharged, he hung his helmet upside down in his garden. He would put fresh water in the helmet every day for the birds. He also placed a birdfeeder nearby. This is my way of remembering departed ones."

Scotty took Tamara around the front entrance. As they entered, she saw Scotty's shoes lined up and got the message that visitors were to remove their footwear. Though tiny in size, Scotty's home conveyed a comfy feel. He gestured toward the kitchen in the back, where the aroma of spicy dishes was still lingering in the air. She could see that a kitchen table provided the eating area.

"The living room in these homes is way too small for a dining table," said Scotty. "Growing up, all the family meals were hosted in the kitchen or outside on a picnic table."

As Tamara walked through the dining room, she noticed some framed photographs placed on the side of the stereo cabinet, above one of the speakers.

"Are these some family photos?" Tamara asked.

"Indeed, they are."

"Do you mind if I look?"

"Help yourself. I have to check that my curried butternut squash soup is still edible."

Tamara walked over to the largest of the photographs and instantly recognized a younger Scotty holding hands with a man and woman. The older man was slightly balding, athletically fit, and smiling in a relaxed, natural way. The woman in the photograph was beautiful, shorter, sporting long hair, and dressed in an orange sari.

"Hey Scotty, is this Gurbeen from the Himalayan, when she was younger? It doesn't look like her."

Scotty came out of the kitchen with a towel slung over his shoulder. He took the photograph from Tamara and brought it closer. He looked at the picture for a few moments in a kind of dreamy way, then spoke. The words tumbled out like a floodgate had opened.

"This is my mother, Sara. She was born in India. Her name means precious or princess. My father met her when he was stationed in Delhi. They fell in love and got married. After that, they went through hell trying to get the proper documents to live in the UK. My father finally decided that they should have a clean start in a new country. They came to Canada and settled in Windsor. My mother gave birth to me in Grace Hospital, where she worked as a nurse. She had a soft spot for Grace Hospital. The Salvation Army opened that hospital in 1920 to handle an overflow from the Spanish flu pandemic."

"Oh Scotty," said Tamara. Her voice was shaking. "I didn't know your mother was from my country." She looked chagrined, as if recalling past exchanges with Scotty. "Ohhh, and I said all those unkind things to you about your obsession with Indian culture. I'm so sorry."

"Look, I heard all kinds of mean things about my mother and me when I was a kid. The thing is… that's over now. She's gone and my dad's gone."

Scotty sighed. He looked up from the photo at Tamara. "You would have adored them both, but especially my mother. She shaped my soul. That's why I didn't stop you from reading the Gita on the car ride home from the Point. The sound of your voice reminded me of her. I miss them both so much."

"I'm stunned, Scotty. I'm constantly learning big things about you. Today I've learned about your mother, a mother you've lost. How are you coping these days?"

"Good days; bad days; awful days… fucked up days."

"Are you able to stay clean?"

"Clean means different things to different people," said Scotty. "There was a period where I had to smoke weed because it calmed me down and kept me from scoring hard shit. These days, my recovery counsellor doesn't want me touching any substances."

"And what about your grief, Scotty? Who do you talk to about the pain?"

Scotty stood still. He didn't answer. He opened the lid to the stereo cabinet and turned it on. He reached over to a stack of LPs and removed

76

one particular recording. As the needle dropped on the first track, Tamara recognized it immediately. It was a recording of sitar master, Ravi Shankar in collaboration with the world class violinist, Yehudi Menuhin. The LP was called *West Meets East*. It won a Grammy Award for the Best Chamber Music Performance.

"I love this recording," said Tamara.

"My mother would have loved it too. It came out after she died. I especially find the alap section soothing."

Tamara knew the term alap, referring to an opening movement in North Indian classical music. That section contains a melodic improvisation that introduces and develops a raga. Except for the tanpura drone, the alap is unaccompanied, unmetered, and improvised. It starts at a slow tempo and introduces the raga's mood. Most importantly, the alap acts like an invocation.

"I mainly talk with Father Jaggs about my recovery," said Scotty. "He knows all the details about the death of my parents and why I got deep into drugs. We don't talk a lot about my grief. Maybe Father Jaggs can tell that it never goes away. Grief and I have become like walking companions."

"Those deep wounds never go away," said Tamara. "I've had my own troubles, although not like yours. I had to get help. My therapist in London helped me to hold my difficulties."

"I don't have to hold anything, my troubles have a stranglehold on me, at times." The duet between Ravi and Yehudi continued in the background, mirroring the conversational exchange between Scotty and Tamara. As the music progressed into a livelier section, Scotty turned the volume down.

"We should eat before my dishes either burn or get cold."

The aroma of Scotty's dishes matched the nuanced flavours of the music. Tamara assumed that her friend had received some level of apprenticeship from his mother and perhaps Binshnu at the Himalayan. Just as Scotty played his horn in an unconventional way, his approach to cooking Indian dishes combined both a fidelity to, and a departure from, tradition. Tamara savoured and devoured Scotty's fusion style.

Scotty prepared a finale of chai. He added a pinch of spicy garam masala powder, a smashed-up nub of ginger, plus a strand of saffron on top. He then impressed Tamara by pouring the tea like a real chai wallah. With great agility, Scotty demonstrated the traditional pour, holding the pot and cup two arms-length apart.

"Impressive stuff, Mr. Chai Wallah."

"You know the weird part?" replied Scotty, "I was often in touch with my mother's family in India. Her sister lived in Windsor for a period of time. In the end, I never made it over to see my relatives or soak in the culture."

"I have to say Scotty, some part of you absorbed your mother's roots. Then again, you and I are alike. We live in between cultures. I've spent as much time outside of India as I did inside it."

"It's still a dream of mine to make a pilgrimage," said Scotty. "I want to scatter my parents' ashes on Mother Ganga."

"May that happen for you in time. I have been to Varanasi and it was life changing. Speaking of big events, can I share something with you?"

"Sure thing."

Tamara took her time but carefully walked Scotty through her experience of sexual abuse at the Academy as well as her therapeutic journey with Dr. Nachmanovitch. Scotty let the story unfold without rush as they sipped on their chai. At the end, Tamara looked pointedly into Scotty's eyes.

"As you might appreciate, sexual intimacy is a loaded area for me. I've been able to move forward and become a confident person because I've been clear about my borders and my boundaries with men."

"I guess that would include me," said Scotty.

"Yes. I feel an attraction to you but I also feel a struggle. We're both wounded people who have a distance yet to go in healing ourselves. I don't want to become your next drug of choice."

Scotty let that last thought swirl around for a moment before speaking. "Are you afraid of opening up to someone beyond yourself?"

"I'm more afraid of projecting stuff onto you that isn't about you."

"Hey," said Scotty, "how about, for now, we just hang out as friends. No serious thing. No big relationship. We can maybe even support one another when times get rough. How does that sound?"

"Hard."

"What's so hard about that, Tamara?"

"Because I feel like I've already dipped more than a toe into the river of *us*. Now I want to dive right in."

Scotty smiled but didn't say anything. Something had been named and they let it remain in suspension. "Bring your chai. Let's check out this new recording of Miles Davis. I just got it. It's called *Miles In The Sky.*" They snuggled on the couch, enjoyed the music and listened to their bodies talking beyond words.

CHAPTER 8

When Nardello surfaced at the next rehearsal, Coyote called a circle. He didn't waste time and spoke directly to the guitarist. "Look buddy," he began, "there's a lot riding on the WSO gig. We covered your ass for the bikers' shindig but we gotta know that you're not going to keep pulling this Houdini shit. Disappearing and then reappearing. What's up?"

Nardello was relieved to come clean and explain his erratic behaviour. He knew his mother had phoned Coyote the first time her son went missing. Nardello's parents were about to get the police involved when they received word from a family friend that their son was alright and would be back in several days. He was not in any danger and had taken a job.

The truth was, Nardello Junior got caught in the drug-dealing intricacies in the Windsor-Detroit area. The facts were simple. If you were a consumer of pot in Windsor, you needed some connection to a grower or distributor. Your contacts could range from a neighbourhood hippie, who provided service with a smile, to the darker dealers who might entice you into trying harder drugs.

The casual consumer didn't have to look too far to find anything he or she needed within the counterculture: the smaller the operation, the simpler the transaction. If you were on the distributing side of the equation you had to vigilantly avoid run-ins with other pushers, or bikers who were aggressively setting up operations. In 1968, you certainly didn't want to draw the attention of the Mafia.

A high percentage of the heroin trade in North America was run by the Mob and directed by the Lombardo family out of New York. The Mafia controlled Detroit's drug trafficking scene and imported its heroin supply through Windsor. One of Detroit's syndicate directors owned a Windsor bakery, which trucked more than bread into the Motor City.

The Italian community around Erie Street was tight and wasn't oblivious to the goods that entered and exited their local bakery. The Purple Gang, before amalgamating with the Mafia, had used the bakery during the Prohibition era for distributing alcohol. Down through generations, the traditions brought over from Sicily continued: you kept your mouth shut, you went to church, and you raised your children to respect figures in the community… and not just the priests.

Nicholas Scarpelli's bakery was situated across the street from the shop run by the Nardello family. When someone from the bakery crossed the street and entered the grocery store, the person was welcomed and shown respect, even though the Nardello family was not involved in the Mob. The only illegal activity that Mr. Nardello performed was to pass along an envelope once a month to a police officer who came in for groceries.

The Mafia ran a handful of gaming clubs in the Windsor area. Three things were required to operate these clubs: clients, capital and an *edge*. The *edge* is an agreement with police to let the club stay in business in exchange for a share of the take. It only took one cop, strategically placed, to provide the *edge*. He could tip the mobsters on any upcoming raids. When the anti-gambling squad of detectives arrived, any evidence of gambling was long gone. The Windsor *edge* worked for the Mafia, picked up the cash and groceries at Nardello's.

The young Nardello respected his parents, loved music, and stayed on the grocery store side of Erie St. He smoked a little weed, drank a little grappa, but led a fairly clean life. Nardello's life moved along hassle-free, until he heard Domenic Troiano play his Telecaster at Massey Collegiate High School with the band Mandela.

As much as Nardello adored Domenic's playing, he didn't aspire to sound like the masterful player. He yearned to channel what he heard in his own head. What he lacked was a conduit for his original ideas. He didn't have his own Fender Telecaster with a maplewood fretboard and Humbucker pickups.

Nardello's family worked hard and provided for their children to attend a private Catholic school. They also saved money for each child to attend university, if they so desired. What they didn't save for was the cost of a Telecaster Custom which listed for $259, plus $58 for a case. A maple fretboard was an extra 5 percent, as was the custom colour. A large gap stood in between what Nardello desired and what he could afford.

An English teacher at Nardello's high school once passed along a quote that stuck with the young guitarist: *"Men go to far greater lengths to avoid what they fear than to obtain what they desire."* In an attempt to do something fearless and obtain what he desired, Nardello hatched a scheme to earn quick money on the downlow. He dubbed the operation *Sweet Deal*.

One case of Nutella holds 64 jars. Nardello's plan was to borrow a case (or two) from his parents' stockpile and pay back the wholesale price to his parents, after he sold his supply. His customers would be limited to senior student classmates at Assumption Catholic High School on Huron Church Road. While any of those students could trek down to the family store on Erie Street for a jar of Nutella, the jars that Nardello retailed would contain an extra ingredient: cannabis infused oil.

He toyed with slogans such as, *"Get high and take care of your munchies at the same time."*

As it played out, Nardello didn't need slogans or promotional materials at all. Several classmates paid the asking price, liked the results, came back for more and brought additional customers to the table. Nardello retailed the product out of the trunk of his car in the parking lot of Assumption and soon sold out of the product. A second case was lifted and altered. Sales were beyond Nardello's expectations.

One of his satisfied customers was Nicholas Scarpelli's nephew. The bakery owner received a call from his sister one night about how strange her son had been acting for a few days. She suspected drugs and wanted the uncle to have a talk with him, to get to the bottom of what was going on. Nicholas brought a good deal of experience in persuading people to spill their guts. Soon enough, Nardello's Nutella, with that special ingredient, was exposed.

While closing his car trunk at the high school, Nardello was abducted in the parking lot by two toughs working for Scarpelli. He and the product were brought directly to the mobster's office at the bakery.

"Have a seat, Bruno," said Nicholas Scarpelli. "We have some serious business to discuss."

"Is it about the Nutella?"

"Bruno, we are practically family. I have watched you and your sisters grow up since you were babies. I've admired how hard your family works to make their business prosper. Maybe it's not for me to say, but I never see you helping out. You seem to take without giving. That's a dangerous attitude, capisci?"

"I understand. I'm not part of the grocery business because I need time to focus on the music business."

"And is selling drugs helping you with that career choice? And for fuck's sake, Bruno, why Nutella? We came to this country with nothing and got nothing in terms of respect. We used our trades, our old country knowledge to build homes, roads and stores. We became plumbers, tailors, restaurant owners, and goddam bakers. Now those anglo 'mangiacakes,' who wouldn't let us rent an apartment when we arrived, come every Saturday to our Little Italy. They buy our tailored suits. They eat our pasta. They come to my little bakery for cannoli. They walk across the street to your parents' humble shop to buy fucking Nutella."

"This was the first time, I swear. I needed some quick cash."

"Goddamitt Bruno! Do you know how often I hear guys say that? Everybody needs quick cash, that's why I have an army of goombahs working for me. You don't seem to comprehend something, despite the fact that your parents are busting their asses to send you to a private school. You may be developing smarts about English history but you don't understand that no one gets something for nothing in this world."

"I wanted a guitar."

"What?"

"I wanted a Fender Telecaster guitar with a maplewood fretboard and Humbucker pickups. It costs a lot of money, so I came up with an idea to earn the cash."

"*Earn* is the key word in that sentence, paesano."

"I play in a band and try to save money, but it's not enough. I would need to work for a year to score that guitar."

"I may not have attended a fancy Catholic school, but I'm not stupido. I know what it's like to want something so bad that you do something bad to get it."

Scarpelli paused and his face shifted from veins popping out to a calmer state of intensity. He got up from his chair and motioned to Nardello to follow him. They walked out into the back area of the bakery where the smell of fresh baked goods filled the air. Scarpelli motioned to a 50-pound bag of flour.

"Bruno," he said, "pick that up and walk over to that Hobart mixer."

Nardello gave a puzzled look then bent over to hug the bag.

"No, no. Squat like you're going to shit in the woods. Then wrap your arms around the bag like this is your goomah. Lift with your legs not your back. Straight up and then over to the mixer."

Nardello followed the instructions and, although lifting and walking with the bag looked awkward, he accomplished the task.

"You'll get better with practice. That's what I'm going to offer you. Two chances to practice. For the next five days you will be staying in my humble bakery. I will let your parents know that I've given you a weeklong job so that you can EARN money and buy that guitar. You'll be getting up at 4 a.m. to assist the baker. He will become your goombadi and you will do everything he asks from 4 a.m. to 6 p.m. Your meals will be provided and there's a shower in the back. You'll sleep on a couch. Afterwards, you will be so tired that you will not have enough energy to pluck your chittare or anything else for that matter. You better stay alert or a guy could lose a finger in a bread slicer or burn your hands in the oven. Capisci?"

"Yes."

"At the end of five days, you will go home, kiss your genitori, go to bed, and wake up a few days later, more of a man. Shortly after all this, a new guitar will appear. After that, you will put in another five days of work. Then, at some point in the future, I will ask you one more time to repay this favour. Meanwhile, you will never sell drugs ever again or I will personally break every fucking finger in your guitar-playing hand."

Nardello was told to write out the name of the guitar. He also scribbled the name *Domenic Troiano in Toronto* beside the information.

The band absorbed the story and Scotty was the first to speak up.

"Nardello, my man, I love you like a brother so I can say this with all my heart – what the fuck were you thinking? Dealing in this town is dangerous enough without getting the Mob involved. I could have loaned you the cash. Coyote could have connected you with Domenic. We're all happy that it worked out but... geez... this could have had a bad ending."

Nardello listened, took in the support and apologized for not being upfront.

The rehearsal that followed was alright but was missing something: Tamara. The group had broken out of a predictable mode of improvising when Tamara played with them. This rehearsal felt like a return to known territory.

"Why isn't Tamara here with us?" asked Sal.

"Cause no one asked her, amigo," said Coyote. "She's been wood-shedding the classical material and meeting with the symphony conductor."

UB spoke up. "I want that magic back. We have a couple more Saturday night performances before playing with the symphony. Why not include her in those two nights? It would help us focus our sound. Plus, I miss her."

"Isn't that going to be anti-climactic?" asked Coyote. "If our crowd hears her play two nights here at the club, what incentive do they have to show up at the Cleary Auditorium. There's no surprise element."

"Well," said UB, "how about we throw in the surprise element of a protest rally hosted by Mr. Pastor and his posse?"

"I just want to know if we can return to that amazing level of playing again," said Nardello. "Let's answer that question on our home turf here at Sotto Voce, before falling on our faces at the Cleary."

"OK," said Coyote. "How about you make that happen, Scotty? Talk to her. If she's in, pick her up for this Saturday. You two lovebirds are probably looking for any excuse to hang out."

The growing relationship between Scotty and Tamara was not as secretive as Scotty assumed.

When Tamara heard the invitation to play on Saturday night, she was euphoric. "I'm feeling like a one-trick pony these days with the violin concerto. I need another outlet before I demolish my violin like Pete Townshend smashes his guitars."

Scotty picked up Tamara for the Sotto Voce gig. He wasn't sure why but he half expected her to be decked out in her hippy attire. He was surprised and pleased to see Tamara turned out in a traditional orange sari. She wore bangles on her wrist and even a bindi. The red dot placed on the forehead symbolized the third eye. In Hinduism, the bindi was also said to ward off bad luck.

"Hmmm," said Tamara, giving Scotty a once-over. "Looks like we need to stop at your place before going to the club."

"What for?"

"Do you have a dhoti kurta set at home?"

"Sure."

"Then you, dear Scotty, are going to bring out your inner Indian tonight."

"Seriously?"

"Oh yeah. Let's get your rig for the gig."

Tucked in his closet, Scotty kept an all-black dhoti kurta that he would wear only on special occasions, such as when a friend or relative of Sara's was visiting. It had been years since he wore the outfit but his size hadn't changed all that much since he was seventeen.

"Let's make it quick," said Scotty.

He pulled outside the house on Bernard Road and they both went in. Tamara had only seen the living room and kitchen inside the house. Off the living room was a small hallway that led to the bathroom and two bedrooms. The one closest to the bathroom is where Scotty headed.

Physically, the room was not that big but it carried a spaciousness. All the furniture had been removed. The bed and dresser of his parents was gone. A window looked out onto the backyard. A Persian carpet occupied most of the floor area. A small shrine sat next to the window. The table supported a small statue of Ganesha, plus a candle and an incense burner. A vintage wall hanging, embroidered with tiny mirrors, was spread across one wall.

Scotty opened the closet door and Tamara beheld a burst of colourful saris. They belonged to Scotty's mother. Scotty reached past the saris. Near the back of the closet, on the right side, he pulled out a garment bag. It contained all the items he needed. The black top, made from a high-grade cotton, boasted hand-stitched embellishments. The white and billowy pants had remained pressed.

Tamara expected Scotty to dash off to the nearby bathroom to change. To her delight, he quickly peeled off his shirt and jeans and stood only in his underwear while undoing the buttons on the kurta. She didn't look away.

"You're lucky this is a quick stop," Tamara laughed.

"Lucky or unlucky?"

"Alright, then let's settle it… here's a kiss for good luck."

Tamara leaned in, put her hands on Scotty's face and pressed her warm lips against his. Scotty didn't let go of the garment bag. Tamara let her tongue slowly circle Scotty's lips and moaned softly.

She stepped back and smiled.

"Trumpet lips."

Scotty opened his eyes, noticed the erection beginning to bulge through his underwear. He slipped on the trousers, shook his head like a lion who had just consumed a tasty meal, and then put on the top. "We'd better go."

When they walked into Sotto Voce, Scotty and Tamara stood out as a couple. Something had deepened. The NADI crew acknowledged it and also applauded their appearance. Everyone withheld comments about the fact that the duo was holding hands, as well as instrument cases.

Once the details of setting up, tuning up, and checking levels had been completed, the band started to head up to the big couch in the second-floor green room. Coyote got their attention. "Do you want me to say anything before you guys play tonight? Should I welcome Tamara and talk about the upcoming concert?"

"Sure," said Nardello. "Let's pack the Cleary. Let people know about Tamara's violin concerto too. It'd be weird if our tribe just came after the intermission."

"I wonder if I could try something different at the beginning," said Tamara. "It might seem strange but, as the exotic guest, I could probably pull it off. There's a form of call and response singing that I know – a chant that I could lead at the beginning."

"Do we have to play anything special to accompany you?" asked UB.

"Nothing more than a D and A drone. We can repeat the chant a number of times and then use it as a springboard into our improvisations."

"Some of the stoners might not dig it," Nardello said.

"On the contrary, it might work magic on them," said Tamara. "They might really get into the repetition. The chant is called *Om Namah Shivaya*. It means... let there be peace, harmony, and love in all the elements."

"Trippy," said Coyote. "Go for it."

By 9 p.m., Sotto Voce was packed. Coyote had spread the word among the regulars that tonight was going to include a musical guest. Those friends told their friends and the place filled to near capacity. To add to the vibe, Scotty had placed Nag Champa incense sticks around the space before the doors opened.

Instead of the band sauntering onto the stage, as they usually did, Coyote went up to the mic alone. He talked eloquently about how music can bring people of all cultures, ages, and religious beliefs together. Scotty looked out on the crowd and didn't see a lot of diversity in age or culture. It looked like a tribe of white hippies who leaned more toward paganism as their religious practice. Regardless, Scotty did appreciate the message Coyote was ramping up and how it tied into the WSO gig.

"As a special addition tonight, Tamara Chandra will be joining the band as a guest player. Would you please welcome her and NADI!"

Inviting people to applaud before a note was struck was another departure for the band. However, in the spirit of what Coyote had created, they walked from the second-floor stairs out onto the stage and acknowledged the crowd. Ron and Brian kept the lights down low and had placed a few candles on stage.

"Namaste," said Tamara, placing her hands together and giving a slight bow. "Thank you for those kind words and for this warm welcome. I am most grateful for all the kindness that I have received since arriving in Canada. We just heard thoughts about how music can build bridges not barriers. I'd like to continue on that theme and teach you what is called a *mantra*. As if you were my echo, please sing back what you hear from me."

Scotty surveyed the audience and picked up an inquisitiveness in the crowd. It helped that Tamara exuded a confidence and beauty that pulled in a focus. He guessed that women in the audience were happy to see a chick on stage. He also assumed that the men were happy to see someone so mesmerizing.

"This chant is called *Om Namah Shivaya.* It is meant to evoke peace, harmony, and love."

UB began with the shruti box Tamara had gifted him. It produced a steady droning sound. Tamara began slowly and was deliberate in pronouncing the Sanskrit words. Scotty was relieved to hear how quickly the audience responded with the call back part. He, and the rest of the band, joined in on their microphones to strengthen the melodic line. The unified voices underscored a sense of community and the repetitive singing evoked a peaceful feeling.

The mantra continued for what felt like several minutes. It was UB who seemed to read Tamara's direction toward a transition. With his left hand pulling the bellow on the shruti box, he used his right hand to contribute additional notes on the Hammond organ with the volume pedal pulled back. As Tamara got softer, UB swelled the chord to introduce a new mode. It was Tamara who responded first and picked up her electric violin. She also pulled back on her volume and let the first few phrases enter like a whisper rather than a shout.

Scotty figured the sound of an electric violin played through pedals and bowed by a masterful player was far beyond what anyone in that audience had heard before. The crowd was enraptured from the first few notes. Tamara must have felt this and began to work her magic, increasing the volume as she sculpted ambient sounds.

Scotty, being familiar with the alap form in Indian music, appreciated that UB and Tamara were setting the mood for what was about to follow. He and the other players listened respectively and didn't add to the duet. Sal must have done his homework, researching more of the rhythmical elements that, traditionally, would be established by the tabla player. Using his hands rather than sticks on various skinheads, Sal entered with a 16-beat teentaal structure. The improvisation kicked into gear.

With a groove established, the audience transitioned from listening with their ears to responding with their bodies. Despite the crowded conditions, the audience congealed into a massive, moving entity that followed the rhythmic undercurrents, the waves of organ swells, and the soaring violin on top. The audience became one body with differing parts. Arms shot upwards out of the writhing mass.

Nardello and Scotty couldn't hold back and dove in with chords, lines, divergent ideas, and ostinato patterns. The volume ramped up as did the complexity. Guitar, violin, and horn took turns supporting and soloing. The band sounded as if music was playing them rather than the other way around. The room got sweaty and hot and the music crackled like a bikers' bonfire.

When improvising, Tamara liked to channel her music while making sensual movements. She dipped and danced in accompaniment to passages she was exploring. As the music got more fervent and euphoric, Tamara's body mirrored the band's passions and tempos. Swept away, she put down her violin and began to dance in a style that combined Kathak movements with freestyle movements. Scotty could not stop watching. He played his horn as if it were a bansuri flute in duet with Tamara.

The audience was drawn in, fascinated by her rapturous expression. This was not so much a performance, it felt more like a personification of what was happening energetically in the moment – in that space. Scotty had read once that Rumi didn't write his poetry down but spun in circles while letting his poetic voice release images and phrases. An ecstatic release was pouring through Tamara right now.

The band and audience watched in amazement as a handful of women pushed through the crowd to the front of the stage. Just as Tamara had led the group in a vocal call and response earlier, the women reflected back the moves they witnessed coming through Tamara on stage. More women joined in and soon the first several rows of bodies were occupied by a group that was both coordinated and free.

Sensing what was happening, Tamara simplified her dancing to include more repetitive phrases that could be picked up, mirrored, and then shifted to a new design. Some of the men in the audience were equally at home with dancing and joined in. From Scotty's perspective, the room started to look like a tribe from some forgotten culture.

Since his last collaboration with Tamara, Nardello had found a

Folkways recording of the gayaki ang style of slide guitar out of India, a genre that was referred to as *singing guitar.* As Tamara danced, Nardello slipped in phrases that referenced the style but maintained his own unique twist. It sparked Tamara, the audience, and the band.

Scotty understood in that moment that NADI could never return to what the group once was. He also knew that Tamara had to become a part of the way forward. They had left a known world and could never return to familiar territory. The audience had also crossed over with the band and had become an active component in the relationship between artists and audience. NADI was no longer a stimulus for tripping out. They had summoned a village feeling, a place in which sound, movement, and interaction confirmed belongingness.

The audience and the band sensed an orgasmic peak. At that point the tempo and intensity began to wind down. The improvisation became simpler yet maintained a feeling of togetherness. As they reached an end point, Tamara returned to *Om Namah Shivaya.* The collective singing became communal. Scotty put down his horn and chanted too. He was getting the sense that he loved this woman more than his head was capable of admitting.

Tamara's presence continued to have a catalytic influence on the band. Prior to her showing up, NADI had functioned in a loose, democratic way. Coyote took care of business and the band worked as a leaderless unit, following their musical instincts. It was a casual approach to governance. Players brought ideas and tried them out without any attachment. Experimentation came and went, yet nothing remained.

After that Saturday performance, Tamara brought more than musical expertise to the band. With her classical background, she brought a disciplined approach to rehearsals. Tamara was careful not to take over like a conductor but guided the group into defining and retaining what she called *building blocks.* These units could then be assembled within the overall arc of improvisation.

Sal had composed a duet for vibraphone and keyboard as part of his university studies. When Sal and UB debuted it at the next rehearsal, Tamara insisted that the piece be included in what she called the growing NADI *repertoire.* Tamara used this new composition as an example of how the band could arrange parts and switch roles. Scotty moved over to hand percussion on Sal's hybrid kit and UB moved to the Fender Rhodes. Nardello and Tamara worked out some complementary parts. After several run-throughs, Sal's composition became a strong component in the set list as well as a springboard for group improvisation.

Other segments equally took on more definition and shape. The band worked on one element that was strictly percussive. They rehearsed definitive entries, calls, group parts, as well as a solo section for Sal. While they were expanding their set list, Tamara and Scotty took time to arrange *Ganesh Mahamantra,* a traditional chant that could involve the audience singing along.

Although it took some encouragement, Tamara coaxed Nardello into owning several minutes in the set to showcase his guitar skills – unaccompanied. In their next Saturday performance, the band walked off to the side of the stage during Nardello's solo. Brian focused a small spotlight on the guitarist while the rest of the stage went dark. It worked so well that the band invested in a stroboscopic lamp. It could be set to a continuous mode and produced a visual effect as if the audience were watching a black and white movie in slow motion, even when Nardello was playing at a blistering speed.

All these components helped the band imagine their shortened performance with the WSO. For the first time in NADI's history, they worked out what they wanted to play and when. The result was a set list that had shape and variation. Although more structure was incorporated, NADI maintained a fidelity to improvisation.

While the band was organizing themselves, so was the pastor and his flock of protestors. Sunday sermons became more fervently focused on the decline of morality in youth and how pagan music – or the devil's music – was abetting a societal slide into drugs and depravity. In one weekend edition of the *Star,* the religious section included an interview with several Windsor ministers. The article focused on their opinions around the contemporary lyrics found in popular music. "Purple Haze" by Hendrix was referenced.

Central to the feature was the juicy tidbit that one particular pastor and his congregation were organizing a protest outside Cleary Auditorium on the evening of NADI's performance with the Windsor Symphony Orchestra. Details of the concert were leaked to the press so someone obviously had an ally at the *Star* newspaper.

Meanwhile, even the hippy crowd picked up on a new wave sweeping through the NADI scene. The Indian import store in downtown Windsor scrambled to supply young women with colourful dresses, tops, and batik fabrics. They almost ran out of red bindis and patchouli oil.

CHAPTER 9

Tamara had practiced and performed both of Bartók's violin concertos as a student in London. When the offer came to perform in Canada, she was really hoping the WSO would ask her to play the Violin Concerto No. 2. This concerto was written in 1938 during a difficult stage in Bartók's life. The composer was troubled about the growing power of fascism. He was both criticized and attacked for his anti-fascist opinions. The concerto, to Tamara's ear, exuded more bravery and dissonance, compared to the more romantic quality of his Violin Concerto No. 1

What Tamara did appreciate about the first violin concerto was the fact that this work was written from Bartók's affectionate heart. The piece was dedicated to Stefi Geyer and never performed until 1958 when Geyer, a violinist, had died. The first movement in the concerto is considered to be a radiant idealization of Bartók's true love. The second movement delivers a more boisterous picture of Geyer.

Two violinists play a predominant part in delivering this portrait and so Tamara had listened extensively to the Sony Classical recording featuring Isaac Stern and Eugene Ormandy, conducted by Leonard Bernstein. Rehearsals with the WSO were a bit stiff at first until the conductor, Matti Holli, pulled out more of an emotive interpretation of the work, explaining to the orchestra members what Bartók was attempting to convey about his true love, Stefi Geyer.

In retrospect, it was perfect that Tamara was performing a Bartók composition rooted in romantic love. Tamara's own heart was softening, releasing old memories and fantasizing about a life with Scotty. While Tamara wanted to deliver all the technical requirements of the concerto, she also wanted her performance to express the heated yearnings and passions she was experiencing.

The afternoon of Saturday, September 7th arrived with a blue sky and the promise of new beginnings. Students had returned to school, summer vacations had finished, and symphony subscribers were ready for a night out. The featured program was to launch the WSO's '68 – '69 season. Already a buzz had been generated. Coyote had connected with the *Star's* rock and jazz critic, John Laycock. A pre-performance interview with members of NADI was arranged. The *Star's* article came out on Labour Day weekend and featured a photo of the group, minus Tamara.

Each member contributed to the interview but it was Scotty who clarified that the program title, *From Bartók to Hard Rock,* was a misnomer. The band was currently fusing original compositions, world music, and what Scotty called *sudden music,* or improvisational elements that couldn't be prepared ahead of time. He discreetly spoke of the collaboration with Tamara saying that *she was an accomplished musician and the band was enjoying their rehearsals with Ms. Chandra.*

Tamara's uncle drove her to the Cleary Auditorium in the late afternoon. She didn't like eating before a performance, although was usually ravenous afterwards. Tamara wanted time to change, warm up and go over some last minutes details around tempo and dynamics with Maestro Matti Holli.

Tamara's uncle was shocked and concerned as he pulled off Riverside Drive toward the stage entrance of the Cleary Auditorium. Although the performance was hours away, a substantial crowd of churchgoers had already gathered and were carrying signs out front of the main doors. The pastor was quoting the Bible through a megaphone and stirring up his flock.

Tamara assured her uncle that it was a peaceful demonstration and that he need not worry. She would see him backstage after the concert. Once inside, Tamara went to her dressing room and used the rotary dial telephone to call Scotty. "I'm glad I caught you," said Tamara.

"Yeah, me too. I gotta leave soon and head to the club. I left some sheet music on the stage – my horn part for Sal's composition. What's up?"

"Well," said Tamara, "I'm down here at the Cleary and the pastor's protest group is gathering. It's early but I get the sense that the audience may have to walk through a sizeable crowd. I know it's speculative, but it might turn some folks off and might turn others back."

"Were you hassled going in?"

"No. I used the stage door entrance. You should too. Can you warn the guys?"

"Let me call Coyote first and then we'll handle it. Not to worry. Just focus on prepping and preparing. By the way, I'm bringing my talisman of Ganesha along...."

"Does the remover of obstacles take care of crowds?"

"That's my least concern," said Scotty. "I've been asking Ganesha to remove obstacles in my heart. I want to be more present for you."

"That's sweet, but for now maybe you should pray to that baseball hero of yours."

"Al Kaline?"

"That's the one. He'd tell you to keep your head in the game."

"Ha!" said Scotty. "I'll see you soon."

The call between Coyote and Scotty was hasty, not well planned. But it changed everything. Their decision was risky. It contained the possibility of causing the entire WSO engagement to generate nothing but bad press. It would likely piss off the Windsor police, the city council, the WSO board of directors, and patrons attending the performance. At the same time, their idea held the potential to knock a homerun ball out of the park. They had a small window to get organized and went to work.

Scotty called John Laycock, the *Star* reporter. He told John to bring a photographer to the Cleary Auditorium in ninety minutes. Scotty then called the other members of NADI and told them to meet up at Sotto Voce as soon as possible. Coyote called the bikers.

A single motorcyclist could cruise down numerous side streets or smaller roads to travel from Sotto Voce on Tecumseh to the Cleary Auditorium on Riverside Drive. If a biker wanted to maintain a low profile, these alternative routes would serve that purpose. However, if a swarm of bikers wanted to turn heads, attract attention and create a scene, the best path would be to ride straight west, across Tecumseh Road, head down Ouellette Avenue, and make a left turn onto Riverside Drive where the Cleary sat a few more blocks down overlooking the Detroit River.

Coyote and NADI had gained two things at the Kingsville biker meet – respect and more respect. Coyote played that card and now cashed in on the fact that bikers from different clubs had become more comfortable with one another, certainly less antagonistic. When Coyote reached out for help on that Saturday afternoon in September, a posse was formed quickly. Their main task was to escort the band and their manager down Windsor's main corridors; their secondary task was to raise a little hell.

The thunderous roar of motorcycles, mainly Harley Davidson choppers, is an invisible phenomenon. Sound can't be seen, even though the air is undeniably vibrating. Disturbing the air can be accomplished by merely one bike. In comparison, the spectre of dozens of revved engines brought a prehistoric rumble to the airwaves. Sound was felt as well as heard.

Only five passengers weren't wearing club colours when the group set off – four band members and their manager. It didn't take too long before several Windsor police cars cut off the posse on Tecumseh Road. It was Coyote who dismounted and spoke to a sergeant in charge. Within minutes, two police cars drove in front of the bikers with their sirens flashing out a warning to pedestrians, drivers, and onlookers. The other cop cars brought up the rear. If the noise didn't attract attention, then the vision did: Windsor police bookending an orderly but dangerous looking crew of bikers roaring steadily down the main streets. Cars stopped; people gawked; horns tooted and children waved. Bikers ramped up the roar.

When the spectacle neared Cleary Auditorium, the protestors stopped their chants, speeches, and placard waving. The growl of motorcycles bounced off buildings and, from two blocks away, gave a sense that Armageddon – the end time battle – had chosen Windsor as the biblical place to duke it out.

The pastor and his protestors were gathered on the Cleary's front lawn just below a garden of terraced bushes. Above them, a gravel path snaked from the side road to the main entrance. Without any obvious instruction, the bikers occupied the side road with their bikes. The beasts rested, four and five abreast, on kickstands. The riders dismounted and formed a human line on either side of the winding path. The protestors remained silent. Once the guardian bikers had formed their channel, the five NADI passengers walked down the gravel path like seasoned dignitaries and entered through the main doors. No words were exchanged with either the bikers or the protestors. The only sound to be heard was a photographer from the *Windsor Star* clicking away with his camera and capturing the entire event as it played out.

Once the musicians were inside the building, the bikers remained in place, arms crossed over their chests. The police sergeant, who had escorted the motorcyclists to their destination, walked over from his patrol car and spoke not to the bikers but to a clergyman holding a megaphone. It was near impossible to hear the exchange, but within a few minutes the protestors were packing up their signs and belongings and dispersed without a fuss.

When the last protestor had left, the bikers returned to their motorcycles and rode off in small clusters in different directions. Hell had indeed been raised and now it had subsided.

CHAPTER 10

The band walked into the main stage area where they could see a group of stage hands coordinating the stage set up with Ron and Brian. Reflective gaffer tape was placed down to mark spots for amps, mics, keyboards, and more. Gear was stacked in the wings, awaiting a quick turn over. There would be no time for a thorough sound check other than during the intermission. Everyone on the Cleary crew was working diligently like worker bees in a hive.

The NADI crew settled into a bright dressing room where a long mirror was rimmed by globe-shaped lights. Unlike the dingy upstairs of Sotto Voce, this dressing room banished all shadows. No one had spoken since their dramatic arrival. Nardello broke the ice.

"That was a surreal entry!"

"Everybody good?" asked Coyote.

"My body's still vibrating," said UB.

"I have no idea how you two organized that escort," said Sal, "but it was like being on a movie set."

"Alright," said Coyote. "Now that we're here and pumped, let's wrap our heads around tonight; time for a huddle."

Coyote's locker room talk seemed more for him than the group. He wasn't on familiar turf. The Cleary Auditorium was a setting unlike most venues he booked or frequented. It was a far cry from Sotto Voce and even further from the Grande Ballroom in Detroit. Coyote was getting his bearings and trying to perform as a manager in an environment that operated on terms much different than the street vibe of the counterculture.

Sal, on the other hand, knew the staff, the orchestra members, and the layout of the building. He knew when to get ready, walk on stage, as well as exit. As a percussionist he was only needed in the opening two pieces of the program and didn't have a role in the violin concerto. When Coyote's pep talk ended, Sal took UB out to the stage area to show him the WSO's organ.

Nardello seemed more concerned with working in a replaced string on his Telecaster. He was also trying out a new look. In the spring Nardello and a buddy drove to Toronto to check out a couple of bands playing in the Yorkville club scene. While wandering the clothing shops and cafes during the day, Nardello had tried on some Hendrix inspired outfits. He picked up a couple of vests, pants, and handmade shirts for performance occasions and was testing a combination out tonight.

Scotty had agreed to not see Tamara until after her violin concerto. He and the band had reserved seats in the auditorium's balcony. They could catch the first half of the program and then slip out at the intermission to prepare for their set. Scotty assumed that Tamara would be feeling confident and calm before her first performance. She used little rituals of warming up, meditating, and playing the piece in her head before going on stage. In contrast, Scotty was so accustomed to just walking on stage without so much as warming up his horn. Taking a page from Tamara's regimes, he had brought his Ganesha talisman along for a little good luck ritual.

Outside the Cleary, symphony patrons were parking and strolling by the river before entering the auditorium. The blue sky had traded places with storm clouds and the air was dense with humidity. Meanwhile, an unusual spectacle was developing on the lawn, exactly where the pastor and his flock had been protesting earlier. A cluster of hippies had spread out blankets and were creating a festival vibe. They blew soap bubbles, shared food, lit incense and passed around joints while watching out for cops.

Coyote had made it clear to his tribe that they could only get a free ticket to the NADI set if they attended the first half of the performance. The symphony had set aside a block of free seats mainly in the balcony section with a smattering of tickets in the orchestra section. Judging by the early-bird crowd, the NADI tribe would be filling out the auditorium.

An explosive bang ricocheted off the riverfront buildings. It was followed by another crackling sound. The thunder and lightning signaled a big storm approaching. Quickly, patrons and hippies moved together toward the main entrance of the Cleary. The once quiet lobby was now flooded with ticket holders and those who needed to pick up tickets.

Women decked out in pearls checked out younger women wearing beads. Balding men looked at younger men with shoulder length hair. Tie dye mingled with tuxes. Brogue shoes shuffled along the damp floor, beside Birkenstock sandals. The density and chaos disgorged as ushers opened the doors earlier than expected to allow everyone shelter from the thunderstorm.

Tamara, alone in her green room suite, found a pad of paper and wrote a note for Scotty. Sticking her head out of her dressing room, she found a volunteer usher standing in the hallway and asked the older woman if she would kindly deliver a message to the door marked NADI. Scotty's name was written on the folded paper.

Coyote answered the knock, received the note and passed it on to Scotty who was looking over his trumpet music.

"Dear Scotty,
I don't know how the Fates have conspired to bring us together but I want you to know that my heart is beating faster as we explore our relationship. Just as Bartók dedicated this concerto to his love, I will dedicate my performance to mine.

With Love, Tamara"

Scotty took in the sentiments and felt his own heart quicken. He wasn't sure of the steps forward with Tamara but was certain that he didn't want to go back to a life before they met. He was unaware of anyone else in the room as he stared at the note. Coyote's voice jolted him back.

"Hey amigo. I just want you to know that the band is wide open to including Tamara in whatever way works for her. Keep that in mind. And... I wasn't going to mention this in case it created pressure, but there are some influential people from Detroit coming to the gig tonight. Let's deliver what we do best."

"Whatever happens tonight," said Scotty, "we wouldn't have arrived at this place without you. Thanks, man."

"We're family... maybe an expanding family? Meanwhile, we

better get the guys and head out to our seats."

The band's seats in the upper balcony were positioned in the last row. From that vantage point, they had a bird's eye view of the audience and could hear the WSO as well as see them. Looking down on the crowd, Scotty noticed how the gathering resembled a Jackson Pollock painting. The regular patrons, seated mainly in the orchestra section, appeared predominantly as black and grey patches. Scattered among these drab colours were splashes of brilliant orange, sunny yellow and bright blue. The hippies stood out with their chatter as well. The lower section of the balcony was filled with audience members that Scotty recognized from Sotto Voce. No one turned around to notice the band sitting in the top row.

The house lights dimmed and the stage lights increased as members of the Windsor Symphony Orchestra took their places on stage. Sal never once looked up to see his bandmates. He seemed at home within the formality of tuning and warming up. Maestro Matti Holli entered to silence from the orchestra and applause from the audience. He bowed, acknowledging the unusual configuration in the seating.

Tapping the podium, he signaled the musicians for the opening piece. Edward Elgar completed his *Enigma Variations* in 1899. This orchestral work is comprised of fourteen variations on an original theme and the WSO had never performed it in public. Maestro Holli chose this composition for the evening hoping that the newer audience members would appreciate Elgar's musical sketches of his friends. He especially hoped the younger listeners would be moved by the "Nimrod" portion, a sketch that Elgar had composed for Augustus Jaeger while Jaeger was suffering from a bout of depression.

The hippies were not familiar with concert etiquette and so, when the first variation concluded, they approached it as if a band had just finished their first song. They applauded vigorously and then looked around at the scowls from regular subscribers. Unflapped by their response, Maestro Holli turned toward the audience and spoke.

"Thank you for your enthusiasm. We have fourteen variations to move through. Perhaps, in keeping with classical music protocols, you might refrain from applauding after each variation and then show us your appreciation at the end of the composition."

The request wasn't fully respected but those occasional shouts or whistles indicated that the hippies were into it and listening. When the *Elgar Variations* ended, everyone was happy to give a standing ovation. The hippies were especially happy to move after sitting still. A few adjustments were made on stage before Tamara's concerto. The timpani and other percussion instruments were rolled off. The players shuffled their music. Scotty could feel his heart pounding and wondered if he was picking up on Tamara's excitement too.

Breaking with more formal customs, Maestro Holli turned to the audience again and spoke. "We are about to perform a special violin concerto for you all. Before we begin, I want to publicly acknowledge our various patrons and sponsors who made it possible to bring you tonight's guest performer. Would you please join me in welcoming to the stage an up and coming violin virtuoso, Miss Tamara Chandra."

The well-heeled members of the audience clapped politely as Tamara stepped onto the stage. The string section tapped their music stands with their bows. The hippies in the crowd whistled, stomped their feet, shouted out cheers, and got out of their seats before a note was struck.

Tamara was wearing one of her traditional sari outfits. Her white linen outfit was offset by a burgundy pashmina over one shoulder. She looked elegant and confident as she took her place next to the conductor's podium. Before his baton went up to signal the musicians, Tamara took a moment to bow, bringing her bow and violin together in a namaste gesture.

From the opening musical statement, it was clear that the audience could breathe with Tamara. Each phrase was understood and imbued with meaning and feeling. While the conductor was presiding over dynamics and tempo, it was Tamara who was leading and interpreting the concerto. Scotty, from his balcony position, could observe hippies swaying to the music as if they were under Tamara's spell. Light seemed to be shining from her as if the stage technician had given her more of a spotlight feature. Scotty had a distinct sense that Tamara was not just playing for the audience and orchestra – she was playing expressly for him.

When the first movement ended, the hippies could not hold back. Instead of the typical silence between sections, they jumped to their feet and cheered as if they had just heard the most beautiful music on Earth. The Maestro turned, let them express their appreciation and then conducted them to sit. Periodically, Scotty would hear an audible "ahhh" from the audience as the hippies journeyed on the waves of sound. Tamara, meanwhile, allowed herself to be more physical in her playing. It looked like her body was playing the music and the violin was giving it voice. Scotty couldn't imagine anyone in the audience closing their eyes to this experience. Watching, listening, and feeling all tumbled together.

When the concerto finished, something unusual happened. A prolonged pause seemed to linger in the air as if the music was rising back into silence – no one clapped. Then, like the thunderstorm outside, the auditorium erupted into an explosion of clapping, shouting, and whistling. Tamara smiled. She and the conductor faced each other and bowed. She gestured to the orchestra in appreciation and they stood up to receive the applause. Scotty felt a nudge in his rib cage. Coyote gestured that the band needed to go now, before the crowd dispersed. The musicians made a beeline for their dressing room.

On stage the turnaround happened flawlessly. The orchestra's setup was dismantled quickly and NADI's gear was rolled into place. Ron and Brian placed microphones, adjusted Sal's drum set and checked volumes on the Rhodes, Hammond, and Telecaster. A Persian carpet was rolled out in front of the band, a place for Tamara, Scotty, and Nardello to stand.

The end of the intermission was signalled by a beeping sound throughout the building. As the band stood in the wings (minus Tamara), the audience filtered in. Scotty noticed that the audience in the front section had thinned out and a number of the regular subscribers were not returning. The ushers picked up on this and signalled to the hippies in the balcony to come down into the seats closer to the stage. The grey colour was gone, replaced now by larger splashes of bright colours.

Tamara then appeared in her same performance outfit, although she was now barefoot with rows of ankle bells tied around both feet. She slipped up close to Scotty and squeezed his hand. Without hesitation, he turned and kissed her. She was radiant.

"You nailed it," Scotty said.

"I'm not sure that crucifixion term applies to classical music," said Tamara. "I did play with a lot of heart."

They waited as the auditorium adjusted to a re-configured seating arrangement. The president of the WSO board walked on stage and spoke to the gathering about having NADI and Tamara Chandra as their special guests. He encouraged those who were new to the symphony to consider returning throughout the upcoming season. He plugged a few of the highlights in the months to come and graciously welcomed NADI. They entered from the wings to enthusiastic applause.

The band took a few moments for final adjustments. Nardello checked his tuning as did Tamara. Scotty played a few notes on the Rhodes to make sure it was working. When the band was about to begin, a woman from the mid-section of the audience suddenly rose out of her aisle seat.

"Shame on you, Miss Chandra!" the woman shouted.

Tamara, like everyone else, was startled and looked out to find the person who spoke. She followed the turned heads.

"Shame on you for playing such beautiful music with the symphony and now defiling the space with this devil music. It diminishes everything you played tonight. Shame on you!"

Tamara watched as ushers moved in on the woman, prepared to remove her as gracefully as possible.

"Wait," said Tamara, into the microphone. "You seem troubled by what you deem to be devilish music. This is not a new accusation. As someone who appreciates classical music, you might note that composers from Paganini to Tartini have received the same criticism. What we are about to play for you actually has more to do with the difficult skill of composing on the spot."

"Shame on you," the woman continued as she was escorted out of the hall.

"And blessings on you," Tamara said in response. Although she had not meant to put the woman down or put her in her place, the audience cheered. It was if they had just witnessed an Al Kaline home run, picked out of a curve ball.

When they settled down, Tamara addressed the audience. "Friends and guests… thank you for staying for this portion of the evening. Newer forms of sound have often challenged older expressions of music. It is the nature of artists, down through time, to evolve and explore fresh techniques, innovative instrument designs, and approaches to performing that push boundaries. Tonight, NADI follows in that tradition of bridging the old with the new. We hope to lift your spirits."

At that moment, a low rumbling sound crept into the room. It took a moment for everyone to realize that UB had slipped away from his Hammond organ and was now seated at the console of the concert organ. He was holding a low drone note that would have shaken the rafters, if there were any. Tamara continued.

"The symbol and sound of OM holds great significance in my home country. As a sacred incantation, it is often sounded during the recitation of spiritual texts, before private prayers, and throughout ceremonies. We invite you to hold a note or a harmony, chanting the sound of OM as we begin this portion of the evening."

UB added a few more octave notes plus a harmony and increased the volume. Spontaneously, the hippies rose from their seats. Some held their hands in the air. Some placed their hands over their hearts. Some linked arms with others. The auditorium seemed to pulse with a collective chanting of OM.

The first instrumentalist to enter was Sal. His midtempo beats, played on various drums, synthesized rhythmical qualities from Africa, India, South America, and beyond. The steady, trance-inducing groove caused those standing up to move around in interpretive ways. A few hippies shuffled out into the aisleway where there was more dancing space.

With both a drone and groove holding steady, the guitar, violin, and muted horn entered in unison on a composed theme that Nardello had written. While the notes came from a Persian Hijaz scale, the phrasing was pure Nardello. As a trio, the three instrumentalists remained perfectly in sync, like a single unit delivering the melody with unique timbres. After playing the head through twice, Tamara stepped forward to explore her variations and improvisations while Scotty played the Rhodes.

Since the last rehearsal, Scotty had added a distortion pedal to give the keyboard more of a gritty sound. It contrasted well with the sweeter violin lines that Tamara was generating. UB allowed the concert organ to cut loose while Nardello comped on some interesting chords. NADI was in the pocket.

The ability to improvise had always been core to the group's expression, but what enlivened their signature sound now was the disciplined way in which they could add breaks, transitions, compositional ideas, and rhythmical shifts on the fly. Sal signaled one of those shifts at the end of Tamara's solo and the entire group effortlessly switched from a melodic focus to a more upbeat rhythmical section. UB climbed down from the organ console and came to the front of the stage where he strapped on a djembe.

The excitation of rhythm brought an unexpected response from the free spirited audience members. As if the percussion signaled permission, they poured out into the aisles en masse; the ushers didn't dare stop the flood of bodies. Tamara, who was playing a kanjira at the time, put down her instrument and began a series of repetitive moves that some of the hippies recognized from the Sotto Voce performance. A dozen or so women moved closer to the front of the stage and eventually up the stairs, onto stage left. Mirroring Tamara, the dancers made it seem as if this element was choreographed and rehearsed.

The band kicked into higher gear, accelerating the tempo and allowing Sal as well as UB to add rhythmic embellishments. Well into the piece, Sal signalled a switch to several call and response patterns. He played both simple and complex phrases, which the other musicians reflected back and finished with a 16-bar phrase that everyone played together. It ended with a roll that swelled to a loud volume then cut off in silence.

UB, who knew what was coming, had already moved over to the Rhodes and started the opening chords to Sal's composition. Scotty traded places with Sal and played the kit softly with a type of drumstick that looked like small dowels wrapped together. Sal faced the audience on the concert sized vibraphone he had borrowed from the symphony.

Sal's composition was called "Undulation" and was dedicated to the Yoruban deity of Shango, the god of thunder and lightning.

Sal was well aware of how enslaved Africans were transported to Venezuela, mostly in the eighteenth century, to work on cocoa plantations. The Nigerian people, with their Yoruban roots, rhythms, and traditions, influenced the folkloric music of Venezuela. Sal wanted to capture those historic stories in his 6/8 time signature and melodic phrases that represented chants.

While Tamara and Nardello had supportive parts, compared to the duet between Sal and UB, those weaving lines added an entrancing component. The younger crowd were more acquainted with dancing to a four-beat pulse but adapted to the 6/8 groove by swaying in time. This undulating response was exactly what Sal had intended.

The composition, towards the end, shifted into a repeating phrase that could be played instrumentally as well as sung vocally. Sal had been careful not to add lyrics but to make it more of an incantation that the band and audience could repeat with open vowels. Sal wasn't sure how many of the older crowd were singing along but he could sure hear the hippies joining in. As the ending approached, the idea was for the instrumentalists and vocalists to soften and eventually sound out acoustically. The last thing heard was a community of voices.

Brian and Ron had given cues to the lighting technicians that they were to soften the stage lights at this section and direct more of a spotlight on Nardello. The effect created a cross fade from Sal's composition to Nardello's solo guitar improvisation. The band, rather than walk off stage, moved over to the sidelines.

Nardello's solo began with long, sustained chords that he faded in and out with the volume control on his Telecaster. Each cluster shifted in terms of intervals or new configurations. They landed on the ear like sonic surprises. The gentleness of this opening passage was then juxtaposed with a firework display of running passages, heavily distorted chords, controlled feedback, note bending trills, and swirling pulses using his wah pedal. Each burst of sound evoked *whoops* and *yelps* from the hippies who were loving the rushes.

Once Nardello had explored and expressed an array of techniques, he reached into his pocket and pulled out his bottleneck device. He steadily repeated the opening phrase, in slide guitar style to call Tamara back into the mix. She joined in the raga-inspired riff, first in unison and then with a harmony part. Next came Scotty on trumpet, UB with innovative chords, and finally Sal with a rhythmic underpinning. The dancers on the stage were up on their feet again as were the hippies in the aisles. As the phrases accelerated and became more complex, the dancing became more frenzied.

Scotty had always enjoyed a convergence of chaos and order in music. He incorporated this idea into the finale of Nardello's improvisation by arranging a section where the NADI musicians diverged far apart, rhythmically, melodically, and harmonically. They maintained just enough coherence to keep things from falling apart. In rehearsals, they called this the *Shiva Section,* in honour of the Hindu god of destruction and restoration.

Sonically, the first part of *Shiva* brought sheer chaos, as if all the unity and artistry of NADI was blowing apart. It wasn't meant to be pretty. The volume got uncomfortably loud and Scotty could see some of the older patrons covering their ears. The hippies loved it. Sal had been assigned the task of playing a percussive cue that would explode the chaos and replace it with silence. He delivered as if he was an eight-armed goddess capable of hitting cymbals, drum heads, a gong, and more.

After the deafening roar, a single *tingsha,* a meditation chime, was struck. This sweet tone indicated that Tamara was to step forward with her acoustic violin. She played it with the body braced against her shoulder, more Indian style, and didn't use the traditional chin rest. Ron and Brian had set a few pillows close to the carpet's edge so that Tamara could sit rather than stand. A microphone on a stand was close enough to pick up her playing without interfering with sight lines.

The band never knew what Tamara would pull out of the air in these solo moments. This time, rather than displaying her virtuosic abilities she chose a style more akin to an alap. The violin took on a singing quality, pulled off by glissando techniques. Scotty could eventually hear where she was heading. She periodically referenced phrases from the mantra of *Om Namah Shivaya* – salutations and adorations to the universal consciousness.

As the theme emerged more consistently, Sal added subtle support on percussion and, one by one, the band members added their voices to the *Om Namah Shivaya* chant. Audience members, mainly the hippies, joined in. The sounding remained gentle and unifying. No one yelped. The sacredness of the chant was respected. Scotty closed his eyes and added his voice. He immediately saw the image of his mother, Sara, smiling. She was the age he remembered from childhood. As the singing softened on stage and in the audience, her vision did not fade.

Just as the sound stopped, Scotty caught Tamara's eye. He wanted to say something to her. Maybe he wanted to declare his love before everyone – witnessed by the audience, the band, the tech crew, and the photographer who was standing close to the stage. Instead, something else happened. As the applause ended, Scotty felt himself lifting, elevating above the scene as if he were a low flying cloud watching the interactions below. He saw hippies coming on stage, hugging everyone. He saw Tamara receiving red roses. He saw himself hugging members of NADI and family and friends visiting backstage.

All the while, Scotty was witnessing each scene from a distance, as if he were sitting in a movie theatre and watching a film. He could discern the emotions being exchanged – comradery, satisfaction, joy, and pride. Everyone he knew, himself included, were players in a scene. Try as he may, he couldn't return back into his body. He heard his mother's voice gently whispering to him.

The backstage gathering was packed with family and friends. The staff from the Himalayan Restaurant had laid out finger food. Drinks, including champagne, were being served by ushers. Joan and Will were laughing with UB and Sal. The Nardello family was circling their son. The WSO Board of Directors, including Maestro Holli, were circulating among invited patrons and guests. Coyote was talking with Jeep Holland and Russ Gibb from the Grande Ballroom. Tamara was surrounded by her uncle's friends as well as sponsors of the evening program. Scotty continued to feel elevated and isolated.

"Hey Scotty, my musical brother," said a voice behind him. Scotty turned around to see Bones, a Windsor blues musician he had known for years. Since entering rehab, Scotty had avoided Bones since they both came from a history of drug abuse. The difference was,

Scotty was currently clean. Bones looked happy and seriously high. It took some effort for Scotty to speak but he managed to connect.

"You OK, my man?" asked Bones.

"Not really," said Scotty. "Something happened on stage and now I'm tripping big time. It feels like I'm floating."

"That's not cool," said Bones, "Here bro, I'm gonna hook you up and help you out. Take a couple of these. They'll help you chill."

Bones reached into his pocket and pulled out some Quaaludes, a sedative drug that works on the central nervous system as a depressant. As a chaser, Bones handed Scotty the glass of water he was sipping. Without thinking of the consequences, Scotty downed the Quaaludes. He had just crossed a line but the world around him didn't crumble. Most importantly, Tamara was still present and as radiant as ever. No real harm was done and, whether it was a placebo effect or not, Scotty started to feel more level.

"Thanks Bones."

"No probs, brother. We should hang sometime. I've moved. Here's my number." Bones handed over a simple business card with a phone number and a picture of a harmonica. Scotty shoved it in his pocket and turned to see if Tamara was still talking to her circle. She was holding court.

"Gotta go," said Scotty, "thanks again."

When Scotty originally pictured this evening, he saw himself offering Tamara a ride home... maybe stopping at his place where, for the first time, they would make love. He had cleaned up his bedroom, selected some music, and put some condoms in a drawer in case his dream came true. As Scotty walked over to Tamara, he got a distinct feeling that a night of lovemaking wasn't in the cards. Her uncle was enjoying the night he had partially sponsored and he wasn't about to let the star of the show slip away.

Tamara caught Scotty's eye and nodded for him to come over and join her. Scotty slid next to her and was immediately introduced to several individuals. He couldn't catch everyone's name but shook hands as they congratulated him on a marvelous performance.

"Thank you all for coming," Scotty said. "This was just the beginning." He let Tamara know that he was going to circulate a little bit and then head back to Sotto Voce to give Ron and Brian a hand unloading the gear.

"Sounds good," said Tamara. "I've got a ride with my uncle so let's meet up tomorrow afternoon. Maybe we can walk or do something fun. I'll call you after lunch."

They both wanted to kiss each other, right there and then, but respected how that might be perceived by Tamara's guests. A smile would have to suffice for now. Scotty walked away and was hoping to gather his belongings in the NADI dressing room when suddenly he was facing UB's mother, Joan.

"A big night for you," she said.

"Yeah, I'm feeling overwhelmed right now, with all these people around. Plus, I'm exhausted. I might check out early."

Joan held Scotty's gaze for a bit longer and then asked a question. "How are things going with Tamara?"

"To be honest, the relationship brings up a lot of things for me. I'm having a weird time sorting through all the feelings."

"Do you want to talk about it?"

"Ahhh… yeah… that would be cool," said Scotty. He was feeling heavy and not wanting to be in this environment much longer. As he was about to leave, Scotty blurted out a question.

"Is it true that upwards of 60 percent of drug addicts relapse?"

"Well, there are statistics that indicate upwards of half of people in recovery will not only slip but relapse, especially former users of heroin. Are you needing some immediate help, Scotty?"

"Nah. I ran into an old friend tonight and I am worried about him."

"Bones?" Joan asked. "I saw you talking to him." Scotty wondered how much detail Joan had seen. He didn't feel like telling the truth to her, or himself for that matter. He just wanted to be alone.

"Yeah. I wasn't expecting to run into Bones here. Our music is not really his thing."

"Dealing is *his* thing. He was working tonight, supplying the crowd."

"Right," responded Scotty. "Anyway, give a hug to Will and tell UB that I'll call him tomorrow. Thanks for coming out tonight."

Joan watched Scotty walk away and every instinct in her body – as both a personal friend and as a professional – sensed trouble.

CHAPTER 11

T he *Windsor Star* photographer showed up backstage wanting to get some casual shots of NADI, Tamara, the conductor, and several sponsors. Coyote, amidst the afterparty chaos, became aware of Scotty's unannounced exit. Other than a quick word to Tamara and Joan, no one knew Scotty had left where he had gone.

"Scotty told me that he was going to help the crew unload at the club," said Tamara. "But then I saw the guys still packing up gear."

Coyote and Nardello were worried. They knew Scotty better than anyone. They knew the distance between how low he had fallen as an addict and how much ground he had gained in recovery. A fall from that height could be fatal. Joan noticed her son and the other band members talking with Coyote and Tamara. She dashed over to where they were huddled. Joan held a piece of the puzzle that might be important.

"I spoke with Scotty just before he disappeared. He asked me a strange question about relapse and the statistics around drug addicts falling off the wagon. I found the question odd, especially in the context of celebrating tonight's performance. He said he was asking because of his concern for Bones, a local dealer."

"I was a bit weirded out when I saw Bones backstage," said Coyote. "I wondered who had invited him or whether he invited himself."

Tamara was troubled and spoke up. "I can't imagine that Scotty would have gotten into any drugs tonight. He was straight when we talked before the show and he was so present during the performance. When would he have even taken anything? Maybe he was tired or needed space. Has anyone called his home?"

"I called a couple of times," said Nardello. "There's a pay phone in the lobby. No one answered."

"Alright," said Coyote. "Let's not freak out. Nardello and I will head out soon and drive over to Scotty's place. Meanwhile, don't jump to conclusions and don't let this bring you down either. You were all amazing tonight. The guys from the Grande were super impressed. They promised some high-profile gigs soon."

Coyote was downplaying what he and Joan knew could be a dangerous scenario. Once an addict has been drug-free for a period of time, especially after going through a formal treatment program, the person is more susceptible to overdose. The individual's tolerance isn't what it once was. A dose of heroin that Scotty may have used on a regular basis could now be fatal.

Nardello and Coyote wasted no time dashing over to the east side of Windsor. When they arrived, Scotty's house was dark and locked. They banged on the front and back doors and peered in through the windows. His car was gone too. The Seminole House wasn't too far away and so they drove over, picked up a couple of beers, and used the pay phone. Coyote called Tamara, Sal, and UB to let them know that Scotty had not returned home yet.

Scotty was still missing on the Sunday. Tamara was invited over to UB's house for dinner, although the food was an excuse for Will and Joan to talk to her. After a pleasant and homecooked supper, where the conversation steered clear of Scotty, the guys offered to clean up the kitchen while Joan and Tamara went to the living room for a heart to heart conversation. The two women liked each other upon first being introduced at one of Sal's recitals. Despite their age difference, they were comfortable talking as if years of friendship had passed between them.

"The subject of addiction is unfamiliar ground to me," said Tamara. "Scotty and I were upfront about his past. It seemed to me that he had come a long way, especially since nearly dying as an addict. He attended meetings, had support from his counsellors and peers. He was getting better at controlling his mood swings. What happened?"

"Well," said Joan, "we're still not sure where he is or what has happened to him but I can tell you a few things about relapsing in general. It happens for a variety of reasons. Not all of them will apply to Scotty but it might be good for you to be aware of them as it seems you two are getting more serious about your relationship."

"Yes, we are. That's why I find it so hard to accept. We never put a name to it, but we were falling in love with one another."

"That is one of the challenges you are faced with. An addict may feel that he or she has gained some control. The addict's flawed thinking says something along the lines of: I struggled with heroin in the past but now I think I can control my use. I can take what I need and stop before the situation gets out of hand."

"That doesn't seem like Scotty. He had a good degree of self-awareness, as far as I could tell."

"I want to be careful with what I say here, Tamara, but I also want to be candid. If you're hoping to be with Scotty for the long haul, you need to know what you're committing to."

"I do want you to be straight with me. I've been in intensive therapy for my own trauma and I only made progress when I was real with my therapist."

"Fine," said Joan. "Stop me if anything gets too disturbing for you. First off, you know that Scotty is carrying a huge amount of emotional pain from the death of his parents. His way of coping with that trauma was to numb the pain with alcohol and progressively hard drugs. In recovery, Scotty came clean about his drug abuse but he didn't fully come clean on why he was covering up his pain."

"I don't know. I have seen him triggered around that awful experience. I've seen him fall apart in deep sorrow."

"Yes, Scotty could go there but he couldn't stay there. You know from your own healing journey that grieving is a long and slow process. In his case, he has to carry that suffering for the rest of his life."

"And I am prepared to walk that long road with him," said Tamara.

"But is *he* willing to walk that long road, Tamara? Scotty needs professional help in dealing with his grief, not only his drug addiction."

"I cannot be his therapist, that's for sure!"

"I'm glad you recognized that. You can't be his new drug either."

"What do you mean?"

"An addict lives in a chaotic state of desperate need and emotional despair. In Scotty's case, he can be fearful of being alone and also separated from the person that makes him feel whole. Ironically, you can offer what he craves – an opportunity for genuine intimacy and a healthy relationship. But Scotty can also be attracted to you for the intense experience of falling in love. You could become the stimulus that gives him another rush… another high! In that scenario, he isn't seeing you as you really are and he is certainly not willing to do the grunt work necessary to develop a real relationship. He is just getting off on *falling in love.*"

It was difficult for Tamara to take in Joan's counsel and to see herself as a mirage in Scotty's world. She wanted to believe that what they had was beyond his experiences with Anita, his tantric lover. The idea of losing a relationship with Scotty hit Tamara hard. She cried and fell apart in Joan's arms.

"I've fallen for him," sobbed Tamara. "I honestly do love him. I want a life with him. I… can't… imagine us not being together."

Joan held Tamara and let her cry.

After three days of not knowing Scotty's whereabouts, Nardello and Coyote were torn about getting the Windsor police involved. If Scotty was injecting somewhere and the cops found him, likely the possession charge would be the end of him. He would be busted, thrown in prison, and become hardened from the subsequent time behind bars.

A call to Nardello changed everything. It was short and came from the bakery across the Erie Street dividing line.

"Bruno," said Scarpelli. "Get a pen. I am going to give you a downtown address. You have less than an hour to get your ass over there. Bring a friend, someone tough. Don't knock on the door, smash your way in. Your friend is in there and he's strung out. It's a trap house and the cops will be raiding the place soon. There's a punk ass guy named Bones running it. Get your friend out of there presto… the cops are on their way."

Nardello called Coyote. Coyote called the muscle. The three of them hopped into Nardello's car and headed to the downtown address. Coyote brought a baseball bat and the muscle carried an axe and heat. It all happened fast. Nardello kept the car running while they smashed in the door, turned the lock and, in less than five minutes, came out dragging Scotty to the car.

Nardello headed directly to Crossroads Rehabilitation Centre outside of Windsor. Father Jaggs was waiting and wasted no time. Once Scotty was stretched out in a private room, surrounded by Nardello and Coyote, he entered the room and spoke to Scotty.

"I only have one question for you," said Father Jaggs. "How you answer will determine how we go forward."

"The answer is YES," said Scotty.

"I still need to ask the question," continued Father Jaggs."The question is: Do you want help recovering from your addiction?"

"I'm so sorry… and ashamed," cried Scotty. "I fucked up big time. Yes, I need help."

Scotty's admittance to Crossroads was just the beginning. It usually takes between 5 to 7 days before heroin completely leaves a person's system. If an individual is more heavily dependent on heroin, detox may last a little longer – up to 10 days. During this process, there would be a constant monitoring of Scotty's blood pressure, heart rate, breathing, and temperature levels. He would have to be kept safe and secure at all times.

Scotty's withdrawal from heroin would be unique to his particular history. Withdrawal is not the same for everyone. Just how dependant the brain and body are to the substance hinges upon how long it was used, how it was abused, and how much heroin was taken each time. The severity and duration of Scotty's withdrawal had to take into account his emotional state and the trauma of loss.

Father Jaggs explained to Nardello and Coyote how heroin operates as an opiate drug. He explained how it suppresses some of the functions of the central nervous system – such as heart rate, blood pressure, respiration, and temperature regulation. More pertinent to Scotty's case was the fact that heroin also binds to opioid receptors, increasing chemicals in the brain that are responsible for feelings of pleasure. When heroin is abused, a rush of pleasure occurs. During withdrawal, the effects are the opposite of an intoxicating effect. Instead of the euphoria, Scotty would have to go through a cycle of low moods, anxiety, insomnia, hypertension, and depression. His cravings for the drug would, however, remain.

Nardello and Coyote offered to stay with Scotty throughout the withdrawal period. They knew the week ahead would be a tough haul for their friend, physically and emotionally. Father Jaggs took them outside into the hallway and was clear with them.

"I appreciate your offer but your support will be more useful on the other side of this first step. The staff at Crossroads are compassionate and trained professionals who know how to create a supportive and calming environment, especially during peak times when his symptoms are difficult to manage."

"How do you think Scotty's going to do?" asked Nardello.

"It won't be pretty," said Father Jaggs. "There are emotional withdrawal symptoms related to heroin, such as depression and anxiety. These can be more prevalent in someone with an underlying mood disorder. When heroin stops being active in the bloodstream, Scotty will have a big dip in his dopamine levels. We think of that as a crash of emotions. Not only do vital signs and anxiety levels spike, but normal things that used to induce pleasure no longer bring the same joy."

"Can he have visitors?" asked Coyote.

"Not during this first phase," said Father Jaggs.

"How long will he need to stay here?" asked Coyote.

"That's a wait and see situation," said Father Jaggs. "When Scotty came to Crossroads the first time, he was so far gone that we had to enrol him in a methadone program. Methadone reduces heroin withdrawal by activating the opioid receptors. It works in much the same way as the drug itself, although with less of the extreme and rapid onset of euphoria that heroin produces. We reduced his methadone doses more gradually and so he was here for a longer time."

"Is Scotty going to take methadone this time?" said Nardello.

"Hopefully not," said Father Jaggs. "As helpful as it was in Scotty's initial stay, a person can develop a dependency on methadone itself. Scotty's relapse was intense. I don't want to downplay it but thank God you caught him in the early stages of abuse. He will have physical symptoms to go through over the next week but the real work will take years. He's deeply wounded."

Father Jaggs agreed to touch base with Coyote midweek. At that time, the Crossroads staff would have a better idea about Scotty's rehab program.

CHAPTER 12

While Scotty was in rehab at Crossroads, his closest friends were facing their own challenges. UB moved out of his parents' home – with their blessing – and shared an apartment near the University of Windsor with Sal. They were busy, majoring in music at the university, and so the break from playing allowed them to dig into their academic workload. They each picked up some extra income from teaching music and accompanying singers, choirs, and soloists. Nothing could replace NADI and they hoped Scotty's sobriety would soon result in a reunion of the project.

UB's parents, because of their connection to Scotty and their years of experience working for Windsor's Addiction Research Foundation, felt it important to call the band, Coyote, and Tamara together for a meeting at Sotto Voce. Scotty was only into his second week at Crossroads. Father Jaggs and the staff had explored the matter of Scotty having visitors. As a result of the discussions, Scotty had requested that his friends NOT visit just now and the news was passed on to Joan and Will.

"I know this can be hard to accept," said Joan. "Truth is, sometimes a person may not want visitors for a certain period during treatment. It's not personal. Even the most well-intentioned friends can create stressful emotions which might hinder the recovery process."

"Would it be alright if I write to Scotty?" asked Tamara.

"I would be happy to ask for you," said Joan. "I can imagine this lack of communication is difficult for you. Feel free to talk with me anytime, Tamara. Part of Scotty's journey in recovery is learning how to cope with the complexities of loss and grief. It's also about him learning how to forge healthy and long-term relationships. A carefully written letter delivered at the right time can help, but it can also hinder. I get the sense that Scotty needs to completely remove himself from his familiar environment and interactions. That way he

119

can focus on healing the wounded parts of himself."

Nardello had been quiet for most of the conversation but then asked a question that everyone was probably thinking. "Do you have any sense of how long Scotty might need to stay at Crossroads?"

"I can tell you this," said Will, "statistics indicate that the longer a person remains in treatment, the better the outcome. The programs at Crossroads vary in length from 28 days to 90 days or longer. In my experience, thirty days in treatment is really just a beginning. It only gives a person a fighting chance at beating their addiction."

"I'll be seeing Father Jaggs in a few days," said Joan. "I can let him know that you all want to participate in Scotty's support. I can ask him for some guidance as to what that might look like. OK?"

Although NADI was taking a hiatus from performing, Club Sotto Voce stayed open. Coyote hand-picked different bands in the Detroit-Windsor area to play in the space on Saturday nights. He focused on jam bands in order to keep the NADI circle returning.

Unfortunately, Sal's complicated percussion setup – including the vibraphone – had to be dismantled and stored upstairs. Also challenging was the fact that the *Star* article, with photos of bikers, protestors, hippies and NADI, generated a lot of interest beyond Windsor. Coyote had to field lots of requests for out of town bookings – one as far away as Chicago.

With no real guarantee as to what the future might look like, Coyote took a lot of names and numbers from club owners and agents. With most inquiries, Coyote claimed the band wasn't booking anything until the spring of 1969.

Nardello continued to work on his guitar skills but with more of a focus on original compositions. The deeper he delved into complex arrangements and harmonic structures, the more he needed mentors to take him beyond the self-taught skills he had attained through practice and a natural aptitude for music. Initially, Nardello bounced his compositional sketches off Sal and UB, who eagerly helped him with an understanding of music theory.

Coyote wasn't able to contribute to Nardello's musical development but he was well connected to the Detroit-Windsor performance scene. On any given weekend, Coyote knew who was playing on either side of the river. One Friday night, Coyote scooped up Nardello and took him to Detroit to hear the McCoy Tyner Trio performing at Baker's Keyboard Lounge on Livernois Street.

The club had given local and touring jazz musicians a home since 1934. It was appreciated for its excellent acoustics and intimacy – seating only 99 patrons. The bar was piano shaped with a keyboard motif. A series of tilted mirrors allowed patrons to view the pianist's hands on the well-maintained Steinway piano.

When Nardello and Coyote crossed over onto the U.S. side of the Windsor-Detroit Tunnel, they were pulled over by a customs officer who enjoyed playing the bully role. They had to wait an hour while their car was being checked over for drugs. The team responsible for this investigation seemed in no hurry to process two Canadian hippies and their car. A so-called *scheduled* coffee break added to the delay. By the time they arrived at Baker's, the club was packed to capacity and they couldn't get in.

Standing outside the club trying to figure out an alternative plan, Coyote spotted a Detroit musician that he knew from her appearance at the Fifth Dimension in Ann Arbor. The club became a legend when Jimi Hendrix played a one-night show there on August 15, 1967.

Coyote approached the young, black musician. "Hey Simone," he said. "I met you at the Fifth Dimension. I really dug your band that night."

"Yeah," said Simone, "I remember you. Don't you work with Jeep Holland?"

"That's me," said Coyote, "and this is Bruno Nardello who plays in a Windsor band I manage. He usually goes by Nardello."

"Cool," said Simone. "What do you play? You don't look like a drummer."

"Guitar," said Nardello. "I'm guessing that you play keyboard, right? You came to check out McCoy?"

"Right on the McCoy bit but I'm actually a bass player. I graduated from Cass Tech High, playing upright bass in the school's orchestra. In June, I completed my music degree from the University of Michigan."

"Are you gigging?" asked Nardello.

"Freelancing," said Simone. "Teaching, recording, subbing, and doing what it takes to survive. My real passion is composing. I've got a ton of ideas but it's tough to get players together for non-paying gigs, just to explore ideas."

"I'd be into checking out your stuff," said Nardello. "I've been playing for a while but just getting into writing. I could use some feedback on my own compositional stuff."

"Do you know Club Sotto Voce in Windsor?" asked Coyote. "That's where my band is based. You two would be welcome to hang there and play some music. I can also keep an ear open for you about gigs on either side of the river."

"Yeah, I've heard about that club but never visited," said Simone. "I like the name. I was hoping to get to Windsor a few weeks ago to check out this violinist from India. Apparently, she played a back to back performance with the symphony and then with this fusion band."

"We're the fusion band," said Nardello. "The group is called NADI and the violinist is Tamara Chandra."

"Yeah, that's her."

Telephone numbers were exchanged and Nardello agreed to call Simone within the next few days to arrange a musical get together. The chemistry felt good.

Tamara started her part-time job teaching violin students at the Interlochen Arts Academy in Michigan. She had plenty of things to do to occupy her time: getting her Ontario driver's licence, learning about the protocols at the US-Canadian border crossing, figuring out the best route and departure times, and borrowing one of her uncle's cars. In truth, Tamara didn't need the income... she needed the distraction.

When Tamara couldn't stop thinking of Scotty, she would invite Joan for "chai and a chat." Tamara would make snacks plus a traditional chai for them both. She would put the drinks in two thermoses and meet Joan on her lunch hour down at Dieppe Gardens. The two women would stroll by the Detroit River, toward the Ambassador Bridge. Joan did a lot of listening and asked a few questions too. Tamara poured out her heart and it was clear to Joan that she loved Scotty and was prepared to wait and do whatever it took for them to have a life together.

After several weeks Tamara got the news through Joan that it was fine to write letters to Scotty. He actually wanted to receive notes from his friends as a precursor to visits. Tamara acquired some linen paper, sprayed it with patchouli oil, let it dry, and wrote a simple note:

Dear Scotty,

I have let a month and a bit pass while observing my heart. I wanted to see if my feelings toward you would subside and become less intense. You need to know that the opposite is true. I love you more than ever and want to be with you for the rest of our days. I don't need a perfect partner. I can't be a perfect partner either. But we can be present for each other throughout our struggles and during our times of sorrow and joy.

If you need to take it slowly, I can be patient. If you need to be quiet, I can listen. If you need to cry, I can hold you.

Please know that I am not going anywhere. These lines of Rumi express more than I could possibly say...

"The minute I heard my first love story,
I started looking for you, not knowing how blind that was.
Lovers don't finally meet somewhere.
They're in each other all along."

With all my love,

Tamara

CHAPTER 13

Each member of NADI had driven out to Crossroads to visit Scotty. Sal and UB went together. Coyote and Nardello travelled several times in Coyote's car. Tamara always went alone. The facility was set on 87 acres of farmland and woods and there were plenty of pathways on the property where the couple could walk, hold hands, and feel alone. They cherished these times of tenderness, often strolling in silence or speaking their hearts to one another.

Scotty's support team, including Father Jaggs, were getting to know Tamara. The couple – and they were obviously a couple – received down to earth guidance on how to move forward in their relationship. Crossroads, like many treatment facilities, provided education for family members on topics such as how addiction works and how to handle stress. Since Tamara had agreed to participate in Scotty's recovery program, this meant meeting regularly with a therapist who taught intervention skills needed at home. They covered topics such as being mindful during tough times or being aware of environmental triggers for the recovering addict. So much came down to practicing honest communication skills; expressing feelings and needs, without projecting blame.

It seemed evident to Tamara, Scotty, Father Jaggs, and the therapeutic team that the couple was moving toward a time when they would eventually be living together. For Scotty and Tamara, the vision of sharing a home together made their hearts race with both excitement and anxiety.

It was mid-November when Tamara spent her first night at Scotty's place. He had returned five days earlier and was happy to see that his friends had tended to his yard and garden in his absence. After stocking the fridge with food, Scotty went through each room trying to remember where he might have stashed papers, a joint, a pipe, or drugs. The few items he did find went immediately in the trashcan out in the alleyway. He dusted, washed bedding, and made room in his bedroom closet.

Tamara arrived for dinner on Thursday night and showed up with an overnight bag. She had to leave early for the academy on Friday morning and had a change of clothes with her. When Scotty greeted Tamara at the front door they both seemed nervous. That dissolved as soon as the kitchen smells reached Tamara. Scotty had prepared a Scottish chicken curry. Having spent time in Aberdeen, Tamara knew that Scottish curry dishes were second only to haggis in the kitchens of Scotland. Unlike traditional Indian curries, the Scots thickened their sauces with powdered mushrooms, flour, and bacon drippings. Most of the recipes included curry powder, turmeric, and a little cayenne pepper.

"You could have ordered in pizza and I would have been happy," said Tamara.

"It's not too late. Trevi Pizza make a good Scottish pizza with fried haggis bits as a topping."

They took their time enjoying dinner and conversation. Tamara hadn't told Scotty much about her teaching engagement and so he enjoyed catching up on the details of her challenges and successes. While enjoying a cup of chai, Tamara asked if they could sit on the couch. She wanted to share something private with Scotty.

As they settled on the couch, Tamara held Scotty's hands in hers. "We're starting a new venture together and we both want a partnership based on honesty. I want you to know me fully. I want you to understand the struggles that have shaped me. I don't want you to hold some fantasy about who I am or where I've come from."

"Do you feel OK talking about some of your past with me now?" asked Scotty.

"Yes," Tamara said. "You know that my parents still live in India but there are some details about my family that I've never told anyone, except my therapist in London."

"I'm listening."

"The story comes with gaps and bits I don't really know. I can give you the basics first and then more details over time. It begins with the fact that I am adopted."

"Adopted?"

"Yes. I was living in an orphanage in Dehradun. I don't know if your mother went over India's geography and history with you but Dehradun is the capital of Uttarakhand, near the Himalayan foothills."

"Yes, my mother always preferred the basmati rice that came from that area."

"The truth is, I don't know anything about my birth parents. I had been at the orphanage for nearly four years. My adoptive parents come from wealth and sponsored the school, especially their artistic programs. The students gave an annual recital to patrons each year and I excelled in the arts program. I was unaware that my parents had been watching me develop as an artist over those tender years. I had been given a few solo spots in that fourth year and, after the concert, my adoptive parents met with me and my primary teacher. Within days, I was sent to live with them in what seemed like a palace. I had private tutoring in dance, violin, and literature. My guardians were devoted to the Hindu deity of Saraswati."

"Were you happy as a child?"

"For the most part. I loved my new parents; I loved learning and I loved the formality that came with their world."

"But?"

"That perfect world came with a dark underbelly. My father's brother, who was years older than me, began to make sexual advances when I was young. I didn't want to go back to the orphanage and I didn't have a clear idea of how this new level of society functioned. He always threatened that I would be sent back if I shared our secrets with anyone."

"He played you."

"Yes. When I reached twelve, my adoptive parents talked to me about going to a private girls' school – a boarding school that specialized in the arts. I would be away from them for months and home only on holidays. I was excited about attending the school but daunted about leaving home. My uncle caught me in that vulnerable state."

Scotty sensed what might be shared next and held the moment carefully as Tamara continued.

"I was raped at the age of twelve, Scotty. I didn't have anyone to confide in, at least I didn't think I could tell my parents. To this day, I don't know how they found out. When it all came out, my uncle left and my father cut off communication with him."

"How did your parents react to what happened to you?"

"The three of us went on a spiritual pilgrimage to the Ganges," said Tamara. "They were and continue to be very religious people. It was never a matter of seeing a therapist or a counsellor back then. I worked through a lot of that other stuff with Dr. Nachmanovitch, many years later."

They held each other tenderly for a long time without saying anything.

Scotty finally spoke. *"Lento."*

"Did you just say *lento?*"

"Yes," said Scotty. "As you know, *lento* is the musical indication to play slowly. I want us to move that way in our relationship – as if we were *slow dancing in fast times.*"

Tamara welled up. *"Lento."* She let the word roll out like a long exhalation.

"I love it. Show me *lento,* my dear."

Scotty led Tamara to his upstairs bedroom where the lights were turned down low. They lay down on the bed, turned into one another, and kissed as if time had dropped into slow motion. Their breathing fell into sync. Although hungry for one another, they moved with restraint and enjoyed savouring each touch and each exploration. Their moans of pleasure seemed like long, musical phrases. From time to time, they would pause and look at one another. Each gaze became an act of intimacy. Neither would rush beyond the cadence they had set.

Scotty reached over to the small transistor radio he kept by his bedside. His intention was to play some classical music broadcast from CBC radio in the background. To his embarrassment, a Detroit sports station came to life. The commentator was broadcasting a Red Wings hockey game with the Toronto Maple Leafs.

"Don't change it," laughed Tamara. *"Slow dancing in fast times."*

Tamara slowly unbuttoned Scotty's shirt. Her hands gradually caressed his chest, exploring each texture of flesh, muscle, and hair. Her lips followed her hands and lingered on his shoulders, his clavicle, his nipples, and his navel.

"And Sawchuck ices the puck to give the Red Wings a change in the line-up..."

Tamara's hands moved to the buckle on Scotty's pants. With a twist, she turned the button on his jeans, pulled the zipper, and peeled away his jeans.

"It looks like Gordie Howe is going to take this face-off..."

Taking charge, Tamara's mouth kissed every revealed part of Scotty's body. She stroked, touched, and licked every part of him.

"Frank Mahovlich passes to Dave Keon and it looks like a break-away..."

Kneeling between his legs, Tamara let Scotty watch as she unhurriedly removed her top, pants, and underwear. She read his mind and let him gaze upon her naked body. Scotty's eyes beheld her fully. She felt like a painting that was being adored. To add to his pleasure, she let her own hands caress her breasts. He drank in every detail.

"Sawchuck stops it and the crowd is on their feet. What a save..."

Tamara let her hands drift down to the mossy hair between her legs. Skilled at self-pleasuring, she showed Scotty the secret ways she aroused and pleased herself. Removing the wet fingers of one hand, Tamara let Scotty taste the juices she had summoned. He licked and sucked her fingers with such sensuality that Tamara felt on the verge of an orgasm as her other hand continued to stimulate her passion.

"Johnny Bower has skated over to the bench as the Leafs' coach is having a word with Tim Horton and Bob Pulford..."

As Tamara crept closer to Scotty, she let go of all restraints. With her legs straddling him, Tamara moved her body until she hovered over Scotty's face. His hands reached up to the small of her back, down her buttocks, and into the wetlands between her legs. Each stroke was delivered with intention.

"... now the score sits at 3 to 4 with the Leafs trailing in the third period. Gordie Howe is facing off with Dave Keon at centre ice."

Scotty lowered Tamara onto his face and let his tongue and hands continue to bring her waves of pleasure. She rocked gently and pulled back a little until a peak of ecstasy filled her body. Scotty drank in her fluids as if they were holy substances.

"...he shoots and scores! That makes it 4 to 4, all tied up in the third period..."

Tamara crawled down and straddled Scotty around his knees. Here she could reach his penis with her hands and mouth. Empowered and aroused, she alternated between stroking and sucking. Her tongue and lips found places that brought forth groans from her lover. Tamara maintained the slow motion of *lento* until, near the end of his release, she quickened the pace. His howl combined the sounds of animal and angel.

"... the crowd is on their feet. What a game. Two rivals going toe to toe in this packed Olympia arena. An amazing display of skill..."

They fell asleep naked, wrapped in the embrace of each other.

When Scotty climbed out of a deep state of sleep in the morning, Tamara was gone. She was already en route to the academy when he rolled over and found the little tent of paper. Opening it, Scotty saw a heart drawn around a single, printed word:

LENTO

CHAPTER 14

Coyote called the meeting for a Sunday afternoon. He wanted to show respect for how busy the members of NADI were with their studies and teaching. Different groupings had seen each other since September. Some had attended dinners with Scotty and Tamara whilst others went to Scotty's support group meetings. Coyote and Nardello took Scotty out for a walk one night. UB had helped Tamara move her things over to Scotty's house.

This was the first time in months that the entire group, including Ron and Brian, were in the circle at Sotto Voce. Coyote, for once, was not pacing the floor. "Great to see everyone," he said. "Thanks for choosing to be here."

"Was there a choice?" said Nardello.

"Nah. But I like to make it seem so. Anyway, I have two important matters for us to discuss… maybe three."

"Can I add a fourth if there's time?" said Nardello.

"Sure. Item one has to do with the expansion of my booking duties. I have partnered up with Nick Caras in a company called Diversified Management Agency or DMA for short. We're now booking most of the major bands in Detroit, including Alice Cooper. The scope has gone beyond supplying talent to the Grande Ballroom. We're managing tours and coordinating FM broadcast concerts with WABX. We're even planning a couple of big summer festivals in Detroit."

"Oh, oh," said Nardello. "Is this the part where the boyfriend says… it's not you, it's *me?* I'm moving in a different direction."

"Just the opposite," said Coyote. "I want to take you guys with me. But I need to know whether we're all on board with what the future looks like."

"What does it look like to you?" asked Scotty.

"Well, it means more exposure to wider audiences by getting you on some concert bills. We'd start with NADI opening for acts like

The Stooges, MC5, Bob Seger, Ted Nugent, The Frost, and more. We'd also play some smaller venues throughout Michigan on our own. Build a following."

"Would these gigs mainly happen on the weekend?" asked Sal. "I'm asking because I am currently under contract with the WSO and some matinees with the Windsor Light Opera."

"Yeah," said Coyote. "We would have to work around everyone's availability."

The circle went quiet as each person was weighing group opportunities against personal responsibilities. Nardello chimed in.

"Hey man, can we come back to this part of the conversation. I'd like to hear the other two matters on the table."

"Sure," said Coyote. "Item number two is still in the works but DMA wants to stage a two-day festival in Windsor this June. We've got word that Toronto's planning a huge, twelve-hour music festival held at Varsity Stadium in September next year. We want to get ahead of that event and mainly feature bands coming out of the Windsor-Detroit scene. We're looking at spaces like St. Clair College for an outdoor festival, or maybe Windsor Stadium for an indoor version."

"Do you want us on the bill?" asked UB.

"You bet," said Coyote. "We're nowhere near headliner status but we could have a decent spot midday."

"Before everyone is totally ripped," said Nardello.

"Speaking of which," said Scotty. "I am still testing the waters as to what I can handle in my recovery. Hanging backstage with the Stooges while they are getting high is not exactly neutral territory for me. Sotto Voce is manageable and safe because, even if the audience arrives stoned, they've smoked or dropped before arriving."

"Are you saying that you can't handle anything beyond this space just now?" asked Coyote.

"I think Scotty's feeling that out," said Tamara.

"I want to hear from Scotty what he feels is doable," said Coyote.

"Look," said Scotty. "I'm still taking things a day at a time so it's hard for me to look at dates and venues several months out. But here's what I do know… we're not a band that fits into the Detroit rock sound. We never will fit in to that scene, and we won't likely appeal to people who want to see Iggy Pop spitting on the audience."

"Are you saying that NADI shouldn't get a slice of the pie?" asked Coyote.

"I really don't know the answer," said Scotty. "What I do know is that we've been evolving as a band. We've gone from being just improvisors to being composers and arrangers. If we get deep into performing, it might take away from writing and maybe even recording."

"So how do I, as a manager, fit into that vision?" asked Coyote. "I'm not a record producer. I'm a booking agent for fuck's sake."

"And one of the best," said Scotty.

"I can't say how this needs to unfold for you, let alone the band, or any of us. I'm just saying that if we start playing all around Detroit, we could lose sight of what we're developing as composers. I would hate to see us become nothing but entertainers."

"I know you've got something special going," said Coyote. "I don't want to put the brakes on it for you. But you guys can't keep hiding out in this little womb. At some point, you gotta bring your sound out beyond 100 people... like you did with the WSO gig."

"Alright, alright," said Nardello. "Can we all give this some more thought? We don't have to decide anything right now. I hear Scotty's point about evolving our sound and I hear the need to reach more people. There's gotta be a way to do both. None of us can see that next step yet. How about we go away and think it over?"

"Well," said Coyote, "while we're all thinking it over, here's another monkey wrench. The owner of this space wants to sell and he's given us a sixty-day notice to clear out. That means we have until the beginning of the new year. I don't have the luxury of time right now to search for another space like this."

"Is that item number three," asked Nardello.

"Fucking right," said Coyote.

"Do we just need a rehearsal space?" asked UB.

"How did we suddenly go from playing auditoriums to squeezing into a rehearsal hall?" asked Sal.

"This is serious, man," said Nardello.

"Shit," said Scotty.

"Is the owner asking a fair price?" asked Tamara.

"Sure, but that's not the point," said Coyote. "Whatever the price, we still have to move."

"Maybe not," said Tamara.

"You mean we try to negotiate a new lease with the new owner?" asked Coyote.

"No," said Tamara. "I mean something else."

"Like what?"

"I become the new owner," said Tamara.

"Say that again?" asked Coyote.

"You don't need to know all the details," said Tamara, "but I have the resources to buy this building. Maybe the space could become something bigger. For that to happen, I would need you all to become partners with a different vision."

"Which is?" asked Nardello.

"Well… the fact is, except for rehearsals and one performance a week, this space sits idle. Why not turn it into a profitable arts space. Sal and UB are already teaching in institutions that take a high percentage of what they charge the students. We could reverse that equation and bring students here. The teachers could keep the lion's share and pay me a portion. We can work out a teaching schedule."

"What about the Saturday night performance?" asked Nardello.

"That could continue. We need a performance context to try out the ideas we're incubating during rehearsals. Also, I might want to start teaching in the space during the week, maybe exploring movement classes alongside music lessons."

"I know we're tossing ideas around," said Coyote. "Just how do you see my role in this plan of yours?"

"I'm making this up as we go along," said Tamara. "Improvising with possibilities. Since you asked, I can see you exploring what the group needs to do in terms of recording options and getting material onto vinyl. You could either find us a label willing to sign us or we could take a more radical approach. Some artists are forgoing the distribution power that a record label brings. That means paying for the production, artwork, and packaging themselves. Artists are finding new ways to distribute their projects at gigs and not just in record stores. We could take ownership of our own recordings."

"Ambitious," said Coyote.

"Does that scare you?" said Tamara.

"Actually, that excites me," said Coyote.

Scotty was taking in the conversation and finally spoke. "Does everyone know the term *lento*?"

"Is that something you order at the Himalayan?" said Nardello.

"It's an Italian musical command... not from your dad, Nardello. It means to play the music at a slow tempo. Tamara and I are applying it to our relationship. I'm applying it to my recovery process. Maybe it applies to our next step as a group. We're living in fast times with fast changes happening all around us. Why don't we set our own pace... a rhythm that suits the band?"

The conversation continued on for a little longer. Coyote and Tamara agreed to look into the possibility of buying the building directly from the owner and not involving a real estate agent. UB and Sal agreed to figure out how many students they could shift to Sotto Voce and what a potential schedule might look like. Coyote said he would contact a guy who had a recording space in Windsor. Nardello said he would hold item number four for the next discussion.

CHAPTER 15

Tamara took possession of the Tecumseh Road building on December 15. The next day the transformation started from an underground club to a dedicated arts space. Local artist, Doug Smith, designed a wooden sign that incorporated the yellow and burgundy colours often seen in Northern India, where Tibetan refugees had settled. Scotty and Nardello painted the dingy walls a warm, buttery colour.

Swooping fabrics were hung just below the ceiling to hide industrial pipes and to add an uplifting energy. Light switches were placed near the rear and front doors. The second-floor lounge became more functional and welcoming. The wooden dance floor was sanded and recoated. The beer refrigerator and circular fans were left running and the ratty couch went straight to the dump.

Coyote was cool with the changes. He could see where Tamara was taking the space and was happy to relinquish his previous duties. His responsibilities with DMA were ramping up as he took on more established bands and bigger events.

Tamara invested in portable wall partitions so that the stage could be blocked out of sight and smaller teaching areas could be defined. Sotto Voce opened in January as a facility offering music and dance classes throughout the week and performances by NADI on Saturday nights. The individual music classes worked well for UB, who brought a used Heintzman upright piano into the space. He also continued to teach music history and theory at the Ursula facility. For the first time, Nardello offered guitar lessons for beginner and intermediate players. He was kept busy and loved developing a methodology not found in the usual Mel Bay instructional books. While students learned about chords, comping, and walking bass lines, they also learned how to improvise and stretch out.

It was easier for Sal to base his teaching of orchestral percussion at the Cleary Auditorium as the Windsor Symphony Orchestra ran a youth music program there. Every Saturday morning, though, Sal led a group class at Sotto Voce that was open to any adult who wanted to learn hand percussion. The group of nearly two dozen students explored the rhythms of West Africa, the samba music of Brazil, and the second-line grooves of New Orleans. Word spread and classes grew.

Scotty stayed out of the teaching focus and helped Tamara with administrative and practical matters – everything from handling fees to fixing leaky taps. He transformed the previously shut down bar area into a little concession spot that carried snacks and drinks. No matter how busy Sotto Voce got, Scotty was faithful in attending his recovery group meetings. Tamara and Scotty, on the encouragement of Joan, started seeing a psychologist together, someone who specialized in grief and trauma.

Tamara's string ensemble program, coupled with her individual lessons, became so full that she let go of her part-time work at Interlochen. What surprised everyone was the exponential rise of Tamara's Sunday afternoon program called Music in Motion. It began as a two-hour session exploring improvisational movement. Tamara wasn't so much interested in instructing Canadian students in traditional Indian styles. She opened classes to the general public and followed a few simple techniques such as mirroring, following and developing group awareness and responding in the moment. For a few weeks, the class worked with the theme of *verbs* in which duos, trios, and larger configurations would improvise to the words *melt, jump, turn, reach, fall,* and *roll* as the impetus for their improvisation.

The movement classes started out using recorded music – and sometimes no accompaniment at all. However, members of Sal's percussion group began showing up at the sessions to provide a live, rhythmical component. The term Music in Motion became more realized as the group began to resemble a troupe. Their material became coordinated not so much by a traditional choreographer but by a co-creative spirit of trying out ideas.

When early February rolled around, Nardello asked for a meeting before the regular NADI rehearsal. Scotty held his breath. The scene at Sotto Voce was developing; his relationship was deepening and his recovery was gaining strength. He was hoping that Nardello wasn't going to announce an exit from the band. Nardello spoke to the group with less of his usual flippant tone. "I want you all to know that I've been seeing someone."

Scotty exhaled.

"Simone and I started out as two musicians sharing ideas and studies in composition. She's a bass player from Detroit and a graduate from the University of Michigan's music program. She's a monster on upright and electric bass."

"I remember that chick," said Coyote. "I introduced you to her outside Baker's Keyboard Lounge."

"Indeed, you did," said Nardello. "We got together at first to check out some tunes and help each other shape our compositions. Anyway, after weeks and months of meeting up, things got more serious. She's met my family already and we've been hanging out."

"Is she black?" asked UB.

"Yes."

"OK, my parents saw you both coming out of Gino's restaurant one night," said UB.

"That's one of our favourite spots since it's so close to the tunnel," said Nardello. "Anyway, I was looking forward to introducing her to you all. And, to be honest, I was hoping that she could sit in sometime, like maybe just rehearsals at first... feel it out."

"Feel it out... because?" asked Coyote.

"Ahhh... I'd like to see if there's a place for her in the band," said Nardello.

"Wait," said Coyote. "We've never had a bass player. That's not been a part of our thing. UB covers the bottom end on the Hammond or Sal on kit."

"I would be open to checking her out," said UB. "No strings attached."

"Any objections?" asked Nardello. He *had* strings attached.

Simone came to the performance of NADI that Saturday. Due to a snowstorm that hit the Detroit-Windsor area, the audience was smaller at Sotto Voce. Simone didn't sit in but stood at the back wall for most of the set and made notes about the band's arrangements, keys, time signatures, and more. To make sure the audience could get home safely, the gig ended sooner than usual.

By the time the musicians packed up and were ready to leave, the roads were treacherous with snow. Scotty suggested that Simone and Nardello let their families know they were safe but that they were going to take one car and stay overnight at his place. Scotty knew that the snow plow would work on the main roads first and so they would be able to get across Tecumseh Road and down to Bernard Road.

Shortly after making it to Scotty's place, Tamara heated up some leftovers, made some tea, and the foursome sat around the kitchen table.

"It was good to hear you all play tonight," said Simone. "Nardello has been showing me some of the tunes on his guitar but there's nothing like hearing all the parts come together."

"We've come a long way from being strictly a jam band," said Scotty. "There's more structure now. The odd thing is, as we've developed more distinct arrangements, we've become more free as players and as a group."

"Why do you think that is?" asked Simone.

"We used to spend a lot of time fishing for ideas," said Scotty. "We would groove on patterns like a surfer waiting for the next big wave. I liked the discipline of not forcing something or resorting to habits. With arrangements though, we're getting better at delivering a compositional idea and then exploring variations on the theme."

"Isn't that the essence of jazz?" asked Simone.

"And classical Indian music too," said Tamara. "Free-form improv holds a special place but even the avant-garde jazz group Art Ensemble of Chicago works with arrangements."

"Those guys are wild," said Simone. "They did a gig in Detroit. As well as playing traditional instruments like horns and drums, they used bells, wind chimes, bicycle horns, even birthday party noisemakers."

"Sal has been getting us to play more hand percussion gear," said Nardello. "We haven't graduated to bike horns yet."

"And then you've got players like Miles Davis," said Scotty. "Those artists value space as much as sound. I love where Miles is heading with a less is more approach."

"Our challenge," said Nardello, "is that we're bringing all these influences from our musical heroes or our cultural backgrounds. We're creating a sound that's hard to nail down. We're *not* jazz. We're *not* rock. We're *not* folkloric."

"You're original," said Simone. "I heard that tonight. Why try to be anything else?"

Scotty spoke up. "It's tricky when a guy like Coyote is trying to get us into festivals. How do you describe NADI? That's why I think we need to get into the studio and capture our signature sound, even while it's still evolving."

"Maybe," said Simone. "What would you call the album?"

"Lento," said Scotty.

"Cool name," said Simone, "but, if I saw that title in a record store, I'd be like... this must be ballads, slow blues, maybe a melancholy vibe."

"I agree," said Tamara. "It's more an organizing principal that some of us are working with right now. As a relatively new couple, Scotty and I are exploring how to take things slower in our relationship and not rush ahead."

"What does that look like for you both?" asked Simone.

"Well," said Tamara, "for one thing, our sexual life includes a lot of time exploring giving and receiving pleasure – without dashing to some orgasmic goal. We savour each other... in *lento* mode."

"What about when you just want to move into *accelerando?*" asked Simone.

"Sure thing," said Tamara. "That's a natural part of lovemaking as well, but the building up to that finale and cadenza can be preceded by... what we would call... *variations on a theme.*"

"Sounds intriguing," said Simone. "I guess I like to mix it up a bit more."

Tamara pushed her chair away from the table and stood tall across from Simone. "Come here," she said. "Let me demonstrate this practice called *tantric*. It's all about coming more fully into the moment through pleasure-centric disciplines. If you want to experience it, just stand up here... across from me."

Simone accepted the challenge and stood facing Tamara.

"We'll start by gazing into each other's eyes. Observe your breathing and notice what comes up as we enter a non-touch form of intimacy."

Nardello and Scotty looked on as the two women stood close together and entered a focus that was less about staring and more about beholding the other person. Their breathing seemed relaxed and their countenance felt peaceful. Tamara spoke gently. "I'm going to shift roles now and become more active as the giver so try to just receive. If it's alright with you I'm going to gently touch your face."

Simone nodded and Tamara brought one hand to Simone's cheek. She stroked her with soft, circular motions that gradually took in more areas of Simone's face – her eyebrows, her temple, her ear, her hair. Tamara's other hand began caressing Simone's neck and moved up to her face. Simone did not break her gaze. Her chest continued to rise and fall with each deep breath. Tamara's right hand grazed Simone's lips. She repeated the motion while her left hand held the back of Simone's neck.

In playing the scene back later in their minds, neither Scotty nor Nardello could say who made the first move: Tamara or Simone? Perhaps it was mutual, but the two women closed the gap between them, their bodies pressed into one another and they kissed.

Simone's hands held Tamara's small back as if to pull her in closer. The kiss itself was languorous and sultry. Both women closed their eyes. When they pulled apart their eyes glistened. A moment of silence hung in the air and then Nardello spoke to Tamara. "How did you know?"

"Know what?" said Tamara.

"That it was alright to kiss Simone," said Nardello.

"I knew," said Tamara. "I attended a boarding school in India with hundreds of girls coming into their sexuality. When I looked into Simone's eyes, I knew that, like me, this was not the first time she'd kissed a woman."

"Thank you," said Simone. "That was a beautiful experience."

Scotty and Nardello left the two women chatting in the kitchen while they went to the spare room on the first floor. The guys started to set out the futon mattress, bed sheets, and pillows. Normally, this room provided a musical space for Tamara and Scotty to practise and so it wasn't cluttered with much more than a piano, a horn, and her violins.

"You OK?" asked Scotty.

"Sure thing," said Nardello. "Once we became intimate, Simone was clear with me that she's bisexual. She loves women as much as men."

"How's that for you?" asked Scotty.

"It's not exactly part of the traditional Italian model," said Nardello. "I dig so much about her that it's not a big deal for me. I don't feel jealous... yet."

"Tamara and I have agreed to be monogamous," said Scotty. "Neither of us need more complications in our lives right now. For the record, I was cool with the kiss. As Simone said, it was beautiful."

That night the falling snow brought a hushed sensation to the house. The sounds of lovemaking could be heard upstairs and downstairs, adding to the eroticism of the evening.

CHAPTER 16

Heavy snow continued throughout the week. Students cancelled their lessons and the regular NADI rehearsal wasn't possible. By Friday, the blizzards stopped and the sun peeked through. The regular Saturday night performance at Sotto Voce was on. The band wasn't sure how it would work out with Simone, since they had missed the mid-week rehearsal spot. Nardello kept assuring everyone that it would be fine. Simone had good ears and was a skilled improvisor.

On Saturday night, a stalled car in the Windsor-Detroit tunnel delayed Simone's arrival at Sotto Voce. She didn't get to the club until closer to 9 p.m. Knowing how picky a customs officer could get about gear coming into Canada, Nardello had already rented Simone a decent rig: one Traynor Bass-Master amp head with a Traynor speaker cabinet holding two 15-inch speakers. Ron and Brian had set up the bass amp between Sal's drum kit and Nardello's guitar amp. Simone was adamant about playing her own electric bass though. She had wrapped her Fender Precision Bass case in a sleeping bag and placed it in the trunk of her car. For the months that she had been coming over to see Nardello, only once was she asked about her instrument. "Just going to a practice session," Simone had told the official.

When Simone arrived at Sotto Voce, she only had time to pee and plug in. While she brought a change of clothes, she went on stage with the jeans she was wearing as well as the thermal top she had grabbed before leaving Detroit. Nardello hugged her and everyone else gave her a smile, a peace sign, or a nod. The audience was seeing a new person on stage with NADI and so Coyote welcomed her over the mic as a musical guest for the evening. She received a warm applause.

Nardello had gone over the building blocks that comprised the

NADI set list. Simone had sketched out chord changes, tempo guides, and unusual scales that Tamara incorporated. All those maps were forgotten in her haste to plug in and tune up. Her sheet music and notes were sitting upstairs in the bottom of her bass case.

One of the favourite ways that NADI liked to start a set was to select a chant that Tamara would lead. The audience would get involved and then the band would develop rhythmical and melodic structures coming out of the interchange. Simone had only heard one example of this opening when she attended the previous performance. On this particular night, with Simone ready on bass, Tamara chose a different chant to lead into the evening.

Other than a supporting drone being played, the chant was nothing more than human voices singing in unison. Sal was ready to add a rhythmical groove once the vocalizing faded. He was about to count that tempo in when, without so much as catching his eye, Simone laid down an opening bassline that emerged out of the chant. It incorporated a fundamental pitch and notes from the chant, yet took the opening volley in a contrasting direction. No one other than Nardello had heard her play before. Each member of NADI was stunned when Simone began with a bassline that was so funky that the audience instantly starting dancing. Sal wasted no time and added a complementary drumming part. The band kicked in altogether, as if they had rehearsed this piece for hours.

Tamara took a solo on top that seemed to straddle East and West. She drew upon classical Indian styles and also sawed away on one note in rhythmical patterns. Nardello couldn't do anything but smile and comp away. UB, who no longer had to work his bass pedals or lower register on his left hand, was enraptured. Simone lit up all his years of studying black musicians – masters of jazz, rhythm and blues, funk, and gospel. She came from that Detroit tradition of Baker's Keyboard Lounge, the Roostertail, Rev. Franklin's Church, The 20 Grand, Lafayette Orleans, and the studio musicians of Motown Records. Some underused part of UB's musical being roared to the fore in response to what Simone was laying down.

NADI had been called many things in their evolution, hybrids that seemed forced such as *psychedelic jazz*. Rarely, in any of those descriptions, was the word *funky* combined with another term. As

Simone continued to percolate and permeate the band, NADI grew roots; the audience could hear it and feel it. The sound had a deep anchoring in Detroit's musical history.

The next piece in the set was usually the transition point where Nardello went solo. He typically developed one of his explorative soundscapes into a song that would eventually include everyone. The lights shifted and Nardello began with an opening texture that sat somewhere between delicacy and rawness. He let it ring out like a church bell announcing Mass.

Before that opening sound had completely faded, Simone used all four of her bass strings to form a chordal response. Back and forth the two musicians traded sounds, explosions, and melodic lines in what became a quickening call and response. When Simone and Nardello reached a pace that held steady, they instantly dropped into a composition they had co-created. It moved along at a blistering speed and they played it flawlessly. On Sal's cue, the band hit shots that accentuated the odd 7/4 meter underpinning the piece.

Tamara found a way in that enabled her to soar like a bird above the intricacies. UB swelled chords on the Hammond, Sal added rhythmical and textural surprises on his kit and Scotty repeated an ostinato pattern on the Rhodes.

Although she had misplaced her map for the rest of the set, Simone had absorbed most of the NADI material, likely with guidance from Nardello. She knew when to support, when to stretch out, and when to play simple. If this had been an audition, the rest of the contenders would have been sent home. By the time the band reached their final note in the performance, Simone had become integrated into NADI. As the saying goes, *the crowd went wild.*

It was Coyote who jumped up on stage after the applause subsided. "Can I get another round of applause for NADI with Simone as our special guest? I'm not sure how we can make it happen but wouldn't it be great to have Simone on a more regular basis?"

The crowd went *really* wild.

After the gig, Simone was talking with a couple of Windsor musicians who were wowed by her performance. The band took advantage of that window and had a quick huddle. Everyone was in agreement that an offer should be made to Simone to join the band... on the spot. What was unclear was how to make that offer practical. Tamara, who was turning out to be an astute entrepreneur, said she could work with Simone and create some financial opportunities. Nardello kept quiet but was bristling with hope.

Simone listened to the band's excited offer but remained cool. When she spoke, it was with less of the passion that poured through her bass performance.

"I loved playing with you all… you gotta know that. The thing is my personal life is not easy right now and that affects decisions I make. Back home I have a brother with Down syndrome. He's a guy with an extra chromosome. When I was away at university, my younger sister helped my parents look after him. Now it's her time to leave the nest and my turn to give support. JJ's getting to a point where he needs more attention than we can give him. But until we solve that next step, I'm part of his care team."

"What are the next steps you can take?" asked UB. With his parents involved in social work, he was aware of both the limits and options to families such as Simone's.

"Fortunately, my mother has dual citizenship," said Simone. "She was born in Canada but raised in Detroit. Some of her family still live near Chatham. They told us of a place for JJ that has a caring staff but an awful name. It's called the Ontario Hospital School for Retarded Children at Cedar Springs."

"Oh yeah… I gave a piano concert there," said UB. "When I was younger, my parents asked me to play some Christmas tunes for the community. I was impressed with Cedar Springs. It has about 800 residents. By the way, I didn't play the typical 'Jingle Bells' repertoire. I included some calmer pieces from the Chopin nocturnes and the residents loved it. The staff was really grateful too."

"Good to know," said Simone. "We're all a bit freaked by the idea of not having JJ close. I guess one scenario for me would be to move to Windsor and visit him a couple of times a week. Anyway, we're checking out whether JJ qualifies for government assistance at Cedar Springs."

"Hey Simone," said Nardello, "tell them about JJ's name."

"Really?" asked Simone.

"Only if you're cool with it," said Nardello.

"Alright. We named my brother after a relative of ours. I'm something like a second cousin to this guy. He's been kind and supportive to my parents. I would say he's the person that got me into music. Any of you know who James Lee Jamerson is?"

"You mean THE James Jamerson?" asked Scotty. "As in the bassist for the Motown session band? THAT guy?"

"You got it," said Simone. "My Fender Precision was a birthday present from Uncle James."

"That explains your funk," said UB. "It's a family trait."

"Hmmm... coupled with a lot of hard work," said Simone.

Simone agreed to come to the next rehearsal and NADI performance. She wanted to take things a step at a time.

"Is that *lento* vibe rubbing off on you?" asked Scotty. Simone smiled and looked at Tamara.

CHAPTER 17

By the spring of 1969, the world was spinning fast from daily headline events. Richard Nixon became the 37th president of the United States. Golda Meir became the first female prime minister of Israel and Yasser Arafat was elected to be leader of the Palestine Liberation Organization. A student named Jan Palach set himself on fire in Prague's Wenceslas Square to protest the Soviet invasion of Czechoslovakia. Two Soviet cosmonauts transferred from Soyuz 5 to Soyuz 4 via a spacewalk. NASA launched Apollo 9 to test the lunar module. In Memphis, Tennessee, James Earl Ray pleaded guilty to assassinating Martin Luther King Jr. but later retracted his guilty plea. Operation Breakfast, the covert bombing of Cambodia by U.S. planes, began a steady campaign. A British rock band called Led Zeppelin released their debut album. The Beatles gave their last public performance on the roof of Apple Records in London and arrest warrants were issued by a Florida court for Jim Morrison on charges of indecent exposure during a Doors concert.

Shifts, changes, and bold directions were also emerging for members of NADI in the early part of 1969. Simone's brother, JJ, was admitted into the residential facilities at Cedar Springs. As Simone was exploring possible living accommodations in Windsor, Tamara's uncle required a live-in caregiver. Simone was given free room and board in exchange for part-time care with some light household duties. She filled the remaining hours teaching bass, visiting her brother, and taking on session work at Polaris Recording Studio – a Windsor facility operated by George Hellow.

Tamara had completed three months of owning the Sotto Voce building and had turned a decent profit with the variety of classes on offer throughout the week. Vocal, woodwind, and brass teachers had approached her about bringing their students to the facility and, although scheduling was tricky, the space was kept active. The police didn't hassle her since it appeared as if Sotto Voce was being mainly used for music and dance lessons (except on Saturday nights). She did receive a surprise inspection from the Liquor Licensing Board of Ontario regarding the serving of liquor but, by then, the concession stand was only selling non-alcoholic beverages. They left her alone after that visit.

Scotty was holding steady and benefitting from the trauma-grief counselling that he attended, both with and without Tamara. Their relationship could have been more difficult since they spent long hours together rehearsing, performing, and taking care of either personal or professional responsibilities. Fortunately, they took comfort in each other's presence.

UB and Sal were doing well in their academic studies and had collaborated on a series of musical vignettes for piano and mallet instruments – mainly marimba and vibraphone. They debuted the compositions at a student recital and were given funds by the Windsor Symphony Orchestra to develop the pieces further, arranging them for soloists and orchestra. *Patterns* was commissioned to be included in the WSO's 1969 – 1970 season.

Coyote was so busy with his DMA talent agency that he wasn't able to attend all of the weekly NADI performances. He was currently a part of the upper echelon of agents handling club bookings as well as managing bands. Punch Andrews was managing Bob Seger, handling the Grande Riviera and starting to develop a new venue called The Palladium. Jeep Holland was also booking, while managing the Rationals and the Scot Richard Case. John Sinclair was busy with the MC5.

True to his word, Coyote had landed the connection with the Polaris Recording Studio. NADI now had a local place to begin work on their debut album. His link to George Hellow also landed session work for Simone as well as some recording opportunities for Detroit bands wanting a better rate on the Canadian side.

By mid-March, with spring energy bursting forth, Coyote felt that NADI needed to get out to a larger audience and try out their material on people who weren't regulars at Sotto Voce. He pitched an opportunity one night at a rehearsal.

"I've been talking with Punch Andrews," said Coyote. "He's managing Bob Seger and they're looking to play more shows in Canada. Windsor's important to Punch because we have CKLW radio. Bob's got this new song, 'Ramblin' Gamblin' Man.' He's trying to get more airplay on AM stations, like CKLW. Anyway, I've got Seger booked into the University of Windsor for Saturday, April 12. It's sponsored by Rick Williams and the student union. They're hoping to sell a ton of tickets. Everyone's on board to have a Canadian band open for Bob. I'm lobbying for NADI to be the warm up act. You'd have a whole hour to play!"

"That's not a great space acoustically," said Scotty. "It's a gymnasium that works well for basketball but sucks for concerts."

"Bob's bringing in his sound system," said Coyote. "Ron and Brian would work with Seger's crew. We'd get the sound as good as possible. Bob's crew are pros, they know how to deal with acoustic challenges – everything from stadiums to clubs."

"This isn't a freebie, is it?" asked Scotty.

"No," said Coyote. "I keep telling you guys. There's good money to be had out beyond these walls. The days of playing for exposure are gone… you're ready to play the big league now!"

"Without a record?" asked Scotty.

"That will come soon," said Coyote. "You know how to get a crowd excited. Bring that onto the bill and Punch will take notice. A great performance will result in more gigs. Plus, there's already a big audience."

"You're aware," said Sal, "that UB and I both attend the University of Windsor – in the music department. If this event flops, we'll have to write a shitload of good compositions to get our reputation back."

"Funny," said Coyote. "Come on guys, I am working in the Detroit scene with bands who would die for that spot with Seger. Why the hesitation?"

Nardello named the elephant in the room. "No one is saying it but everyone's thinking it," said Nardello. "Scotty… are you prepared to get back on the horse?"

Scotty looked around at his friends in the circle, each one waiting for his answer. Scotty knew that whatever decision he made had to come from a place of conviction not obligation. The band wanted to know if he was ready to step up into the majors. Scotty didn't weigh in until he caught Tamara's eyes. She looked steadily at him as if to say… *it's your call, my love, not mine.*

Scotty spoke up. "Look, we'll be performing to an audience who mainly wants to hear the Bob Seger System play his songs from *Heavy Music* to the newer stuff. I don't know if we'll win over a mob of new fans. But can we deliver a memorable performance? Yes. Am I totally confident that we can give the audience a full serving of NADI? Yes. That's not the issue, as you all know. What's at stake is the fact that I'm not only a musician but also a recovering addict. For me to pull this off, I can't have anyone in the crew or band getting high. I can't be in a dressing room where the other band is getting high. I will need to stay close to Tamara before, during, and after. I'll play the gig and probably not stick around for Bob. Can you live with those conditions?"

"As long as you take me home after the gig," said Tamara. She winked.

It was agreed that NADI would update their promo photos since Simone was now an official member and they could use a fresh look. Coyote said he would try to score a pre-concert interview in *The Lance,* the university's student newspaper. Gord Gilmour was running it now as editor. The gig was on.

Closer to the concert, Sal came up with an idea that he ran by Tamara and Scotty. "I've been working with my percussion ensemble each week," said Sal. "We're really sounding tight and it's got this festive energy that might work at the Seger gig. It could involve the dancers that have been studying with Tamara."

"Hold on, buddy," said Scotty. "We were able to fit the hippies on stage at the Cleary because of the size of that orchestral space. There's no way we can get drummers and dancers on the university stage. Our gear will be pushed forward, ahead of Seger's band. It'll be tight enough up there."

"Ahhh," said Sal. "You didn't let me finish, amigo. My idea doesn't involve the stage. My idea involves the whole space."

"Go on," said Tamara. "I'm intrigued."

"The audience will be seated in three sections in the gymnasium," said Sal. "Two thirds will be in the bleachers used for basketball games. The rest will be on the floor level, with a large aisleway going up the middle. They have to leave a big pathway to abide by the fire marshall's code. That pathway is a space waiting for something to happen. I propose that NADI doesn't enter from the stage but struts from the back as a dancing and drumming phenomenon."

"A spectacle of sight and sound," said Scotty.

"Exactly," said Sal. "The MC announces us from the stage. All eyes are forward then... POW! An explosion of drums comes from the rear as we parade in with the dancers. A total surprise, wouldn't you say?"

Sal's vision grew as the gig approached. The dancers and drummers rehearsed the parade entrance. Additional woodwind and brass players came out from the university's music program. Sal orchestrated a gumbo of musical ingredients that looked and sounded like a Mardi Gras parade mixed with a Brazilian carnival.

On the night of the performance, Scotty was in a good place. He and Tamara had spent part of the day doing practical things – shopping at the farmer's market, raking the grounds at home, and preparing a light meal in the afternoon. They even managed a short meditation before they left. Ron and Brian brought the gear down from Sotto Voce. They didn't need a sound and lighting system since Seger's crew had that together. Sal decided to leave the vibes at the club. The biggest items were the Hammond B3 and Leslie speaker cabinet.

Bob Seger's band didn't request a sound check and so NADI had the luxury of adapting their sound to the gymnasium. Everyone was delighted with how clear the sound was, especially since the Seger crew supplied them with stage monitors. While the sound bounced around a bit in the gym, everyone knew that hundreds of bodies would absorb those soundwaves.

An opening act always runs the risk of playing to a smaller crowd. The main act draws the audience and sometimes people skip the opener unless the band or artist is well known. NADI was somewhat known through reputation, helped by articles in the *Star* and *The Lance*. By performance time, the gym was packed with a curious crowd.

Organizer and MC, Rick Williams, had been forewarned about

NADI entering from the back and so gave an introduction as if the band was about to rush the stage from the side. His last words were: "Ladies and gentlemen… give a warm welcome to Windsor's own… NADI!"

The audience applauded. Suddenly, out of the sound of hands clapping, came a thunderous element. Djembes, shakers, cowbells, horns, cymbals, bass drums, and more sonic colours flew onto the airwaves. Heads turned and were greeted by a splash of energy as dancers and musicians grooved up the aisleway. The audience leapt to their feet in response. Hands clapped in time. Bodies swayed to the rhythm. The gymnasium walls and floors amplified the sound.

With all the heads turned toward the back, and some people standing on chairs for a better look, no one noticed what was happening on stage. Two members of NADI had entered the stage and plugged in their bass and guitar. It was perfectly timed. The parade reached the two-thirds mark up the aisleway and started a roll that began so softly that some in the audience thought the players were finished. Instead, they were just beginning a crescendo of sound that went from the quietest rumble and graduated to a deafening roar. On Sal's cue, the ensemble cut off cleanly and passed the spotlight to Nardello and Simone who screamed out an amplified volley of sound.

The crowd cheered so loudly that all of Seger's band, including Bob, came out of the dressing room to see what was going on. Just as they had rehearsed it, Nardello and Simone ripped into an opening guitar and bass duet that sounded like Hendrix was sitting in with James Brown. The groove was contagious. The parade progressed to the front of the stage, while dancing and lightly drumming along. Sal, UB, Scotty, and Tamara peeled away from their place in the parade to run on stage behind their instruments. The audience yelled again as they realized how much their involvement was a part of the opening act. Rather than being mere spectators of a performance, they were being invited in as participants.

From the start, the unusual nature of NADI connected with the audience. Within the first few minutes of the set, the band broke into an instrumental composition that kept everyone on their feet. That opener cooked along with solos and breaks until, on Sal's cue, all the instruments cut out to reveal each member of NADI on a microphone singing a funkified version of *Radhe Govinda,* a traditional chant. Tamara gave the audience a few simple gestures and they quickly got the idea that they were being invited into a call and response form of singing. The effect was energizing and unifying. The dance crew from Sotto Voce remained in front of the stage. Rather than face the musicians, they turned out toward the audience. They became an additional colour in the collage of sound, music, and movement.

Each composition in the set list landed well with the audience. The band built toward their prepared ending with everything from modal music, featuring Tamara's violin, to a rhythmic component, featuring everyone on percussion. Scotty announced that this would be NADI's last song and that the group was grateful to be opening for Bob Seger. He thanked the audience and turned to Tamara who typically started the section with her vocal part. Just as Tamara stepped up to the microphone a guy in the audience yelled out.

"Hey, I like your music but can you play something we all know?"

Since NADI wasn't a cover band, they looked a bit stunned in response. To everyone's amazement, Simone stepped up to her microphone and responded.

"Hey guy, we'll take up your challenge if you promise to sing along."

"I ain't much of singer," he replied, looking a bit wasted.

"Can you dance?" said Simone.

"Can you play something I can dance to?"

"Sure thing," she said. "You look old enough to remember this one."

Simone started with a groove that was vaguely familiar to the audience but had been simplified down so she could talk over it. "First, I'm gonna tell you a story about a secretary who was working at Motown Records. One day the company's biggest star, Marvin Gaye, walks in. He was working on a new song. When the secretary heard it, she loved the tune. Marvin invited her to try it out in the studio. She brought in two friends, Rosalind Ashford and Annette Beard. The trio hit it on the second pass. That secretary's name was Martha Reeves. So… here's that hit from 1964 by Martha and the Vandellas: 'Dancing In The Street.'"

Having finished her talk over, Simone laid down a funky version of the bass part from the Motown classic. The band vamped on the opening chord and then, to everyone's amazement, including the members of NADI, Simone starting singing.

"Calling out around the world
Are you ready for a brand new beat?
Summer's here and the time is right
For dancing in the street
They're dancing in Chicago
Down in New Orleans
In New York City
All we need is music, sweet music
There'll be music everywhere
They'll be swinging and swaying and records playing
Dancing in the street..."

There couldn't have been a better song choice to ignite and unite the audience. The gym was filled with a majority of people who grew up singing or hearing that Detroit anthem. By the time the chorus had been sung out and the band was entering the second verse, out onto the stage ran Bob Seger. He stood with Simone at the mic and joined her singing:

"It's an invitation across the nation
A chance for folks to meet
They'll be laughing and singing and music swinging
Dancing in the street
Philadelphia, PA
Baltimore and DC now
Don't forget the Motor City
All we need is music, sweet music
There'll be music everywhere
They'll be swinging, swaying and records playing
Dancing in the street...."

What happened next could not have been planned. The drummers, instrumentalists and dancers at the front of the stage joined in. Sal,

UB and Scotty scooted down the stage stairs to join the musicians on the floor. The only amplified sound left on stage was Nardello comping away on guitar. Simone started a repeated vocal phrase that looped onto itself and caused the audience to sing along.

"Dancing, dancing, dancing in the street
We'll be dancing, dancing, dancing in the street."

Bob and Simone's voices harmonized. They cut to a two-bar phrase and let Tamara respond with a two-bar solo. Back and forth it went. The drummers and dancers on the floor began to parade back from where they started at the back of the gym. The audience was clapping in time and singing along. Bob Seger moved to the MC's microphone just as the parade of drummers and dancers was exiting.

"Come on Windsor!" he shouted. "Let's hear it for NADI. *Amazing!*"

Nardello, Tamara, and Simone hung out on a final chord that grew with the audience's applause. They ended with a sharp cut off on the down beat. Seger's lighting technician pulled down all the stage lights so that nothing but darkness remained. All the musicians exited instantly to the continuous roar of the audience. By the time the house and stage lights came back on, the players had disappeared like magicians. It was a long time before the clapping ended.

CHAPTER 18

N ADI won a huge fan base with their set at the U. of W. gig. They also attracted the attention of the guy who had managed Bob Seger from his early days in a band called The Omens. Punch Andrews knew something special when he saw it. Although he didn't fully understand what he heard from NADI, he knew they were unique. Punch called Coyote a few days after the gig.

"I've got a proposition for you," said Punch. "Bob's doing a small tour to get his 'Ramblin' Gamblin' Man' record out to audiences beyond Detroit. Bob and I really like the way NADI warmed up the crowd at that university gig. What are the chances of taking them on the road for three nights? It would be Friday in Toledo, Saturday in Grand Rapids, and Sunday in Lansing."

"Thanks Punch," said Coyote. "We're honoured that you'd think of us. Can you hold the spot? I'll talk with the band today and confirm as soon as possible."

"Cool. I gotta say, they don't sound like anything else from this area. That's a good thing but tricky too. Have you thought about getting them into the studio? Maybe they could turn out some stripped-down material that could get radio play?"

"We're on it," said Coyote. "We're probably going to use Polaris Studio in Windsor."

"Alright. Hey… Bob sends his regards too. He really dug the show."

Going on the road was a foreign concept to NADI. The group had never played three nights in a row. They had never tackled the routine of sleeping each night in a different hotel room, eating fast food, driving for hours to the next city, and striving to make each performance feel fresh. Crossing out of Canada and into the States would require Ron and Brian to compile a list of gear, including serial numbers. This would prove to be a daunting task for Sal's percussion gear since many of the pieces were crafted by artisans who didn't bother with serial numbers.

In preparation for the first gig in Toledo, the band agreed to bear down more on vocal arrangements – harmonies, lyrics, plus English versions of call and response. NADI didn't have any material that fell into a typical song structure and, outside of their home turf, they couldn't rely upon a core of friends or fans to cheer them on.

Scotty took an initial stab at writing some lyrics. He had been reading a book of poetry by the German poet, Rainer Maria Rilke. Scotty was taken by a particular image around how darkness can envelop everything, whereas light from a fire only illuminates a small circle.

"You darkness, that I come from,
I love you more than all the fires
that fence in the world,
for the fire makes a circle of light for everyone,
and then no one outside learns of you.
But the darkness pulls in everything:
shapes and fires, animals and myself,
how easily it gathers them..."

While Scotty had an initial sketch of the lyrics, he was struggling to find chordal progressions and rhythms to support the words. He called up Nardello to see if they might meet up that afternoon. Unfortunately, his family was celebrating the 80th birthday of Nardello's nonna. Likewise, Tamara, Sal, and UB were all busy teaching. Nardello suggested calling up Simone. "She's a natural when it comes to compositional ideas."

Simone was happy to come over to Scotty's. She brought her bass and some fresh bagels. "I always get the munchies when I'm writing music. Not sure if it has to do with stimulation or distraction."

Scotty got out his Rilke poem and read the passage that inspired his song. Sitting at the Heintzman, he put his own lyrics on the piano and sang the first two verses and choruses that he had written so far.

Calling out to darkness, come into my room
Wrap this night in silence, spin a winter's moon
Shape shadows into dreaming, bring the curtain down
Make a place for things unseen; a womb, an underground

Oh. Oh.	*Darkness falls.*
Oh. Oh.	*Darkness calls.*
Oh. Oh.	*Darkness grows.*
Oh. Oh.	*Darkness holds us all.*

Calling out to blackness, cloak this quiet night
Fill my soul with presence, take away all sight
Weave wonders into dreamtime, curve the spiral down
Cast a spell half whispered; a hymn to mystery found

Oh. Oh.	*Darkness falls.*
Oh. Oh.	*Darkness calls.*
Oh. Oh.	*Darkness grows.*
Oh. Oh.	*Darkness holds us all.*

He didn't have anything else beyond the first two verses and the chorus. Scotty finished what he had written and turned to Simone.

"What do you think?"

"It needs a bagel."

"What?"

"It needs work or it needs to be parked."

"How so?"

"Look," said Simone, "you're in recovery so naturally you're introspective. But the audience coming out to hear Seger isn't interested in a meditation on darkness. Have you listened to 'Ramblin' Gamblin' Man'?"

"Yeah."

"To quote…

Yeah, I'm gonna tell my tale come on
A come on, a give a listen

158

'Cause I was born lonely down by the riverside
Learned to spin fortune wheels, and throw dice."

"Not exactly Chaucer," said Scotty.

"Bingo. But it moves people because the song develops into a story. I hate to say it but, for all your love of poetry, there's more of a narrative in Seger's tune. That's why we need bagels. We gotta start fresh."

"What do I do with this song then?"

"Put it in your personal journal, where it belongs."

Whether it was a symbolic act or a ploy to nudge Scotty in a fresh direction, Simone toasted up bagels; she slathered them with peanut butter and bananas. When they sat at the kitchen table, Simone asked a question about a threshold moment that had happened in Scotty's life, a turning point.

Scotty described a particular low point when his drug addiction caused the end of an important relationship. A woman he loved walked out on him. The breakup caused Scotty, for the first time, to contemplate suicide. Late one night, he headed down to the Detroit River with the intention of climbing up the Ambassador Bridge and jumping off.

"What stopped you from doing that?"

"It's hard to explain. I felt like some energy had my back. Some presence was watching out for me, guiding me back from the brink. This is weird... but I remember hearing a sound. It was almost choral, like something singing me home... or bringing me back into myself."

"Now that's a story. I got shivers listening to you describe it. Think you could shape that into a song?"

"Not sure. I don't want to get all self-confessional. We might have to eat more bagels."

"What. You don't like my bagels?"

"I like your bagels. I like working with you. I like that you're pushing me."

"Not pushing. Maybe drawing out what's already there. How about we try to put that story into music?"

They sat at the piano. Scotty pulled out a yellow pad of lined paper. He forgot that Simone knew her way around on keyboards. He also assumed that the musical vibe they might start with would be similar to the modal nature of NADI's music. He found it strange, therefore, that Simone's opening chords came more from a gospel feel. The tempo was pulled back... not too fast... so that the words could breathe.

"Tell me the story."

The first lines came tumbling out as if Scotty were writing a book.

She left their home in Motown
Headed out the door
Now he's standing on a downtown street
Hoping for a score

Simone looked into Scotty's eyes and could sense that he was drawing a bucket up from a deep well of pain.

"Tell me what happened next."

"I don't want to get too literal."

"You don't have to make it autobiographical, but don't shy away from what really went down."

Scotty closed his eyes. He was recalling the scene from his memory. Simone kept playing the sequence of chords and the groove from the first verse. Scotty jotted down a few lines, crossed out some words, and then sang the next verse with a similar melodic shape to the first.

He found a bar on Woodward
Closed the joint at one
Took a cab straight to the river
Had his demons on the run

"Keep it coming," said Simone. "I'm going to alter the chords a bit here so as to introduce a change of mood. Just listen for a bit and then write without editing."

Simone kept the rhythmical energy but softened the volume and varied the intervals within the chords. Again, Scotty closed his eyes and took in the transition. When he put pen to paper, his lyrics flowed without any need to drastically change them.

So send an angel down to the waters
Tell her to bring some wings
Someone's standing on the bridge tonight
While somewhere a choir sings

"This is the turning point," said Simone. "Something wants to get through. It doesn't have to be complicated but what you say does have to have heart. Just start singing what that choir might sound like. Put it out there."

Scotty hummed some lines. He was searching. The first attempts edged him closer to where he wanted to go. Scotty lifted the melody above his mid-range voice so that it was more emotive and plaintive. Simone could feel a quality coming through that was different, as if another part of him was singing out. When he landed the melody, he sang it over and over again... like a prayer.

So hold on... hold on
Hold on to your soul
Hold on... hold on
This night will make you whole

Simone harmonized with Scotty, adding some gospel embellishments that were a little bluesy as well. They repeated the chorus over and over again, refining the notes but working emotions into the music. Without saying anything, Simone went back to repeating the chords she used in the first verse, as an invitation for Scotty to return to the plotline.

"I want you to flip the focus," said Simone. "Try to put yourself in the woman's position, the one who walked out. Where did she go? What happened to *her* broken heart?"

The prompt from Simone caused Scotty to return to that tender connection with his former lover. It took him a long time to find the words. Then they came. He scratched them out, closed his eyes and let more lyrics emerge. As he tweaked them further he sang:

Well she went down to the gospel church
She fell down on her knees
She prayed to the Sisters of Mercy
To come and set him free

She felt an angel fly to the waters
She heard the swell of soothing strings
She saw him stand by the waters deep
Then she heard a choir sing

Hold on... hold on
Hold on to your soul
Hold on... hold on
This night will make you whole

"From the top."

Over and over they repeated the song, each time making adjustments in the vocal and instrumental elements. When they both knew it was finished, they stopped. The music turned into silence.

"I heard this story when I was a kid," said Simone. "Check it out. Long ago there was a poet who'd be labouring in the fields. She could feel when a poem was coming. If she was fast enough to fetch a pencil and paper, she could capture the poem as it moved through her. If she didn't get it she felt sure that it would land somewhere else – with someone else."

"Amen," said Scotty.

They sat quietly on the piano bench. The act of creating together had brought a degree of vulnerability and intimacy into their friendship. Nothing more needed to be said but it was clear that a deeper bond had formed.

At the next rehearsal, Scotty and Simone asked if they could share the song they had co-written. They wanted to see if it could be included in the set list for the Bob Seger shows. Fortunately, Coyote was present that night. Simone used the Fender Rhodes to play the piano part and Scotty stood at the front of the stage with no instrument other than his voice. The band sat in the audience section to listen.

Both musicians had memorized their parts. Scotty didn't need his lyric sheet and Simone knew the chords and arrangement by heart. They played it through once and didn't hold back on the emotional content of the song. Both the lyrics and supporting keyboard part were simple enough to carry the song. What made it work was the soulful blend of their voices when they sang together.

Instantly, everyone in NADI, including Coyote, knew that the song worked on different levels. Most important, it moved them. Spontaneously, they all stood up and clapped. Coyote was the first to speak. "Holy shit," he said. "That song is a motherfucker… and I mean that in the most complimentary way. I hope you have more where that came from?"

Scotty tried not to have any expectations but he secretly wanted to hear what Tamara would say. He deliberately didn't look at her but was relieved to hear her speak next. "That touched me so deeply. I was transported. Thank you both for writing that song. YES, it needs to be included in the set list. Beyond that… it also needs to be recorded."

UB, Sal, and Nardello all chimed in with complimentary comments as well as suggestions about how the band could fill it out. It was Nardello who would lift the song to another level. "I have an idea," he said. "In the final verse, the lyrics highlight the woman's experience – something about her going to the church, praying to the Sisters of Mercy and then hearing a choir sing. I wonder what it might feel like if Simone sang that part and the listener gets to hear a woman's heartbreak and hope."

"I'm happy to try that out," said Scotty. "I'm open to experimenting with all kinds of possibilities. Ultimately, I want the song to have our group energy and sound."

The bulk of NADI's rehearsal that night was focused on ways to fill out the orchestration without taking away from how it worked best – featuring the voices and gospel keyboard. They tried expanding it with a guitar solo but dropped that arrangement. They experimented with UB playing the Rhodes with Simone laying down a bass part. That approach also got dropped. What worked in the end was a configuration of sounds that built up as the song developed.

Sal added a light rhythmical ingredient with Simone's entrance on the Rhodes. Nardello switched from guitar to bass and played a tasteful part that Simone had sketched out for him. UB didn't come in with the Hammond organ until the turn-around verse.

So send an angel down to the waters
Tell her to bring some wings
Someone's standing on the bridge tonight
While somewhere a choir sings

During the chorus, everyone except Sal sang harmony parts. It took a while to work out the dynamics but eventually the women's voices stood out more and the guys' voices became supportive. Intentionally, Tamara didn't play violin until closer to the end when Simone sang the lyrics:

She felt an angel fly to the waters
She heard the swell of soothing strings

Tamara worked out a violin part that, the more she refined it, became the identifiable hook that would stick in the listeners' ears. It was memorable and added the final spice needed to complete the song. The only remaining question had to do with the ending. Coyote wanted to hear two versions and it took some time to get them both right. The first arrangement was for the live performance. It allowed Tamara more room to develop a solo part over top of the vocalists singing the outro. This stretched out the song and could expand as long as needed in a live performance.

The second arrangement involved Coyote timing the song and making sure that a stripped-down version clocked in at three minutes – perfect for a radio version on a 45-rpm single. That second approach worked best with more of a fade out exit, as if the chorus could keep on singing in the listener's mind, after the music stopped.

Coyote would not be persuaded from his insistence that NADI record the song as a single. When it became a non-debatable matter, the group turned their attention to what could be recorded on the B side. They didn't have a second vocal song. Nardello suggested that they edit one of their instrumental compositions called "Monkey." The piece was inspired by a Frank Zappa song called "Peaches en

Regalia," a jazz fusion composition released that year on Zappa's album *Hot Rats*.

"Monkey" was typically used in their set list as a transitional composition. It gave the group a tightly arranged piece with well-rehearsed parts. They usually played it as a bridge into a percussion improv but sometimes passed around solo parts between Nardello and Tamara.

The group agreed that "Monkey" could fit into a three-minute format without compromising the playful spirit of what was essentially a group composition. Popular AM radio stations rarely played instrumental songs anyway. A few emerging FM stations, such as WABX in Detroit, were going way beyond the AM norm. They not only played instrumentals but would let a song like "In-A-Gadda-Da-Vida" by Iron Butterfly go on for the entire 17 minutes. NADI was less concerned about recording "Monkey" and concentrated their energies on the new composition, which they called "Motor City Angel."

Simone had logged plenty of studio hours at Polaris. George, the owner, was happy to donate an afternoon recording session to NADI in exchange for them mentioning on the 45 that the songs had been engineered and recorded at Polaris. George also had an outstanding favour from a record pressing company and was able to get the mastering, printing, and shipping to NADI at a decent price. It all happened quickly. The first run was modest – one thousand copies. The plan was to distribute the first 100 copies to radio stations in the Windsor-Detroit area. They could sell what was left in a few record stores but concentrate on having it available offstage, at concerts.

Before the Seger string of engagements, Punch Andrews introduced Coyote to one of the most influential music directors in the Detroit-Windsor area: Rosalie Trombley. In 1963, Rosalie worked part-time as a switchboard operator and receptionist at Windsor's CKLW, a popular radio station. After figuring out how a Top 40 station functioned, Rosalie accepted a position in the music library. In the fall of 1968, she was offered a full-time position as CKLW's music director. Her main job was to find the songs that listeners liked best. Her decision to add a song to CKLW's playlist could determine whether the record would become a hit, or not. Rosalie was respected for her instincts and good ears. More often than not, she could predict when an album track might climb up the charts.

When Coyote took the freshly pressed "Motor City Angel" to CKLW, he brought Scotty and Simone along to meet Rosalie. The meeting was brief. Rosalie was cordial yet professional. She didn't play the song in front of her visitors but asked questions about the nature of their music, the upcoming tour with Seger, and why they chose an instrumental song for the B side. She took Coyote's business card and made no promises. It wasn't company policy to let artists know whether she had put their songs into rotation. However, as a favour to a local Windsor band, she would give Coyote a heads up if she intended to play it.

A few days later, Coyote got a quick call from Rosalie. She liked the song and wanted to give it a shot on Tom Shannon's show. He was a popular DJ at CKLW and had a large audience who listened in. Uncharacteristically, Rosalie suggested that Coyote let some of NADI's fans know that "Motor City Angel" was going to be aired that night. It wasn't a rehearsal night so Scotty and Tamara invited everyone over to their place where they could listen to the station through Scotty's stereo cabinet and enjoy some snacks prepared by Tamara. UB and Sal couldn't make it over to Scotty and Tamara's place but tuned in from their apartment.

Admittedly, the members of NADI rarely listened to AM radio. The playlist was eclectic and some of the more popular tunes were far from what the musicians preferred. Tom Shannon's list that night featured a mix of hits. Sometimes they sang along with tunes such as "I Can't Get Next to You" by The Temptations, "Honky Tonk Women" by The Rolling Stones, and especially "Everyday People" by Sly and the Family Stone. When it came to "Sugar, Sugar" by The Archies or "Dizzy" by Tommy Roe, they ate and joked around about how they would spend their millions after becoming famous.

They nearly talked over the DJ's announcement after he had played "Crystal Blue Persuasion" by Tommy James and The Shondells.

"Shhh," said Coyote.

"So, here's something new for you... an exclusive right here from CKLW. You heard it first on our station... our pick of the week. A

Windsor band called NADI. Check out their debut single, 'Motor City Angel.'"

Scotty cranked up the volume. It was an odd experience hearing themselves over the radio. They had grown accustomed to rehearsing the song and recording it with a fuller sound. Despite turning up the volume, Scotty felt the dynamics had been squashed. Still, the thrill of feeling their music coming out of the speakers made up for the loss of high-fidelity sound. No one spoke. Scotty and Tamara looked wide-eyed at each other. Scotty and Simone smiled. Coyote couldn't stop nodding. Nardello, with his eyes closed, played an air bass along with the song.

"There you have it," said Tom Shannon. "'Motor City Angel' by NADI. Call in if you want to hear that one again… right here on the Big 8."

Coyote was tempted to phone in as an anonymous listener and rave on about "Motor City Angel." Tamara persuaded him to let the song have a life of its own. If it was meant to be… callers would decide.

Nardello raised a beer and spoke. "I want to acknowledge the two people here who gave us something NADI can be proud of. Here's to Scotty and Simone."

Glasses of water, wine, and beer were raised. Scotty and Simone embraced. Scotty made a silent wish that more material was waiting in the unseen realms – just waiting to be birthed.

CHAPTER 19

NADI, and especially Coyote, waited for "Motor City Angel" to climb higher in the Top 40 playlist. Surprisingly, the B side of their 45-single got into the hands of a Detroit TV producer. He needed a theme song for a pilot television project called *What Do I Do?* It was a 30-minute program in which a panel of celebrities had to guess the occupation of a mystery guest. There were rules as to what questions panelists could ask. The interaction between the host, the guest, and the panelists added a comedic element to the show. To match the playfulness of the program, the producer wanted a quirky theme song. He only needed a section for the intro, the outro, and as a stinger when the show returned from commercials.

A copy of "Monkey" got into the producer's hands. He liked the mix of something peculiar and playful. Through a copyright lawyer, royalties were worked out and payments were to be sent to NADI for the right to use their intellectual property. Fortunately, Tamara had worked out all the publishing requirements for both songs before they were pressed. It wasn't a ton of money, but within weeks the first cheque for "Monkey" appeared in the mail.

The CKLW airplay was intermittent. However, a surprise came out of left field. Every Sunday night a radio program was broadcast out of Detroit called *Martha Jean's Gospel Hour.* While a lot of religious music filled the time slot, Martha would occasionally play a James Brown song or a blues track that seemed inspirational. For some reason, she loved "Motor City Angel." Martha began to play it on a regular basis.

One thing led to another and a second Detroit station picked up the song. Simone's old neighbourhood, in the city's Cass Corridor, was home to WDET-FM, a station licensed to Wayne State University. At least once or twice a day, the track was getting airplay from DJs. This exposure led to a third Detroit station picking it up. WABX

– The station that glows in the dark – was respected as an influential radio station that specialized in freeform and progressive rock music. Although the song was less edgy than what WABX usually played, the hometown nature of the lyrics and music resonated with listeners and programmers.

With a handful of stations airing the one vocal song NADI recorded, the group faced a problem. They had only pressed several hundred copies of the song. Rather than place these in record outlets, and receive a fraction of the sales, the group decided to go with their original plan of selling individual units off stage at their concerts. The Seger tour would be a good litmus test. If they came home with empty boxes they would go ahead and press more records. Although rarely discussed, the pressure was on to follow up one song with a dozen more tracks needed to complete an album.

The first night out with Bob Seger was set for a Friday at the Masonic Auditorium in Toledo, Ohio. The roadies left late morning from Windsor to avoid heavy traffic in Detroit and accommodate the predictable delays crossing into the States. Coyote drove UB and Sal mid-afternoon in his car. Scotty volunteered to take Tamara, Nardello, and Simone in his station wagon. The two couples had prepared a cooler of food and non-alcoholic drinks for the trip. Once the suitcases and instruments were loaded in the trunk, Scotty hopped into the driver's seat. He expected Tamara to join him upfront but to his surprise, Nardello squeezed into the passenger's seat.

"We're shit outta luck buddy," said Nardello. "The women decided to sit together. We're stuck with one another. At least we get to control the radio."

Sure enough, Tamara and Simone climbed in the back with pillows and blankets. They were already talking up a storm before the car pulled out. Scotty turned on the radio as they cruised along. The women seemed oblivious to what was happening in the front seat and the music muffled any exchanges between Scotty and Nardello.

"How are you feeling about tonight?" asked Nardello.

"It's weird," said Scotty. "We're expanding our fan base more through radio play than performing. It'll be interesting to see how a fresh audience responds to us – especially people who have come to hear Seger and not us."

"I had this strange idea about starting off with 'Monkey' tonight," said Nardello.

"Yeah. Why?"

"The TV show has been out for a couple of weeks now. There's a chance that some of the audience would have caught it. They might recognize our song from the opening and closing theme."

"Sure. It's a cool tune. Might be fun to stretch it out as a way of getting us and the crowd going."

"Where do you want to put 'Motor City Angel?'" asked Nardello.

"Definitely way back in the set. I was thinking about somewhere in the last third. That way we can end with something more upbeat."

Laughter came from the back and the guys turned around to see Tamara and Simone snuggled up against each other looking at a photo album. It was a compilation of photographs that Tamara took when she was living in London, England. Scotty had seen it before. There were some fun shots of Tamara partying with her friends in the Chelsea Gardens pub scene.

"Hey," said Nardello, "I wanted to mention something that UB told me last week. Sal's been worried about some phone calls they've been getting at the apartment. When UB picks up the phone, he can hear someone breathing on the other end. The person sometimes says that he knows where Sal is living and then hangs up. Sal told UB to not say anything. Let the caller speak first, even if it's one of UB's parents."

"That's strange," said Scotty. "What's that all about?"

"Well UB was getting freaked out by the calls and finally Sal shared a part of his life story that none of us had heard. You know Sal came from Venezuela on a music scholarship."

"Yeah."

"Well, apparently the back story is way more complicated. Turns out that Sal shot somebody and had to get out of town before he was arrested. He hid out in Colombia initially and then, through a conductor friend, applied for a music scholarship and student visa to Canada. He was sure no one from Caracas would look for him in Windsor, Ontario."

"Wait. What does UB know about the shooting part?"

"The first part we already knew. Sal was going out with this guy whose father was high up in the military. The father found out about his son being gay and that Sal was his lover. Sal was given a strong message to stop seeing the son and to leave the city while he was still alive."

"That's a little different than what we first heard."

"The part that none of us had heard before, including UB, had to do with a soldier showing up at Sal's place in Caracas. This happened the next day when he had planned to disappear. I guess the soldier was sent as an enforcer to make sure Sal got the message to leave *el pronto*. The guy roughs up Sal a bit and then puts the barrel of a gun in his mouth. He gives him a choice: Suck on the barrel and take a chance that the gun might ejaculate a bullet. Or, suck on his dick and swallow a wetter bullet. The guy drops his pants and he's already hard. Sal fears for his life but takes the guy's dick in his mouth and starts to give him a blow job. As Sal is sucking him off, the soldier is whacking him in the head and calling him a fucking fag."

"What did Sal do?" asked Scotty.

"He could sense that things were going to get more violent and felt that as soon as the guy came in his mouth, he would probably get the shit beaten out of him… or worse. Now the guy has grabbed Sal's hair and is ramming his dick into his mouth as he's getting more excited. Sal can sense the guy is near orgasm and so he has to do something quick. He chomps down hard on the guy's dick and the soldier jumps back in pain. Sal, in the confusion, grabs the soldier's gun from the table, cocks the trigger, and shoots the guy in the thigh."

"I bet he was aiming for the groin."

"The wounded guy is bleeding and screaming. Fortunately, Sal had already packed and had a knapsack ready with the basics: some clothes, cash, and his passport. He grabbed the knapsack and bolted."

"Did the guy survive the gunshot wound?"

"UB didn't say," said Nardello. "What Sal suspects is that someone in the military intelligence has tracked him down. He's worried that there might be a hit put out on him… to keep him quiet."

"Jesus. Why didn't Sal come to us sooner? He must be worried sick."

"UB thinks that Sal was protecting us. Didn't want us to get involved

171

or have us worrying before the Seger gigs."

"Does Coyote know?"

"UB encouraged Sal to talk about the whole mess with Coyote while they drive to Toledo."

"I can't imagine a guy like Sal shooting somebody," said Scotty. "But I get that his life probably depended on it."

"I don't know jack shit about the world of contracts and hit men. But I do know someone who swims in those waters every day."

"You mean the baker across the street from your folks' store?"

"Mr. Scarpelli isn't someone I want to cozy up to," said Nardello. "But in a case like this, I would trust him to deal with the situation more than the cops."

The lack of laughter from the back seat indicated that the women had heard most of the conversation and were taking in the gravity of what Sal was facing. To switch the mood, Scotty turned the radio until he found the afternoon broadcast of the Tiger-Boston baseball game in Detroit. Scotty needed some Al Kaline mojo.

The stage at the Masonic Hall in Toledo was all set by the time the band arrived. Seger's gear was pushed behind NADI's set up, ready for a quick change over. The soundcheck didn't take long and everyone was pleased with the acoustics – not too *boomy.* NADI had their own dressing room separate from Seger's crew. It was small but leagues up from the second floor at Sotto Voce. Ron and Brian had ordered in some pizza for everyone so there was no need to go anywhere.

Before talking through the set list or arrangements, Coyote requested a huddle.

"Let's take care of some family business first," said Coyote. "By now we're all aware of the stressful circumstance that Sal and UB are facing. There's a very real possibility that Sal is being tracked. This is some serious shit and so the guys are going to stay with me for a bit, until we can sort this out. I'll put some feelers out to see what anybody knows. There's no point in getting the cops involved. The last thing we need is Sal getting deported back to Venezuela."

"When we get back," said Nardello, "I was thinking of asking the owner of the Erie St. Bakery for some advice."

"You mean Scarpelli?" asked Coyote.

"Yes," said Nardello. "I'm cautious about asking him for a favour but there's nobody in Windsor who would be more connected to the underworld than him."

"Shit yeah," said Coyote. "He's the fucking mayor when it comes to that world."

Sal was quiet. UB sat beside him with his arm around his shoulder. Finally, Sal spoke. "I should have been upfront with you all from the beginning. I've been carrying around this part of my past hoping that it would go away. I was so ashamed of shooting someone, I didn't even tell my partner until last week. I didn't want anyone to get involved."

Nardello broke the tension. "Well, brother, I gotta hand it to you in terms of what to do in a life-threatening situation when a guy has his dick in your mouth. I'm not sure Batman would have been that resourceful. The guy's just lucky that you didn't chomp down *harder.* You can recover from a bullet wound but losing an important appendage could have been a lot worse."

Sal laughed. "It was a long time before I could give a blowjob again." His tone then became more serious. "Being with UB helped me to heal. When we were intimate he didn't even know how that image would replay in my mind. It was his gentleness that changed me."

"Here's to the healing power of sex," said Nardello raising a glass.

"And love," said UB.

Tamara and Scotty smiled at each other.

As planned, NADI's performance that night began with an extended version of "Monkey." From the start the band needed to raise their energy. It was as if they weren't playing for the audience but for one another – especially for Sal. They took liberties with the arrangement and even threw in a section that featured Sal on percussion. When they finished they were amazed to hear some people in the audience chanting the identifiable chorus to the TV show: *What Do I Do? What Do I Do? What Do I Do?*

The ice was broken and a connection made. The band relaxed and dropped into a spirited exchange with one another and the crowd.

Solos got wilder and the energy got higher. When they came to play "Motor City Angel," Scotty stepped up to the microphone.

"We really want to thank Bob Seger for having us on this mini-tour. The timing is perfect because we just put out our first single. It's getting some airplay in the Detroit area and we want to bring it to you tonight in Toledo. If you like it, we're going to sell copies during the break. It's called 'Motor City Angel.'"

Simone jumped in right away with a keyboard intro that set up the opening chords. Some people must have heard the song already because the closer she got to the identifiable arrangement, the more the audience cheered. Scotty had always believed that a particular song could soothe your soul or stir your heart, so singing "Motor City Angel" was becoming a form of therapy for him. He could feel how far his life had fallen and measure how far his journey in recovery had taken him. The more he sang out the story, the more he realized that Tamara was that angel in his life, helping him to grow his own wings and rise above what could again pull him back down.

Tamara was on fire during her solo and the band drew out the improvisation longer than they ever had. The crowd cheered her on. NADI's live arrangement required the band to soften after the violin solo, and for the voices to carry out the song with everyone singing.

Hold on... hold on
Hold on to your soul
Hold on... hold on
This night might make you whole

As the band started the chorus, the audience joined in. They had never intended to create an anthem-like arrangement but, spontaneously, it was happening. The singing and emotions kept building and suddenly the crowd started cheering as Bob Seger came out onto the stage, stood next to Tamara and joined in with everyone else singing the chorus. It wasn't grandstanding and certainly didn't detract from NADI's performance. Seger, like everyone else, just wanted to be a part of that massive Masonic Temple choir.

With all the unplanned soloing in the first half of the set, coupled with the surprise singing, Scotty realized that their set had reached the time limit. He thanked Bob for joining them on stage, the crowd for singing along, and the sound crew for doing such a great job. The band stood together at the front of the stage and bowed. Everyone, including Bob Seger, cheered them on.

They sold a shitload of records that night.

CHAPTER 20

The rest of NADI's mini-tour continued to deliver, both musically and socially. The comradery between the musicians deepened over meals, driving stretches, and going for walks together in down times. Sal was more himself again and not preoccupied so much with possible troubles. Tamara and Simone had become more openly affectionate, holding hands during strolls and snuggling in the back of Scotty's car. One afternoon, while driving to Dearborn, Tamara fell asleep on a pillow in Simone's lap. Simone stroked her hair, held her close, and also drifted off.

The radio was playing. Scotty and Nardello felt safe to talk about the deepening relationship between the two women. "Does it concern you?" asked Scotty.

"What?" said Nardello.

"That Tamara and Simone are getting closer. They're clearly fond of one another."

"Fond?" said Nardello. "Wake up, brother. They *love* each other. Surely you can see that?"

Scotty thought about what Nardello was saying. He had not admitted the obvious to himself. Nardello named it.

"I don't want to pry man," said Scotty, "but does it threaten you... that your partner is bi-sexual and attracted to Tamara?"

"Attracted? There you go again! Scotty, my man, these two women are soul mates... they love each other. And, they love us. I've talked to Simone. She's not going after Tamara with the idea of taking her away from you. Simone is just being herself, open about who she is and who she loves. You need to understand this. Simone respects our partnership and she certainly honours the relationship you and Tamara have. Just let them love each other without fear of losing the best thing you've ever been given."

Scotty listened to Nardello's straight talk. He relaxed a little, although he was not quite prepared for Nardello's next statement.

"And while we're being honest with one another, brother, you can open up with me. I get that you've done a lot of therapy with counsellors and recovery specialists. But sometimes, Scotty, it's not about spilling your heart out to professionals. It's about talking up-front to the people who love and care for you. I've learned that from Simone."

When Scotty heard those words, he realized how much he had insulated himself from those closest to him. On a number of occasions, Scotty had avoided collaborating further with Simone. He didn't want to bring more complications into a band made up of layered relationships. He liked being with Simone, but his long-standing friendship with Nardello was precious. He didn't ask Simone to meet up for another songwriting session in case that stirred a jealous reaction in Nardello.

Scotty had been sidestepping his connection with Simone, imagining that being alone with her would be an infidelity in his partnership with Tamara. As Nardello pointed out, Scotty often steered clear of talking about his feelings and fears with those who cared deeply for him. No one had been fooled – except himself.

On the last night of the tour, the couples each enjoyed a hotel room to themselves. Even Coyote had found someone from the gig to spend the night with. Scotty and Tamara talked until 2 a.m. about everything that had gone unspoken. They were too tired to make love but their conversation felt like an expression of intimacy. Sal and UB also poured their hearts out to one another. They discussed what they would need to do in terms of moving from the apartment to Coyote's place. They professed their love for one another. UB provided a safe space for Sal to land that night. Simone and Nardello got naked and naughty together. They laughed and teased one another; they showered and played a game that involved asking the other person for five-minute cycles of pleasurable offerings. They fell asleep exhausted and happy.

Coyote didn't do a lot of talking that night.

When the band got back to Windsor, a good portion of their singles

177

had been sold. Uppermost in Scotty's mind was the need to write more original material. During the last evening on the Seger tour, NADI had landed an interview with an emerging Detroit music magazine called CREEM. The interviewer gave a good review of their show. In the article, Scotty had promised that the band would be going back into the studio soon to work on their debut album.

The day after he got home, Nardello went across the street to the Erie St. Bakery. He wasn't interested in buying biscotti. He wanted to talk with Nicholas Scarpelli about Sal's situation. Scarpelli listened to the whole story, made a few notes, and asked for details on Sal – where he lived, who he lived with, how he arrived in Canada, what he was doing at the university. It all seemed straightforward enough until Nardello got up to leave and was ready to thank Mr. Scarpelli.

"Before you go, I want to ask if you know this phrase: *Ogni mali nun veni pri nòciri.*"

"Yes," said Nardello. "It means: *Not every pain comes to harm you.*"

"Your parents have taught you well, Bruno. You can leave your problem with me. Now I have a favour to ask of you. I have a niece who is about to get married. Your band has a song that she likes."

"'Motor City Angel.'"

"On the day of her wedding, during the reception, you and your band will dress nicely and come play that song for her and her partner to dance to. Capisci?"

"Yes."

"Someone will contact you with the details."

Nearly a week passed before Nardello heard from Scarpelli. He was summoned to the small office at the back of the bakery. Scarpelli was on the phone and so he waited by the Hobart mixing machine, the one he got to know well when working off the debt for the Nutella incident. Scarpelli had quietly sidled up behind him.

"Do you miss your part-time job here?"

"I'm grateful for the lesson you taught me. And I am in your debt for the guitar too."

"Consider the books balanced. And now… two things you need to know. Here's the date for my niece's wedding reception." Scarpelli passed over a piece of paper. "It's being hosted at the Caboto Club. Be there after dinner. Be ready to play around 9 p.m."

"You know that's the Victoria Day long weekend?"

"Look at me," said Scarpelli. "Do I seem like someone who will be celebrating Queen Victoria?"

"No sir."

"Good answer. The second matter concerns your friend from Venezuela. This was a complex negotiation. As we say, '*Ntra greci e greci nun si vinni abbraciu.*"

"There's honour among thieves."

"Yes. Here's what you need to know. A person in Venezuela hired a hitman here in Canada to take out your friend. In other words, this was serious business. In order to fix it a contract had to be bought to neutralize the original agreement. That came at a high price."

"I'm not sure I fully understand."

"A killer had to be paid not to kill. Then, a message had to be sent back to some people in Venezuela… to back off. That also cost money, because people don't work for nothing. I've taken care of those two matters. I won't tell you how much money was involved in all this but you need to know that debts will need to be settled. Understand?"

"I understand but, as you know, I don't have much money."

"This I know. What you do have is a band, a connection to a recording studio, and maybe a lucrative niche in the music business. As a business man I need to diversify. My colleagues and competitors in other parts of the country have been getting into clubs and casinos. You're smart enough to know that lots of artists have financial backers… people like myself who have invested in their success."

"I know about Sinatra and others. But my group isn't exactly a Las Vegas act."

"Do you think I care about what music you play? My interest is in operations where I can move cash around without drawing a lot of attention. Let's just say that I am interested in small, independent record labels and performers who wouldn't appear to be connected to my… family business."

"I don't know what to say, Mr. Scarpelli. I can't speak for the band."

"I would suggest that you not mention it to them. It's enough for you to know that a family friend has just saved the life of your bandmate and it came at a high cost. What you can say to your friends is that an investor is interested in backing the band's career. Think it over. You know where to find me."

Nardello nodded. The meeting was over. Nicholas Scarpelli was not someone you negotiated with and so the two men shook hands. Nardello crossed the street to his parents' place and wasted no time calling Coyote. They met at the Seminole House for a beer and an important conversation.

"Shit," said Coyote.

He heard Nardello tell the whole story. Coyote sipped on his beer with mixed emotions and ruminated out loud.

"It's complex. The good news is that Sal will be safe. If anything happened to him, Scarpelli's deal would be off the table. The bad news is that we become involved in the Mob's money laundering operation. Once they get their hooks into you, there's no getting out of that relationship."

"Damn right it's complex," said Nardello. "Scarpelli made it seem like we have a choice but we're really on the hook for blowing off Sal's murder."

Coyote took a long swig of beer and then spoke carefully.

"There are only three people in this group that would get what's at risk here. Two of them are sitting here in the Seminole House. Who's the third?"

"Scotty."

"He's been around the music business and the dealers too. He knows that the scene of sex, drugs, and rock 'n' roll isn't run by hippies. It's an old, worn story. The Mob first ran the clubs and the speakeasies, and made it possible for white audiences to hear *race music.* They gave breaks to artists from Louis Armstrong to Charlie Parker. But they would shake these artists down too."

"I'm not sure what you're getting at," said Nardello.

"Tell Sal that he's safe. Then we only tell Scotty about the so-called investor. Everyone else is kept out of the picture as to who is backing the project… for their own safety. We also don't need them getting freaked out going into the studio."

"Do you know the story of Sinatra? He was under contract to sing exclusively for the Tommy Dorsey Orchestra. Frank wanted out of the contract. A Mob guy shows up and puts a gun to the bandleader's head. Frank was free from one contract but tied to a more binding one."

"Your point?" asked Coyote.

"Just know who we're dealing with. Scarpelli works for the Lombardo family out of New York."

CHAPTER 21

After a week of living in Coyote's house, Sal and UB were relieved to hear that a friend of Nardello's had straightened out the whole matter. They didn't know the details, only that they could return home without any more concerns. Just to be on the safe side, the couple found a new apartment. It was closer to the university and they moved in at the end of the month, as the school term was winding down and students were moving out of rented spaces.

NADI's weekly rehearsals were replaced by workshop sessions that happened two or three times a week. Sometimes it was just Scotty and Simone deep into songwriting mode. Other times, a few more bandmates would be present, helping with compositional ideas and arrangements. Once a week the full band would gather to refine parts or try out transitions from one song to another.

As a group, NADI was impressed and influenced by the Beatles approach to *Sgt. Pepper's Lonely Hearts Club Band.* As a concept album, the Beatles used everything from circus music to classical Indian music and held the recording together with a storytelling thread. The group wanted NADI's debut album to also be eclectic. They wanted it to feel like their live set at Sotto Voce, with extended solos. They also wanted to include elements that weren't possible in the live shows. Tamara, for instance, was writing parts for her string ensemble. Sal was rehearsing his percussion group to come into the studio. Simone had met with some gospel singers she knew from Detroit to add backup vocals.

Scotty stayed focused on writing lyrics and composing music. He knew, from his conversations with Nardello and Coyote, that Scarpelli was funding the project. However, he didn't want to start obsessing about a mobster being involved with a musical project – that could become a huge distraction. As Nardello had said, Scarpelli wasn't all that interested in the content. It was more about a way to launder money and make it look legitimate. If something could make money, Scarpelli took notice.

Scotty's lyrics tended to lean toward themes relevant to the times. He didn't give a shit if the songs would piss off Scarpelli. In his opinion, the Mob was just another version of the *Establishment.* To provide a metaphor for washing away all the slime of corruption and manipulation, Scotty wanted the recording project to be called *NADI – The River.*

Their first recording session in the Polaris studio came off easily enough as the group decided to make a longer version of "Monkey" – the way they played it in concert. They also wanted a fuller arrangement of "Motor City Angel," one that would feature Tamara's solo. They arranged a finale section in the song with more voices, supported by the string ensemble. Simone's vocalist friends aced their part and brought so much soulfulness to the recording.

During a Sotto Voce rehearsal, the conversation turned to how their writing could incorporate more of that Detroit gospel feel into the recording project. It was agreed that Simone, UB, and Scotty would compose a piece written in a slower 6/8 rhythm. It could be sung by Simone and backed up by her friends. UB sketched out an organ part that would be used for the verses. It had the right feel and combo of church meets blues.

When it came to lyrics, and what Simone might want to sing, she talked about the hardships young mothers face when fathers are absent from raising the children. The image caused Scotty to re-imagine the old biblical story of Mary and Joseph. What if Joseph was not a caring father? What if the setting was moved forward in time and Bethlehem became Birmingham?

NADI had played the Birmingham Palladium, just on the outskirts of downtown Detroit. That part of the Motor City area seemed desolate to Scotty. It personified a place where shelter would be difficult and the streets could be mean. The trio spent numerous hours trying out possibilities. Eventually they came up with a song called "Birmingham." Scotty wrote the lyrics while UB and Simone composed the music.

A streetlight shines down on this shelter tonight
Mary so tender and Joseph so wild
She rocks her baby as he hits the bars
It's a cold one again in Birmingham

Three kings of the street followed her here
One offered gold the other just leered
A third made a gesture a fist and a slam
It's a dark one again in Birmingham

Sleep child in motherly peace
Rest in my arms, safe in my love
Sleep child in motherly peace
Rest in my heart, safe in my love

She cradles him sweetly in arms that can hold
May courage bring comfort to suffering untold
Nurtured in love is Mary's sweet lamb
For there's a haven tonight in Birmingham

Pray for the Marys and infants so mild
Pray for the men who follow no star
Pray for the sisters who do what they can
For it's always so cold in Birmingham

Sleep child in motherly peace
Rest in my arms, safe in my love
Sleep child in motherly peace
Rest in my heart, safe in my love

When Tamara heard the piece, she gave herself the challenge of writing out a string arrangement for "Birmingham." She included a part for Nardello, as if the guitar were a natural part of a string ensemble. It took some experimenting to get an effect that worked but eventually Nardello added a quality that brought a grittier contrast to the softer strings.

Simone's voice was ideally suited for this song, and the recording happened effortlessly. The one glitch was the fade out and transition at the end of the song to the next track. It lacked imagination. UB came up with a brilliant solution. He pictured a Salvation Army band standing on a downtown street corner during the Christmas season. He subsequently wrote a five-part, instrumental hymn for brass players. The idea was that the brass quintet would fade into the mix while the vocal chorus was fading out. UB called in his university classmates to play on his composition which featured trumpet, French horn, trombone, euphonium, and tuba. When they hit the recording session, it only took a few takes to get it right.

After the recording, UB was captivated with the brass ensemble sound. The image of playing outside, be it on a street corner or in a parade, gave him the incentive to write more music for a brass section. While he had never visited New Orleans, UB was familiar with Second Line music – a crowd of dancers with parasols and handkerchiefs following a street band. They would move in a spirit of community called *second-lining*. UB's vision was to shift the staid brass quintet on the street corner – sounding like a Salvation Army band – and transition them into a parade band in the New Orleans tradition. Sal and the percussion group could fill out the rhythmical element. When UB ran his proposal by his bandmates, everyone remembered the high energy entrance at the University of Windsor concert with Bob Seger. They wondered how they could recreate a similar vibe.

UB said he could write out some brass parts in the parade tradition and Sal offered to collaborate on some percussion possibilities. Meanwhile, Scotty pulled out one of his writing journals, filled with poems and lyrics. He scribbled some opening lines in rough draft form and asked the band to improvise on a funky, shuffle groove. Working from sketched out lines, he sang.

When moonlight and magic slip into this town
Lipstick and saxophone just wanna get down
Call up the brothers, call the sisters too
Drummers and dancers y'all know what to do

It really doesn't matter if you're young or gray

Come to the party, come on out to play
Got rhythms in your body, got grooves in the street

One tribe One vibe
Celebrate the night
One tribe One vibe
It's gonna be alright

The feel was rough and the lyrics basic, but the heart of it was present. For now the band just locked into the energy, they could refine it later. It was Tamara who picked up on the activist potential of the song.

"I get the celebratory spirit," she said, "but this song could become more political, more of a rallying song for the gay rights movement."

"How so?" asked Sal.

"I know these are rough-hewn words," said Tamara, "but with a few rewrites we could slant it differently. Imagine singing: *It really doesn't matter if you're straight or gay.* Or, instead of referring to the *Second Line,* the lyric could say *Catch the vibe... the Rainbow Tribe beat."*

"Is it our place to speak for the Rainbow Tribe?" asked Scotty.

"In this band of six," said Tamara, "only two people have strictly followed the heterosexual path. Plus, *Rainbow* can stand for the counterculture community too."

Scotty crossed out some lyrics, added some new words and the band tried the next version.

When moonlight and magic slip into this town
Lipstick and saxophone just wanna get down
Call up the femmes, call the fairies too
Drummers and dancers y'all know what to do

It doesn't matter if you're straight or gay
Come to the party, come out to play
Bring rhythms in your body, bring grooves in the street
The Rainbow Tribe is about to meet

One tribe One vibe
Celebrate the night
One tribe One vibe
It's gonna be alright

Scotty did a decent job singing but looked troubled when they finished.

"I gotta tell you, this is not working for me. It's not my place to be singing these lyrics. I'm a white, straight guy singing about things that I support but… it's just not authentic. UB should be writing the words and singing the lines."

The band turned at once to face UB. He didn't miss a beat.

"Give me until tomorrow to come up with something."

That night, Tamara and Scotty lay in bed, talking about how the album was evolving. The night was humid and they could hear freighters signalling as they passed each other on the river.

"How are you feeling about the project?" asked Tamara. She stroked Scotty's forehead.

"I'm glad you asked. It was a difficult day for me. I have lots of questions about our direction. When we play live, there's an excitement about taking risks and surprising one another. When we get in the studio, it becomes more controlled. Arrangements get fixed. Each take might be slightly altered but we already know what's going to happen. And at the writing session today… I felt like I was dumbing down our musicianship."

"How do you mean?"

"Just think about it," said Scotty. "You, Sal, and UB are trained classical musicians. You can cut everything from medieval music to the avant-garde yet we spent all today messing with elementary music and really bad lyrics."

"Ease up there cowboy. Remember that *lento* principle? Not all good compositions come quickly and fully formed. Even classical composers might have nothing but a simple melody as a starting point. Over time, with perseverance and skill, a well-crafted symphony might be created."

"Yeah, I suppose. It's just that I worry whether NADI, in the long haul, is going to be rewarding and challenging enough for everyone?"

"We can't see that far down the road but what we do know is

that the lives of seven people have become woven together. We are wrapped up in one another."

Scotty was quiet then turned into Tamara. "I don't want our story to ever unravel, Tamara. I always wanna stay wrapped up in you."

"I'm not going anywhere, my love. Want to slow dance?"

Tamara slipped off the t-shirt she had been wearing as a pyjama top. Scotty never tired of seeing her naked and was instantly aroused.

"Let's play a musical game," she said. She reached over to Scotty's transistor radio and spun the dial until she found the CBC's classical broadcast. They were playing Samuel Barber's *Adagio for Strings.*

"We have to make love to each other with the opposite energy of what we hear," Tamara said. "If the piece is slow, we go fast. If the music is fast, we go slow. Wanna play?"

The andante nature of *Adagio for Strings* proved to be a perfect backdrop for a facet of their lovemaking they had not fully explored – more assertive energies. Tamara ripped off Scotty's shirt and pinned his wrists down with her hands. She mounted him and bit into his neck and ears. He bucked her trying to get free but she rode him like an old cowhand. When he did free his hands, he flipped Tamara onto her back, wrapped her legs around his neck, and entered the well that was already wet.

As they throbbed against each other, moaning and shrieking with pleasure, the CBC announcer introduced the next Samuel Barber selection – the 3rd movement from Barber's *Violin Concerto.* The dramatic piece moves at a hyper speed, like *Flight of the Bumblebee.* It took tremendous effort for Tamara to switch gears and shift away from a deeply satisfying primal mode. She hadn't experienced this animalistic side of herself in a long time and she loved Scotty's passive, yang energy as well. Still, a deal is a deal. Both paused, took deep breaths and switched positions. Tamara, straddling Scotty, arched her back and rocked on top of him as slowly as she could. They laughed… hoping that the next recording let them swap tenderness for wildness.

When UB showed up at rehearsal the next day he was not alone. The brass players and some of Sal's percussion group came along. UB took charge and asked Scotty to read the trumpet part. He then facilitated an initial rehearsal of his arrangement, including the entire brass quintet. The tempo had been pulled back, without sacrificing any energy.

Sal's crew spent some time getting the rhythmic parts tight. Throughout the instrumental portion of the rehearsal, UB got very specific about dynamics: when he wanted the full ensemble or when he wanted the sound to be stripped down to fewer percussionists. In addition to the instrumental building blocks, UB had written out harmony parts for everyone to sing on the chorus.

"I want the overall feel to be slinky," said UB. "Imagine a New Orleans trad band at night, playing under a full moon. It's hot and humid. No one wants to push. There's a sexy feel to the music and lots of space with a laid-back mood."

UB asked the brass players to not sit down. He wanted them to stand in one place while they played. The sound engineer strategically placed a couple of microphones to capture more of an overall effect. To prevent sound bleed, they positioned the percussionists in an arc behind isolation partitions.

"This song is about a gay man dressing up as a woman," said UB. "He loves to dance and join in Second Line parades. His life has been hard but he, being Wishbone, is strong and determined. Brass, I want you to enter with the A Section. I've marked it as a repeat until the lyrics come in. I just want bass drum, snare, and triangle off the top."

UB stood in the middle of the circle with a handheld microphone, prepared to sing and conduct. Simone, Tamara, and Nardello had a lyric sheet and hovered around a single microphone, ready to harmonize on the chorus. UB conducted the instrumental entrance and then sang as if that's what he had done all his life.

He puts on his stockings and his lipstick too
Wishbone's heading out to dance away his blues
Straighten the wig, slip on the dress
Tonight he's gonna fly from the nest
Tonight he's gonna fly from the nest

He gets his high heels on and his parasol pink

189

Puts glitter on his eyes and sips a little drink
Beads around his neck and a gun in the purse
Tonight he's gonna shoot down that curse
Tonight he's gonna shoot down that curse

Chorus
Some people just want to play in the band
Some people just want to clap their hands
Some people just want to lay down the groove
Some people were born to move
Some people were born to move

His mama made him pretty, his papa made him hurt
His sisters showed Wishbone how to slip into a skirt
Now the band is getting ready and the crowd is getting hot
The moon is gonna shine on everything he's got
Yeah the moon is gonna shine on all that he's not

Some people want to play in the band
Some people want to clap their hands
Some people want to lay down the groove
Some people were born to move
Some people were born to move

When they came for Wishbone they grabbed his figure
Nobody thought that he would really pull that trigger
Never underestimate a man in high heels
'Cause he can show you just how freedom feels

Some people want to play in the band
Some people want to clap their hands
Some people want to lay down the groove
Some people were born to move
Some people were born to move and move and move

When everyone came to the final chorus, the musicians kept playing. The brass players retained a connection to the original parts but improvised new riffs. The singers messed around with the repeating line:

Some people were born to move and move and move

UB closed his eyes and took it all in. His face looked like a man in a state of rapture.

CHAPTER 22

Scotty admired Tamara's work ethic. She kept her hand on the administrative details of Sotto Voce, taught her string students, visited her uncle, and practiced her violin at least two hours a day. She always found time for their relationship and he never heard her complain about the workload. Still, he was cautious about laying another burden on her shoulders. "Hey Super T," he said. "I know you have powers beyond us mere mortals… don't you ever get overwhelmed?"

"I'm living that Spencer Davis song – *Keep on Running*."

"Alright, then I won't feel bad running this by you. I'm hoping that you can re-arrange one of the first instrumentals we worked out with you at Sotto Voce. I like a lot of the new compositions on the recording project, but I also miss that original structure of a drone, a rhythm, and then a defined melody. I was wondering… could you re-arrange one of those earlier pieces? Maybe include a combination of a string ensemble with Nardello's edgier sound. Oh… and could you also work in a call and response chant too, one that someone listening to the album could instantly sing back."

"Do you want naan on the side?"

It took Scotty a second to realize that Tamara was teasing him. She was actually honoured to have more of a lead on one of the tracks. How she found the time wasn't clear to Scotty. By the next rehearsal, which included the string players, Tamara had composed and arranged "Kali Ma" – a tribute to the Hindu goddess of time, creation, preservation, and destruction. As Tamara explained to the group, she may appear fearsome but, in essence, is a compassionate goddess.

The band loved playing the piece. It took them back to their roots while including new branches of development. "Kali Ma" paired a traditional sound with Simone's funky bass and Nardello's burning guitar. Regrettably, when they took the composition into the studio, they couldn't reduce the track below a ten-minute mark. The best take, where Tamara and Nardello traded licks back and forth, rang in at twelve minutes.

"Not exactly radio friendly," noted Coyote.

"Screw it," said Nardello. "It's pure NADI. We're not being self-indulgent. There's no way we could chop this down and feel good about an edited version. I say we make a statement with this album. We're asking the listener to come along with us for the ride. Think about it… music from older cultures can go on for hours and even days in some cases. Why the hell are we fussing over a twelve-minute piece?"

Tamara held back. She didn't want to sway the decision. In her mind, she recalled how a concert of Carnatic music could last upwards of 240 minutes.

"The track stays as it is," said Scotty.

"Damn right," said Simone.

"Escucha a tu corazón," said Sal.

"That means listen to your heart," said UB.

Coyote knew the band was united. He played the last card that might persuade their choice. "How do you think our investor is going to feel? We're writing songs with lyrics that will never get airtime on any radio station and now we have a track over ten minutes long. Is this album just for *you* guys? How about the person putting up the money who ends up with a product that only a handful of college radio stations would play?"

"Are we ever going to meet this investor?" asked Tamara.

"He's a silent partner and prefers to keep it that way," said Nardello.

"Then let's take a cue from his silence," said Tamara. "If he doesn't speak up, we're left speculating as to how he might vote."

Scotty didn't want more questions surfacing about the silent partner. He wanted the group to remain focused on the recording project.

"I say we continue writing and recording… both for ourselves and for the following we're starting to build. As musicians, we can step out of the prison of the three-minute song. Maybe it's time for radio stations to get with the times. It's formatted music that has to go."

"That may be so," said Coyote, "but this is our debut album. We want *more* stations to play it, not less."

Nardello chimed in. "Have you heard Hendrix's recording of 'Voodoo Child'? It clocks in at over fifteen minutes."

"That's fucking Hendrix," said Coyote. "Nobody knows who we are yet."

"We may win or we may lose," said Scotty. "But we will give all our heart. To quote W. B. Yeats:
He that made this knows all the cost,
For he gave all his heart and lost."

That night, as Tamara and Scotty were cleaning up after dinner, they reflected on the day's recording session. Despite artistic differences with Coyote, the band remained happy with the "Kali Ma" track and stood united on leaving it full length on the album. Scotty thought they had covered all the necessary details about the day. That's when Tamara dropped the bomb.

"Hey Scotty, can you tell me more about this silent investor? I'd really like to meet him. There are lots of publishing and copyright matters to discuss."

Scarpelli. There was no getting away from him. Scotty felt profoundly conflicted. On one hand, he wanted to protect his bandmates from getting involved with a dangerous guy like Scarpelli. As he had agreed with Coyote and Nardello, the rest of NADI could forge ahead with their recording goal – undistracted and unaffected. What was to be gained by getting anxious about something or someone they couldn't control?

At the same time, Scotty and Tamara had repeatedly heard from his addiction recovery counsellor that keeping secrets from one another would eventually erupt into some dysfunctional behaviour. As the counsellor put it, *"Secrecy pervades all aspects of our lives. It can silently erode the bond of trust in a partnership."*

In this respect, half the band was hiding secrets from the other members and carrying on as if the silent investor was a neutral partner. What literally came from the underworld would eventually erupt into the light of day. It was only a matter of time.

"Can we sit down?" Scotty asked. "There's a long, messy story I gotta tell you."

Scotty rolled back the story to Nardello's first arrangement with Scarpelli: the Nutella-Telecaster deal. Tamara knew a little bit of how the debt was repaid. She had not heard the particulars of who Scarpelli was and his role in the Detroit area Mob. What was even more difficult for Tamara to hear was information about the hit job on Sal and how the contract had to be bought back.

At times, Tamara possessed a deductive mind and would have made a good detective. In certain circumstances she could remove the reactive emotional veil and look squarely at the facts from a detached point of view to a possible solution. Scotty attributed this to her years of practising mindfulness meditation. He wasn't surprised, therefore, when Tamara asked for whatever details Scotty knew about the back off message sent to parties in Venezuela. She also pressed him about what Scarpelli had quoted or implied around the cost of calling off the hit. Scotty could sense that she was laying out particulars like a forensic investigator – not merely for her understanding, but to determine the band's possible options.

Once she had pieced together as many bits of the story that Scotty could provide, she turned her attention away from Scarpelli and wanted to comprehend why the trio of Coyote, Nardello, and Scotty chose to keep everyone else in the dark.

"What was your rationalization behind not telling me or the rest of the group for that matter?"

"I didn't want to freak everybody out," said Scotty. "Sal and UB were already stressed and we were writing and working on an album. I guess I wanted to keep the whole thing chilled. It's been hard for me to keep the album upfront while dealing with all this background tension."

Tamara took Scotty's hand and spoke calmly.

"You're in recovery, my love. We've been guided by people who have your back – everyone from Father Jaggs to your addiction counsellor. They use the same mantra over and over: be honest with yourself and be honest with your loved ones. If not, you know what will happen."

"I get it! I just… I don't see a way out of this predicament with Scarpelli. On the plus side, Sal is safe and our album is being financed."

"By a mobster! You know that once you pay the Pied Piper, he can lead you wherever he wants to go... including in a lethal direction."

Scotty exhaled his frustration. Perhaps for the first time he was not sidestepping the facts. The group was indebted to a gangster who had no investment in NADI other than as a source of making dirty money seem clean. Scarpelli was also gambling on the possibility of cashing in on the band's success. He was *not* a silent partner.

"Let's say we put all our emotional reactions to one side," said Tamara. "We're left with a very difficult problem to solve. As bad as the situation is, and as bad as the characters are, it *is* possible to find a solution. No one has reached a dead end yet... so to speak."

"Go on. Because I don't see a way forward."

"First, there's an assumption that Sal's life was actually in danger. The story revolves around the premise that a hit had been contracted by someone in Venezuela. When we strip away the assumptions and possible illusions, we don't really know if the story is true or not. I, for one, am a little suspicious that, after all these years, someone from Sal's past would surface and have the financial resources to pay for a killer. For what purpose? To shut up an incident that no one really cares about?"

"Well," said Scotty, "how would we even begin cut through *that* Gordian knot?"

"It may be impossible to prove but imagine for a moment that Scarpelli, like his counterparts in New York, wants to get into the entertainment business. He wants to take the underground gambling scene and turn it into something legitimate. His peers have shown how the formula works. You own a few clubs, take a slice of the recording industry and launder money. Finally, there are artists who owe money because you funded their success."

"We know all this. How does this relate to Sal?"

"Let's just say that Scarpelli's foot soldiers beat the bushes, to see what would fly into the air. Sal was scared and intimidated."

"Wait a minute," said Scotty. "How would Scarpelli even know about Sal's past? Other than Nardello, he doesn't know anything about NADI."

"I don't know," said Tamara. "We could speculate that someone had dirt on Sal and wanted to use it... maybe to get him sent back to Venezuela. Somebody wanted vengeance, that's for sure. It could be anyone from a jealous musician to a pissed off pastor who felt humiliated by the treatment he got from bikers."

"So, someone wants revenge but doesn't want to get their hands dirty. That person then gets connected to the Mob with the intent of getting Sal deported from Canada."

"Yes. So Scarpelli sees a soft spot, a way to get into the music biz. He's not interested in Sal. He's not even interested in whether NADI succeeds or not. He couldn't care less about Sal or helping Nardello out, for that matter. Organized crime works like a corporation; they acquire small operations and gradually expand their influence. Hustling Polaris studio and NADI is simply one step in a bigger scheme."

"Let's say that you're onto something. That still leaves us in a situation where Scarpelli has the upper hand. How do we deal with that?"

Tamara thought for a moment. Her reasoning mind had been stimulated and now her calculating mind kicked in. "We could make a terrible album and record a parody of all that's sacred in the rock music world. We could play all the clichés and become caricatures of ourselves. Think about it... we could mock the rock spectacle in a way that would make Alice Cooper look like a golf-loving suburbanite."

"Wicked," said Scotty. "However, Scarpelli has zero interest in the artistic merits... or lack thereof... of our band. We're a washing machine to him. Come tax time, he claims that his investment in a Windsor band didn't produce any return. He writes off a whack load of cash but stays on track with the end game of procuring Polaris, opening some Detroit clubs, and distracting those who want to investigate his illegal operations. To him, NADI is just like a batch of bread that got burnt."

"I suppose you're right. And... we'd lose our chance to release all that innovative music we're making."

"Do you have a backup plan?"

"I do," said Tamara. She paused and thought for a moment. Like rain clouds gathering, Scotty could sense that something big was coming. Tamara laid out her devious scheme and they both challenged it together, playing devil's advocate with one another to the point where they felt confident enough to bring it to NADI and the crew.

Scotty was about to wind down and get ready for bed when Tamara unveiled another scenario.

"I've asked you to be honest with me," she said. "Now it's my turn to be upfront with you. There's something that I've kept hidden from you. I don't know why. Maybe I am more like you than I care to admit. I wanted you to focus on your recovery and I wanted us to concentrate on our relationship without complicating things. Truth is, maybe I didn't want to deal with questions I haven't fully processed myself."

"You're not having an affair are you?" asked Scotty. He could feel an uncomfortable wave of anxiety wash over him.

"It's not that simple or complex, Scotty. I've been faithful to you even though I've had moments when I've wanted to make a move on Simone."

Scotty watched and listened to every word and gesture coming from Tamara. He loved this woman with all his heart and couldn't bare the slightest thought of losing her. He had never doubted her integrity and knew she wouldn't lie to him. He was somehow comfortable with the uncomfortable fact that she was about to share something she had kept secret.

"Early on in our relationship, I told you about my adopted parents. I told you about the awful rape that happened when I was young."

"Yes," said Scotty. "Your uncle was the monster and was sent away by your father… or he went into hiding?"

"My family never heard from him at all while I was attending private school in India and we never had any communication from him while I was studying in London. As you know, a second attempted rape happened during my first year at the academy. It was trauma upon trauma, Scotty. I would have fallen apart had it not been for Dr. Nachmanovitch and her therapy."

"I remember you sharing some of her techniques with me."

"After working with her for several months, I broached the subject of forgiveness. One of my best friends and classmates had asked me whether or not I had forgiven my uncle or the school's teacher."

"What did your therapist say?"

"I remember her response clearly. She shared how some survivors of sexual abuse try to go straight into forgiving the perpetrator before addressing their own outrage and woundedness. She talked about how clients had prematurely attempted to forgive as a means to get back to living a 'normal' life. She also warned me that, by not attending to the pain and hurtful memories, I could spiral down into depression. Or, turn to addictive behaviour to stifle emotions."

"I can relate to that path."

"In our sessions, we flipped the forgiveness theme back onto myself. I don't know if you're aware of this but it's common for survivors to blame themselves for the abuse. In my case, relative to my uncle, I had blamed myself for arousing him. I carried a degree of guilt all through private girls' school and only got sexually involved with women when I was sure that the feelings of attraction were mutual. Anyway, it took a long time to realize how mixed up I was, how much guilt I had carried, and how much I needed to have compassion for myself."

"I'm following you. But it feels as if there's something that you aren't saying."

"Here it is, my love," said Tamara. "The man who made it possible for me to come to Canada, to play with the WSO, and to eventually meet you... was my uncle here in Windsor – the same uncle who raped me."

Scotty took time to register the information. Tamara didn't break her gaze as she let Scotty process the content. When he seemed ready, she spoke again.

"I was in a good place when my uncle reached out. My life at the academy was fulfilling. I had a good circle of tight friends. I was playing experimental music as well as the classical repertoire. Most important, I was seeing Dr. Nachmanovitch weekly. All the support was in place when I got my uncle's letter out of the blue."

"How did he find you?" asked Scotty. "What did he say?"

"Years ago, he had moved to Windsor. He had some initial investment money and, because of his engineering background, he became successful with a tool and die company he had developed. He later sold his technology to the Ford Motor Company and retired early as a millionaire. But, for all his wealth, my uncle was a guilt-ridden and depressed individual. He had to face the terrible wound he had inflicted on his niece."

"Did he reach out?"

"He reached in first... in a spirit of repentance. In the Hindu Dharma, it's believed that unresolved emotions affect a person's present as well as future life. If someone has wronged another, forgiveness is to be sought from the individual wronged. You also seek forgiveness from the community at large. This period of healing requires acts of charity, purification, fasting, rituals, and introspection. My uncle undertook all of these steps before reaching out to my father."

"What was your father's response?"

"Maybe you would know this from your mother. In Hindu Dharma there are two forms of forgiveness. One comes through the feminine figure of Lakshmi. The other form is explained in the masculine form of Lakshmi's husband, Vishnu. Even when the one who does wrong does not repent, Lakshmi forgives. In contrast, Vishnu forgives only when the wrongdoer repents. My father was more aligned with Vishnu. He had to feel deep down that my uncle had genuinely come to see the impact of his behaviour on the family and on me. It took many months and exchanges for my father to register the real remorse and understanding from his brother. When that became clear, my father suggested that my uncle contact me in London. I received an initial letter that, honestly, rocked my boat. I had to sit with it for a long time before responding."

"What did your uncle say?"

"The first letter was more of an invitation to communicate. He wanted me to know that he was deeply troubled by the harm he had caused. He asked if I would be willing to write back and forth. I think he was giving me a safe context to share the impact his actions had on my life. Although I was slow to respond to my uncle's request, I did work with my therapist to create specific boundaries and rules of engagement. I couldn't risk being re-traumatized by anything flirtatious or ingenuine."

"What made you decide to correspond?"

"In the sacred text, the Gita, there's a principle that states: *to be free from negative karma, you must seek forgiveness every day.* It's a constant practice – whether you've committed any offense or not. The truth is, when you live in this world it's impossible to avoid hurting or harming others. Intentionally or unintentionally, anyone's actions are bound to affect others. I could sense that my uncle was suffering from his selfish and violent actions. Like me, he had paid a hefty price."

"So, you began to write to one another?"

"Yes," said Tamara. "I brought each letter to my therapy sessions with Dr. Nachmanovitch. We explored my reactions, my responses, and my decisions going forward. The letters became raw material for practising self-awareness. They also became central to my own healing journey and to my understanding of the psychological wounds inflicted on the perpetrator. I arrived at a place where I could forgive but not forget."

"So how did you find it possible to meet with your uncle face to face here in Canada?"

"I needed proof that the acts of penance he professed were grounded in action. Independent of my uncle's letters, I had to find someone in Canada that knew him and that could vouch for his character. A small number of Hindu families resided in Windsor. They met at each other's homes to observe religious events, celebrate festivals, and conduct prayers. As the group grew in size, their participation in cultural activities increased. They needed a temple and a group of the devotees acquired an abandoned church. My uncle paid for the building and it was soon converted into the Hindu Mandir. Through a couple of contacts, I was able to anonymously inquire about my uncle. The man they described was a transformed person from the one who raped me."

"Still," said Scotty, "that was a huge risk for you to come over to Canada, meet this man, and then stay at his house?"

"Well… there's the jewel in the story. My adopted father accompanied me from England to Canada. It was an emotional week. The real test came when he had to return and I was left alone with my uncle."

"What was that like?"

"When my father was visiting we saw that my uncle was not well. While he attended collective gatherings at the Hindu Mandir, he lived by himself and would have to return home to an empty house. He had no support for his wellbeing. Through the Hindu community we arranged for a housekeeper to live in and provide care. It was beneficial for my uncle and it gave me a direct contact if anything got weird."

"Is that what Simone is doing these days, looking after your uncle?"

"Somewhat. My uncle's physical health has been declining for years. He suffers from bradycardia. His heart tissue has been damaged from a heart attack and chronic heart disease. After years of caring for her brother, Simone knows how to give care when needed."

"I'm glad we got our hidden stuff out in the open."

"Me too," said Tamara. "There's one more piece of this that I need to complete with you. It has a bearing on us and maybe a bearing on this clusterfuck with Scarpelli."

Scotty laughed. He liked hearing Tamara swear from time to time.

She continued. "When my father and I talked about a potential trip to Canada to see his brother, he cautioned me about something. My uncle being a person of wealth and also a very sick man, knew his days were numbered. Long before I even agreed to visit, my uncle had made me the sole beneficiary of all his assets. He has designated me sole heir to his estate. My uncle's lawyer will act as his executor."

"Do you think he was trying to assuage his guilt?"

"I wasn't sure how to respond when my father explained the beneficiary part to me. I didn't want *my* forgiveness to be bought. My first step was to discuss the matter with my therapist, then I was upfront with my uncle. I wrote him about the issue of shame and how money couldn't buy back my innocence. We had a number of good exchanges. I finally realized that, since he left India, my uncle wrestled every day with his sexual abuses. I was never removed from his thoughts and feelings. His niece, more than anyone in the world, occupied a central place in his broken heart."

"I can't imagine how tortured he felt."

"We've had some deep conversations since I've been here," said Tamara, "and I think he's made a degree of peace with the past. Still, there's a wound that he and I both will carry for the rest of our days."

202

"You said something earlier about this having a bearing on us. How so?"

"When you and I went to the Point together," said Tamara, "my being and body said YES. I felt more than a kinship with you. That was obvious to me and it brought a caution too. We came into this relationship with many broken bits. When you relapsed we were both tested. I had to know in my heart that I could be with you in sickness as well as health. The matters of *for better, for worse, for richer, for poorer,* were there for me to be certain about. I had to know that, regardless of what happened, we could go the distance."

"Did I pass the test?"

"I love you and could love you every night, Scotty. You need to know that I will hold you close when our twilight years arrive. As I've said before… I'm not going anywhere."

"Ditto. I am grateful to be wrestled to the bed… anytime… and I love being with you in our simple ways too."

They kissed.

"One more reflection on the clusterfuck…" said Tamara. "Do you have any idea as to what amount of money Scarpelli was dangling in his little extortion scheme? He's made an assumption that we're all starving artists who could never meet the price tag. Even if it wasn't bogus, there's a fixed amount that he's holding in his head. What if we got Scarpelli to claim how much he's talking about and then paid him off?"

"I don't know. These Mob guys, if they smell money they don't back off. It could backfire on us."

"Is it worth a shot?"

"Coyote and Nardello might have a better idea," said Scotty.

"Let's not stop there. Why not come clean with everyone? We're in this mess together. Let's talk it through… no more secrets."

"Are you willing to disclose your financial details as well?"

"The group knows that I have some resources. They know that I bought the Sotto Voce space as a business opportunity. I think it's enough for them to know that I'm willing to call Scarpelli's bluff and pay him off."

"That part makes me nervous."

"I don't know yet how we can play this out with Scarpelli. What

I do know is that I trust the principle of honesty. In the Gita it's written that truthfulness includes multiple layers: *To be honest in our thoughts; to be honest with our words; to be honest with our actions.*"

"Nothing better than the Bhagavad Gita when it comes to addressing clusterfucks with the Mob," laughed Scotty.

CHAPTER 23

Nardello was assigned the awkward job of inviting Scarpelli to visit Polaris during one of the recording sessions. The group had been alerted as to who Scarpelli was and also his part in the so-called protection of Sal. Everyone listened, asked questions, and agreed to help find a way of dissolving the agreement with Scarpelli. There were no guarantees that a solution could be negotiated. As a band of improvising musicians, they were willing to play the conversation by ear and let the scene play out. Coyote had offered to bring along a biker friend, in case some muscle was needed. No one felt comfortable with the threat of violence. Tamara quoted Gandhi and Nardello reminded everyone who they were dealing with – a key player in the Mob.

On the day Scarpelli was to visit Polaris, the band was feeling good about the progress on the album. Other than adding two more tracks, the end was in sight. The final tasks of mixing and mastering wouldn't involve most of the group, although Simone wanted to have a hand in how those stages were developed. She had become highly conversant on what was needed on either side of the glass – working as a session musician and picking up engineering tips. The guys at Polaris had taken the time to mentor Simone. They recognized her natural talent in the studio in being able to understand the technology and the aesthetics of sound.

When Nicholas Scarpelli arrived at the studio, the band was laying down a bed track for their new composition called "Invocation." The rhythmic backbone of the piece required multi-tracking large and small percussion parts. Later, the instrumental and vocal pieces would be added. Scarpelli was let in the side door by the owner of Polaris. He was dressed impeccably, as if he were going out for an evening of fine dining in a high-end restaurant. George ushered the mobster into the enclosed room where the engineer was hovering over a large console, tweaking knobs and raising or lowering levels.

The band didn't notice Scarpelli until the engineer leaned over to his talkback microphone and spoke. "Thanks for that take. We might need to do one more. The djembe part was riding a bit too hot. Why don't you take a break… you've got a visitor anyway. I'm going to step outside for a smoke. Let me know when you're finished and we'll get the levels right for a final recording."

The band looked up to see Scarpelli in the booth and put down their percussion instruments. George turned out the lights in the console room and showed the guest to the main recording space. Nardello brought out a folding chair for Mr. Scarpelli and shook his hand.

"Hey everyone," said Nardello. "This is Mr. Nicholas Scarpelli. He's the silent partner in the recording project. I invited him down to meet you all and to hear what we're up to."

"Good to meet you," said Scarpelli. "I wanted to connect with the band before you perform at my niece's wedding reception. She's a big fan of your song on the radio."

"'Motor City Angel,'" said Nardello.

"Yes. That's the one. So… how's the recording going?"

"We're getting near the end," said Scotty. "Just two more tracks to go."

"Bene," said Scarpelli. "Guess I should have brought my cheque book down for George. I don't know much about the costs to make a record but I'm sure he will give me a hefty bill at some point."

"Well," said Scotty, "the project comes with costs above and beyond making a record."

"How so?" asked Scarpelli.

"There's the price tag on saving my life," said Sal. He looked directly at Scarpelli with an unemotional poker face.

"Ahh… I see," said Scarpelli. He turned to Nardello. "I thought this was a private matter between you and me; one friend helping out an old family friend."

"True enough," said Nardello, "but the arrangement involves everyone and, as a band, we try to be upfront with one another. No secrets."

Scarpelli's demeanour visibly changed. He shifted from amiable and relaxed to concentrated – like an animal preparing to attack. Before he could respond, Scotty spoke up.

"Mr. Scarpelli, we do appreciate what you've done for us. Sal's situation was... complex. We couldn't have gone to the police for help, Sal could have been deported... or who knows what? You have resources and connections that we needed and we are grateful for your help. Sal is still here and we appreciate you backing the project."

"Alright," said Scarpelli, "it sounds like you're all aware that fixing Sal's problem came at a high price. In return, I require two things: One, the matter of helping your friend out stays in this room. Don't be talking with anyone outside about our arrangement. Understand? Secondly, the cost of doing business with me is the recording project. As musicians, you are creating an album for *my* company. This will be considered as work for hire. That means as a limited liability company I own the content and the copyrights. You can continue to put your artistic energies into how it sounds and even how it looks but in the end... the whole package is mine. You benefit from exposure, concert gigs, and bigger opportunities than you get from hanging out in your little bunker on Tecumseh Road."

"You drive a hard bargain," said Coyote. "And we are at a disadvantage. The cost of calling off a hit on Sal, and footing the bill for this project... requires deep pockets."

"More than you can imagine," said Scarpelli. "But that's what I bring to the table. I have a long history of taking risks and... I'm gambling on you. Maybe I will make some money? Maybe you'll get famous? Maybe nothing happens and nobody gets hurt?"

"I know this is a speculative request," said Scotty. "But let's say that somehow we raised enough money to pay you back for resolving Sal's problem and to cover your investment costs. What amount would we owe you?"

"Even if you could pull that kind of cash together, which I doubt is possible," said Scarpelli, "the arrangement is non-negotiable."

"Surely we could work something out with you, Mr. Scarpelli?" said Coyote. "The band just wants to have ownership of the album... our debut album."

"Think of it as a stepping stone," said Scarpelli. "To climb higher up the mountain, you have to make some sacrifices. You've put time and creativity into this first effort. You've learned some things in the process and it hasn't cost you a dime. The next couple of steps along the journey will be up to you – unless you need some help again. At that time we can start with a new arrangement."

"But…" said Nardello.

"No. Nothing more needs to be explained," said Scarpelli. "I am part of an organization that has shaped the entertainment industry for decades. You might imagine that successful entertainers in the business just arrive, get a lucky break here or there or have God-given talents to offer. Wake up! The people I work for own major clubs, have their hands all over the recording industry and have an even bigger say as to who gets to be the next Tony Bennett. Play the game… and perhaps good things will come to you too."

He got up, ready to leave the meeting with his upper hand in tact.

"Good luck with the rest of your sessions," he said. "I will be seeing you soon enough."

"Before you go," said Coyote, "I just have to ask something…" Coyote looked past Scarpelli to the console booth where the sound engineer had turned on the lights.

"Did you get all that?" asked Coyote.

Through the main room speaker, everyone heard the words. "I recorded every single word."

Scarpelli stiffened. He didn't look back to the booth but cast his eyes around at each person in the band, registering their faces.

"You little fucks," he said. "I helped you out and this is how you show your appreciation? Do you have any idea how difficult I could make your lives? Hand over the tape or bad things will happen."

Just then a new voice came through the main room speaker. It was not the engineer or the owner of the studio. The person speaking was now visible in the console room. He was a large man dressed in a plain suit and was holding up a badge. Detective Bill Raven spoke.

"Mr. Scarpelli, on behalf of the Windsor Police Force, I will hold onto this tape. The rules of engagement have changed a little. Here's how it's going down: You will walk away from this business deal. Consider it an investment that didn't yield any return. The Polaris studio is not for sale and neither is the band. If anything happens to anyone here the tape will become a prominent piece of evidence in a serious investigation. Is that clear? I think you have enough to attend to in the bakery. You may leave now."

Nicholas Scarpelli was smart enough to not retaliate or negotiate. He was well aware that a combination of Windsor and Detroit detectives, including FBI agents, continued to keep tabs on his interests: gambling, loan sharking, extortion, narcotics, and labour racketeering operations. Scarpelli wasn't about to be brought down by a handful of hippie musicians. He turned and left the building.

CHAPTER 24

The Windsor police were happy to have a tape of Scarpelli making incriminating statements. Detective Raven checked in regularly with Nardello to make sure everyone, including his family, were safe. Scarpelli disappeared from their lives yet continued to linger on the periphery of everyone's thoughts. Without going into details, Detective Raven let Nardello know that the net around the mobster was getting tighter. He was confident that it was only a matter of time before the Mafioso leader would be behind bars. Needless to say, the band did not play at his niece's wedding reception.

George at Polaris was also happy to be free of the Mob. Scarpelli had been leaning heavy on him and giving little ultimatums in terms of selling the studio. In return for how it worked out, NADI was getting a financial break on the recording project. Tamara picked up all the additional expenses for recording and packaging *The River.* She enlisted a seasoned entertainment lawyer who was familiar with copyright and publishing matters. Along with members of NADI, a fair payback arrangement was laid out. Individual and group song writing credits were clearly spelled out. The lawyer made it possible for NADI to become a limited liability company and explained that by incorporating or registering as a formal business, they could gain certain tax advantages and avoid liabilities, should NADI ever be sued.

The album was in line at a pressing plant, waiting for bigger runs to be completed. It was during this slow phase that Tamara got the news about her uncle. Simone found him lying in bed one morning, not breathing. She called the emergency number and while waiting for the ambulance to arrive, she let Tamara know. The death of her uncle was not unexpected. Still, his passing brought to the surface sharp fragments in their troubled history. Tamara imagined the story between them as consisting of three chapters: Incident; estrangement;

and reconciliation.

Tamara returned to Riverside Drive for a few weeks. In keeping with the Hindu tradition, her uncle's body remained at the family home until a cremation could be organized. Following custom as a symbol of purity, Tamara dressed her uncle in white clothes. She also reached out to her uncle's circle at the temple. Over the next 13 days after the cremation, members of the Hindu community came by to express their grief. Tamara spoke with her adopted parents and everyone agreed that it was not necessary for them to travel to Canada. They would say prayers and enact rituals in India.

During the mourning period, Scotty spent a good deal of time with Tamara. Scotty's mother didn't school him in the Hindu teachings of life after death. Subsequently, Tamara helped fill in the gaps. She explained how, in the Hindu tradition, the belief in reincarnation is foundational. Most Hindus believe that humans are in a cycle of death and rebirth called *samsara*. When a person dies, their *atman* is reborn in a different body. Some believe rebirth happens directly at death. Others believe that an atman may exist in other realms for a period. Tamara wasn't fixed on any one belief. "I only *know* what I don't know," she said.

Despite the fact that her uncle's home could accommodate six people, Tamara and Scotty left the Riverside Drive mansion after the mourning period ended. They returned to Scotty's humble Strawberry Box House on Bernard Road. The garden, kitchen, bedroom and practice room all felt more like home to her. Once her uncle's estate was settled, Tamara would inherit the Riverside house, and much more. This choice of what to do with her uncle's house also impacted Simone who had been caring for the uncle in exchange for rent. After a few open discussions, it was agreed that Nardello would move in with Simone. Together they would look after the property and maintain a presence in the house. For the couple, this trial period of living together was the next step in a committed relationship.

"What happens if I fail the test?" asked Nardello.

"I will kick your ass to the curb," said Simone.

Nardello was happy to move in with his girlfriend and equally delighted to move away from Scarpelli across the road on Erie Street.

The pressing of *The River* album was out of their hands now. They could only wait and figure out possible distribution options. Coyote headed up the task which left the band space and time to focus on other matters such as teaching schedules at Sotto Voce, rehearsals to keep the album material fresh, regular Saturday night performances and personal time for practising and/or composing. Coyote was lining up engagements in Michigan. NADI was ready for a full roster of summer festivals and smaller concerts where they would be the featured act.

Sal had just completed a week at the WSO's summer camp for young musicians. He was in charge of teaching all the percussion workshops except for one day dedicated to West African music. As a classical musician and a South American, he didn't feel qualified to teach this component and was able to persuade the WSO to bring in a Nigerian artist who happened to be performing and teaching that spring in New York City.

The elderly musician's name was Bamidele Bajowa from the Yoruban culture of Nigeria. As well as being conversant in the ritual drumming and chants of Yoruban music, Bamidele had lived in Mali, Ghana and Senegal, where he had expanded his multi-instrumental skills. In his WSO workshop, Bamidele demonstrated his proficiency on djembe, African thumb piano (mbira), talking drum, balafon, and a stringed harp-like instrument called the kora.

Bamidele emphasized to the young students that African music was first and foremost a communal and ritual practice. Unlike Western music, where a receptive but passive audience listened in their seats, African music was about engagement through collective sounding, singing, drumming, and dancing.

Bamidele explained that ritual music in his culture could evoke the presence of orishas, the deities of the Yoruba people of southwestern Nigeria. In the spiritual and musical practices of his community, the orishas were respected as spirits. They were sent by higher divinities as guides for all creation and humanity. Bamidele would not teach the students any sacred music that was meant to call in the orishas. However, he was able to share a wealth of interactive processes that opened the ears and hearts of all the participants.

After the camp when Bamidele attempted to cross the border and return to NYC, he was denied re-entry. A customs officer claimed that Bamidele's visitor's visa had expired. The musician would have to apply for an extension. This would require letters of support from the institutions that brought him over from Nigeria. He would also need to show proof of residency from the individuals hosting him in America. Bamidele's station wagon, full of African instruments, was turned around and sent back to Windsor.

When UB explained the circumstance to his parents, Will and Joan immediately went to work. They found Bamidele a place to stay with a host family that had a spare bedroom. They contacted a US immigration lawyer based in Windsor who helped Bamidele obtain and file the necessary forms or letters of support. He was told from the outset that this process of applying for another visitor's visa could take several weeks.

Despite the complexities involved, and the loss of income from teaching or performing in the States, Bamidele remained calm. As a Nigerian in his late sixties, Bamidele carried himself as an elder. He accepted difficulties and sought out solutions and possibilities. He refused to waste energy in getting frustrated or despondent.

While immigration matters were being sorted out, Sal and UB took care of Bamidele. They showed him around southwestern Ontario, shared meals by the river, attended concerts together and even took Bamidele to the movies. Their guest graciously received the attention and, in return, generously shared stories of life in Africa.

It was Sal's idea to devote a series of Sunday afternoon drumming workshops at Sotto Voce. These gatherings would be facilitated by Bamidele. Sal was certain his percussion students would come to study with this masterful musician and he could spread the word to others who might be drawn to the communal experience of music making. It didn't take long before all the chairs were occupied and Bamidele was guiding a group composed of people from different ages and backgrounds. Without feeling any sense of obligation to the visiting maestro, every member of NADI attended the sessions.

On the second week of Bamidele's stay, Sal suggested that the master be invited to open their Saturday night Sotto Voce set. The elder agreed to participate and envisioned two parts. To begin, he would play the kora – perhaps tell a story – and share some traditional music. Secondly, he would include anyone from the Sunday percussion group to join him.

The usual hippie crowd that gathered on Saturday night was intrigued by Sal's announcement. The evening would begin with a special guest visiting from West Africa. Everyone respected Sal's request that the audience find a comfortable place to sit on the floor. Bamidele was warmly welcomed as he walked on stage carrying the kora.

Once Bamidele was settled – with one microphone amplifying the kora and another projecting his voice – the elder spoke about the first instrument he was about to play. He explained that the kora could be thought of as an African harp, designed by the Mandinka people.

"Kora players," said Bamidele, "have traditionally come from *Jali* families. They are historians and storytellers who pass their skills on to their descendants. The instrument is played in Guinea, Mali, Senegal, Burkina Faso, and the Gambia. The word *Jali* means something similar to a bard or oral historian."

He turned the instrument around so that the audience could see how the resonating body was built from a large calabash gourd cut in half. He showed how the front was covered by cow skin to further project the sound. A long hardwood neck was attached to the resonating body and supported by two handles. Finally, 21 strings were added. Traditionally, the strings were made from thin strips of hide, either cow or antelope skin.

"Today," Bamidele said, "most strings are made from harp strings or nylon fishing line. The strings run in two ranks and are held in place by notches on the bridge."

Bamidele showed how the player plucks the strings in polyrhythmic patterns with four fingers. The remaining fingers secure the instrument, by holding onto the two hand posts. He then took a moment to demonstrate two playing styles: ostinato riffs called *Kumbengo* and improvised solo runs called *Birimintingo*. With ease and dexterity, Bamidele then played both styles simultaneously.

The audience made audible whoops and claps to indicate their appreciation.

"Thank you," acknowledged Bamidele. "I am now going to play

a song called 'Jarabi.' It is about love. I invite you to join in with this hand clapping pattern of 1-2-3 and 1. We must stay in time together. Then there's a chorus where we all sing *Wee ohh wee ohh Jarabi.*"

Within minutes, a sense of village was created. As the piece got steady, Bamidele motioned to Tamara, who was standing off stage with her violin, to join him. Their unrehearsed collaboration sounded as if they had been playing together for years. No one could sit still and the audience was soon on their feet, clapping, singing, and dancing.

After several more minutes of "Jarabi," Bamidele invited the percussion group to join him near the front of the stage. He encouraged the audience to make a semi-circle so that anyone who wanted to dance could enter the space. The percussionists had worked diligently for a couple of sessions with Bamidele and had obviously practiced their parts in between. Bamidele gave out several short phrases on his drum and the percussionists answered as best they could. He ended with the cue to come in together with their first pattern called *Kuku.*

From time to time, Bamidele would point to a section of percussionists, and give them a hand signal to stop while the rest of the group continued. He would then play call and response exchanges with them for a bit, then cue them back into the ensemble. The musical offering included high energy moments when Bamidele would indicate that the larger group should soften their sound. Over top of interweaving parts he would give the audience a taste of how a masterful drummer can play with time and tell stories through drumming.

At one point, several women were dancing in the space, seemingly lost in a state of ecstasy. With his djembe strapped around his waist, Bamidele stepped off the stage and moved close to the first dancer. With a series of slaps, rolls, and flams on his drum, Bamidele became a puppeteer who could pull a string that lifted an arm, caused a right hip to snap, or inspire the dancer to shake her booty. It all happened in a spirit of play. The result was sensual without being lascivious. He moved from dancer to dancer letting each individual enjoy a cycle of interaction.

Toward the end of the drumming circle, Bamidele interjected one final round of call and response. It was followed by a rehearsed cue that signaled the last phrase. The crowd cheered and the elder rolled the skin of his hands on the skin of the djembe, in a gesture of appreciation. A simple chant arose from the audience in unison:

"Bamidele... Bamidele... Bamidele..."

The members of NADI took to the stage. Scotty whispered something into Bamidele's ears and he nodded. Scotty used his hands to indicate a quieter moment from the audience. Then over the microphone he spoke. "We are so grateful to be hosting this wise elder. We have all benefitted from his teachings and his connection to a wealth of musical knowledge. As you know, for as long as he's here, we will host regular Sunday afternoon drumming classes at Sotto Voce. You can talk with Sal about the details. Meanwhile, Bamidele has agreed to sit in with our group tonight. So, once again, would you please show Bamidele some love from our Windsor village."

The applause was thunderous and could have established a starting point for NADI that was wilder than their usual entrance. Tamara sensed this and immediately began with a quieter violin passage. Because of her prior improvisation with Bamidele, she knew the notes in the scale of his kora. Without saying a word, Bamidele picked up his instrument and entered with a slow yet repeating refrain. It gave the collaboration a set rhythmic pace. One by one, members of NADI joined in. The elder, through decades of interacting with musicians beyond his Yoruban background, knew how to find common ground. By adding a repeating vocal part, not rooted in any African language, he invited harmonies and developments from the band.

As NADI dug deeper into their repertoire, the African musician flowed through the setlist effortlessly. Sometimes he added a simple percussion part, or he would leap forward with an intricate contribution. He watched over the crowd and the band like a benevolent mentor.

CHAPTER 25

Three lawn chairs formed a triangle in the backyard of Scotty's house. Tamara and Scotty had invited Bamidele over for dinner. They were now enjoying the softening qualities of dusk. Each person was sipping on a warm chai made by Scotty.

"Can I share a dream with you?" asked Scotty.

"I am a lover of dreams," said Bamidele. "I am a keeper of stories and a carrier of poems. My father would say that dreams, stories and poems arrive like messengers. They visit our house of belonging to share something significant. Each speaks in a unique tongue."

"Perhaps you can help me translate the language of the dream," said Scotty. "It came to me several months ago and returns from time to time in my imagination – as if to remind me that I have yet to unwrap the gift."

"I cannot unwrap it for you, my friend. However, it might land freshly with new insights by you sharing it with me."

"Ok, it begins like this: I am standing alone on the bank of a blue river. I look across the water and see a small group of... beings that embody wisdom and love. Without a word spoken, they make this beatific sound... a pure vibration. Instantly, in my heart there's a longing to join them. I look at the river and know I can't cross it. Suddenly, I look up and see a monarch butterfly hovering above the river. I watch it and sense that it is telling me how to cross the river. Just then, I wake up from the dream."

Tamara sat quietly, her mind returning to the butterflies they saw at Point Pelee.

"You have been given a wonderful visitation," said Bamidele. "It is not my place to decode it for you. I am confident that you will grow into the dream's message. In my Yoruban culture, we have a saying: *Omi yi iay'a a mon e e san gb'onen e.*"

"What does it mean?"

"It is difficult to translate exactly. In English, you could say: *The water one is destined to drink never flows past him.*"

"One riddle explained by another riddle," said Scotty.

"Maybe. For me the saying means that the timing of a mystery or a gift is always perfect," said Bamidele.

"And what mystery is at work in your life?" asked Tamara.

"A good question. Here's one thing I know. I was in New York waiting to meet an old friend from Nigeria. His name is Fela Kuti. He's a fascinating and smart man. Both his brothers are well known doctors. Fela was sent to London to study medicine. Once he got to the UK, he switched his focus and studied music instead, at Trinity College of Music."

Bamidele stretched his legs from sitting, got up, and poured fresh chai in everyone's cup.

"Fela's preferred instrument was trumpet, like you Scotty. While he was attending Trinity, he formed a band called *Koola Lobitos*. They played a mix of jazz and a type of dance music called highlife. A few years ago he returned to Nigeria and Ghana to create a more sophisticated version of *Koola Lobitos*. He named the style of music *Afrobeat*. It mixes highlife, funk, jazz, and traditional Yoruba music. Fela sings about the usual themes of love and loss, although lately his lyrics are becoming more social and political in nature."

"Are you a part of his band?" asked Scotty.

"No. Fela and his band are much younger than me. I am more of an advisor and friend. The band is coming to the States to perform and record in Los Angeles. He wanted to meet in New York to discuss a vision he has for a community. He wants to call it *The Kalakuta Republic*. His idea is to form a modern type of village, a commune with a recording studio, nightclub and a home for people connected to the band. He wants me to be a part of *Kalakuta*. He sees us officiating together and performing traditional Yoruban ceremonies."

"Does that call you?" asked Tamara.

"I am intrigued with the possibility of bringing music, community, and spirituality together. There is one hesitation, though."

"What's that?" asked Tamara.

"I receive visions. I cannot control when they come. Just as Scotty's dream arrived as a message from the unseen world, my visions can be forms of guidance for me or others. One night, before I left Africa, I saw the image of a handmade pouch attached to the waist of Fela. As I fixed my gaze on the pouch, the name *Anikulapo* came to me."

"Does that name have any significance in Yoruban history?" asked Scotty.

"It means – *he who carries death in his pouch.* I felt strongly about sharing the vision with Fela and wrote to him immediately. I took the vision as a serious warning. But Fela, who is a confident and sometimes difficult man, read it differently. He interpreted the vision to mean: *I will be the master of my own destiny and will decide when it is time for death to take me.*"

"Do you fear for Fela's safety?" asked Tamara.

"Nigeria can be a dangerous place, especially if you are not aligned with the controlling powers. My friend, Fela, can touch the soul of many people through his music... just as your group can. As his music becomes more political, he will inevitably cross paths with those who want to silence him."

"Will your life be endangered too?" asked Tamara.

"Not that I see. I will always be a friend to Fela, but in the end our destinies are different."

Scotty was relieved to hear that Bamidele would not be put in harm's way. He also felt an affinity with Fela's vision of community and of bringing people together through music. Sotto Voce was a small version of that village experience. Unlike Fela, though, Scotty preferred to keep a low profile and avoid the attention of those who might try to shut down his cultural experiment.

Scotty was curious as to whether Bamidele had received any insights or visions relative to NADI... or even himself.

"Bamidele," said Scotty, "I respect you as a wise man and elder. I understand only a little about shamans and medicine women. From what I have read some older cultures have people who receive visions. Is that a part of your culture?"

"It is not strange that you ask," Bamidele said. "My father and grandfather were great diviners. I possess a small fraction of their talent. In the Yoruban community we practise a system of divination called *Ifá*. My father was deeply respected for his abilities with the divining chain known as *Opele*. Even greater was his ability with the sacred palm, or kola nuts, called *Ikin.* He would cast them on a wooden divination tray, *the Opon Ifá.* Families would come from far away because of his accuracy in prophesizing someone's future."

"Did your father or grandfather school you in *Ifá?*" Tamara asked.

"Whatever raw abilities might have been there, were schooled out of me. I attended a learning institute in Jos, Nigeria. My parents sent me to live with my aunt during the school months. Practices such as *Ifá* were discouraged at the school as superstitious beliefs."

Scotty nodded. "Many First Nations children of this country have gone through a similar harsh experience with schooling. They're taken away from their parents and placed in residential schools where they aren't allowed to speak their native language."

"Yes, all my school lessons were taught in English. Fortunately, some small ability to foresee remains in me. While I don't cast *Ikin,* visions come to me… from time to time."

"Have you had any visions when you've been with Tamara and me?"

Bamidele looked at the couple as if he were discerning how to reply or how much to say. Then he spoke.

"Playing with your band that evening at Sotto Voce made me very happy. That night a vision came to me. I was standing in a circle within a clearing in a wooded area that I do not recognize – it certainly was not in Nigeria. There were four holes marked at each of the cardinal directions. When I looked at each one, I could see two small trees growing up. The trees appeared to be healthy and strong. When I looked at the hole in the south, the dirt was being pushed aside as the smallest saplings were barely visible. Although these two trees were still breaking the surface, I could tell that there was something different to them than the ones that were further along. The vision dissolved at that point."

Tamara and Scotty listened intently, as if expecting Bamidele to say more or interpret the vision for them. He remained silent.

"I can relate to the image of two trees coming out of each hole," said Scotty. "Our group is unusual in that we are made up of three couples. Tamara and I are in a relationship, as are Sal and UB. There's also Nardello and Simone. Could the fourth hole, in the south, be Coyote and someone else who is yet to appear?"

"That I do not know," said Bamidele.

"Could it be *you?*" Scotty asked. "Your presence in NADI last week felt so natural... like you belong with us."

"That I do know," Bamidele said. "Sharing time and playing with you all has brought great joy to my life. I will always be grateful for how and why we met. My path, however, will take me back to Nigeria at some point. This is clear to me."

Bamidele could tell that Tamara was still reflecting on the vision. He wondered if an interpretation had come to her and whether it was his place to ask. Fortunately, Bamidele did not have to inquire as, unprompted, Tamara began to share her perspective.

"I got the same sense as Scotty. The trees growing beside each other represent the couples in our group. My feeling about the hole in the south comes with some tenderness – like the emerging saplings. There is a fourth relationship among us that is less manifested. It is younger and hasn't received the same amount of energy as the others. The pair that is surfacing could represent the loving relationship I have with Simone. She and I are more than sisters – more than friends. We could be lovers and a couple. That relationship has not developed fully because we have agreed to focus on our present partners. Nevertheless, our relationship and love for one another is very strong."

Scotty could detect an underlying mood in Tamara as she spoke. He wasn't sure if he was picking up a longing in her or a grieving – as if she had accepted what couldn't be, yet was living with the loss. Before he could even process his thoughts, a question surfaced. "Do you think it would be possible for your heart to hold us both? Could you love Simone *and* me... maybe not equally, but differently?"

"I am already doing that," Tamara said. She spoke the words without edge or judgment. "Nothing has lessened in my love for Simone and I would guess that it is the same for her. What we haven't been able to do is express our love intimately."

Scotty saw the dilemma in that moment. Both he and Nardello clung to a belief that if they allowed Tamara and Simone to explore their relationship – as women who obviously loved each other – there was a risk involved and they could well lose their partners. Scotty could not speak for how Nardello might be challenged by this arrangement, but his own foundation was deeply shaken.

Bamidele was quick to read what was not being said. "Do you know the poet Pablo Neruda?" he asked.

Both Scotty and Tamara nodded their heads.

Bamidele continued. "He wrote a line that has remained with me over the decades. The poet said: *You can cut all the flowers but you cannot keep spring from coming.*"

The trio let the poetic line hover, like a butterfly over a deep blue river.

CHAPTER 26

When Tamara entered the living room, her husband was looking out past the fields of alfalfa to the maple bush in the distance. His eyes were red from crying over the last few days.

"Are you thinking of Nardello, Scotty?"

"Off and on… I was thinking of Bamidele and was remembering something he said to me decades ago."

"Back in Windsor?"

"Yes. It was the time when he got his immigration papers in order and was heading to New York City. He and I went for a walk along the river. Bamidele was always having visions and so I told him about one of my own. It was a dream in which I walked off a stage; the lights were dim and the audience went quiet. When I woke up, I felt complete."

"How did he interpret that dream?"

"You know Bamidele. He would never give a straight answer. In typical fashion, he asked me a question that I never forgot."

"Which was?"

"Are you who you are because you do what you do? Or, do you do what you do because you are who you are?"

"What do you think he was getting at?"

"Our band was everything to us back then. I defined myself as a musician. I couldn't imagine doing anything other than performing music. Based on that perception of my identity, I would be nothing if I didn't play. I don't think Bamidele was ever suggesting that I stop making music… I think he was inviting me to know myself beyond the definition of a musician. Then whatever I did in the world would not define me. It would become a medium for my own expression."

"Do you think Nardello came to that same understanding?"

"In his own way. Right up until last year when he got the diagnosis, he had musical projects on the go. But… yeah, Nardello knew earlier than me that NADI was a great ride but that the band wouldn't always be on the road. That understanding let him explore other interests. If you had asked me in my twenties what was in store for Nardello, I would have never imagined his success in the construction business. I probably would have pegged him for some role in the music industry – session player, producer, or songwriter."

Their conversation was interrupted when a beautiful young woman walked into the room. She walked directly over to the window and hugged Scotty.

"How are you doing Dad?"

Scotty looked at his daughter, Sara. He felt his heart lift.

"Thanks for coming over, sweetie. Your mother and I are expecting the others shortly."

Sara turned to see her mother in the room and ran into her arms.

"Oh Mum," she said, "I knew Uncle Nardello's day was coming but I imagined I would be stronger. I'm a mess. How are you both?"

"Everyone's a mess, dear." Tamara held her daughter. "It's fine that we're barely holding it together. We can cry; we can tell stories; we can be sad; we can eat… we can be quiet too."

"Is Auntie Simone coming over?" Sara asked.

"Yes," said Tamara, "UB and Sal too. The only one we're missing is Coyote. He had to fly back to Florida this morning. He's on the planning committee for this year's MusiCares benefit. We stayed up late with him last night. He sends you his love."

The room went quiet for a moment and then Sara commented, as if she was replaying the previous day's memorial.

"Uncle UB did a great job conducting the service."

Scotty walked away from the window to join his daughter and wife who were standing near the doorway. He looked at them both, feeling a deep sense of gratitude for their presence in his life.

"Your uncle was painfully shy when we were growing up. He never struck me as religious back then, although he did play the organ at a downtown church and, in his younger years, studied with the Ursulines. Some of those nuns were really kind to him… others… not so much."

"He and Sal have found a good place in the United Church," said Tamara. "They've been tireless advocates for human rights. UB gets that from his parents. I'm so glad that they've been able to keep their musical passions alive too."

Sara walked a few feet over to where her father was standing and hugged him again.

"Your eulogy was so moving, dad. I felt Uncle Nardello's spirit when you read that poem."

"He always loved Pablo Neruda. When I said that one line, I lost it...

Take bread away from me, if you wish,
take air away, but
do not take from me your laughter."

Sara held on to her father while he welled up and cried a bit longer. The silence was broken by the sound of someone ringing the front doorbell. Tamara left to answer it. Scotty could hear that the rest of the group had arrived – Sal, UB, and Simone. He and Sara waited as they entered the living room. Hugs and kisses were exchanged as tenderness filled the air. Everyone seemed poised to either cry or laugh.

"Scotty and I have prepared a lunch for us all," Tamara said. "We thought it best to start, though, by gathering in the living room and opening this letter from Nardello." They all still referred to Bruno as Nardello.

Scotty sat in his comfortable armchair. It was the place where he read, made phone calls, and where he was now prepared to open the brown envelope left behind by Nardello. Sara sat between Tamara and Simone on the larger couch. The two women entwined their fingers around Sara's hands. Sal and UB sat together on the smaller couch.

A small altar had been created by Tamara on a low-lying table in the middle of their semi-circle. She had placed Nardello's meditation bowl next to a beeswax candle that had already been burning, along with a stick of Nag Champa incense. When everyone was comfortable, Tamara spoke.

"Welcome everyone. Our hearts are full with every possible emotion and our cups overflow. I would invite us all to sing a particular mantra for Nardello. The purpose of this mantra is to bring peace to

Nardello's soul as he makes his way back to *Source*. It is also meant to bring peace to those of us grieving. In our home we will sing this mantra for the next ten days."

Tamara led the group in chanting *Om Namo Narayana'ya*. When they finished, Sal leaned over and gave the meditation bowl a gentle tap. The brassy tone rang out and then faded to nothingness. The significance was not lost on anyone.

Scotty waited in silence until it felt like the right time to open Nardello's letter. As he sliced open the envelope with his brass letter opener, he envisioned Nardello's smiling face – long before the condition of Hodgkin lymphoma had been detected. Scotty half expected the document inside to have been handwritten but he quickly realized that Nardello had suffered through significantly low energy times. Even the act of typing would have been extremely difficult. Perhaps Simone had typed for him as he dictated his last words.

Scotty pulled the papers out and let his eyes connect with each friend and family member in the gathering. As a group they had remained remarkably close, regardless of the geographical distances with Sal and UB. Together, they had attended graduation ceremonies, marriage celebrations, the ordination of UB, and the naming-blessing ritual for Sara. A year ago no one would have imagined that they would gather to remember Nardello.

Scotty's hand was a tad shaky when he pulled the papers out. His voice trembled but got stronger as he read.

"My dearest friends,

By the time Scotty reads these words, I will have slipped out of my cocoon and found my wings. Please know that I made peace with my mortality. During my illness, some days were extremely hard but I received each extra day as a gift, another chance to be with Simone.

The group of us have travelled a long road together and each of you has left an indelible imprint on my being. I am grateful that we each had times to be together and say goodbye over the past several months. My daily practice as a Buddhist gave me the discipline of staying present in the moment. Recently, I have been wrapping myself in the memories and stories we made together.

There's nothing left unsaid between us. The word secret often implies something hidden away – concealed. Our family, though, retains what I would call sacred secrets. You all know these confidential matters but I want to recount a few of them, especially for Sara who may not know the full picture. She can ask more questions of those who remain.

Sara, darling one, you are the child of this unusual family. You were birthed by your mother and you were loved into beingness by each of us. Labels are too small. Your parents made Simone and me your godparents and you called me uncle from very early on. Although these terms were convenient for us all, in the end Simone and I always thought of you as our own beloved. We have no other children... only you.

I want to recall a sacred secret that defines who you are in this grouping. It comes from a much earlier time when we were making music and living in Windsor. A seer came to us from Africa and stayed for several months. His name was Bamidele. One night he shared a vision with your father and mother. Bamidele's vision defined our relationship to one another. Here it is again.

In a wooded clearing, there's a circle. The four cardinal directions in the circle are marked by holes in the ground. Out of each hole grows a pair of trees – young, yet sturdy. The hole in the south contains two trees that are smaller and just emerging.

Bamidele's vision predicted an important outworking in our family. Your father and I knew from early on that Tamara and Simone deeply loved one another. They were upfront about it with us. At the same time, they also respected how threatening their relationship could be to your father and me. Scotty and I went for many walks along the river together, sharing our struggles to get to a place where we could let go of our small ideas around partnership and monogamy.

Your mother and Simone never pressured us. They found countless ways to express their love for one another without being sexually intimate or enjoying trips away together.

In retrospect, I can see how long it took your father and I to get free of our conditioned beliefs. Our marker is June 28, 1969, when the police raided the Stonewall Inn in Greenwich Village, New York – known more as the Stonewall Uprising. This was a key moment when the gay liberation movement got organized. One year later, on June 28, 1970, the first gay pride marches took place in New York, Los Angeles, and San Francisco.

This date stands out as a turning point in the history of our extended family. Your uncles, Sal and UB, were going to New York to partake in the parade. Scotty and I, like a couple of stubborn turtles, had finally crawled to a place where we could celebrate the loving relationship between our partners. While your dad and I stayed home, Tamara and Simone went to New York. They marched in the Pride Parade, loved each other passionately and returned home as a couple. They emerged as the two sturdy saplings growing out of the fourth hole in Bamidele's vision. From that day onwards, Tamara and Simone have remained faithful to one another as much as they have remained loving partners to Scotty and me.

Some of this family story is familiar to you. I mention it because, in the spirit of Bamidele's vision, you are the one who stands in the centre of this loving circle. You are our beloved. I hold such precious memories of those annual cycles when your mother and Simone would go off into the world for a stretch of time together. Your Dad and I would take you camping, canoeing, trekking, or on some exotic adventure.

Now I come to a part in the story that has a twist in the plotline that you haven't fully heard. It's my honour to break the silence.

On the night you were born, your father and I were attending a Hindu temple service in Windsor. An old friend, Bishnu, died. He was the owner and chef of the Himalayan Restaurant, a place we loved. It's also the site where most of the band first met your mother.

While we were attending Bishnu's service, your mother was pregnant with you. We felt it was alright to be away because you weren't supposed to arrive for another few weeks. Also, your father and I were only four hours away from our homes in King Township – just outside Toronto. Before we left Windsor, we called home to let Tamara and Simone know we were heading out to the highway. Simone and Tamara were together that night and everything seemed fine. Your mother didn't have any signs that you were coming. There were no contractions.

Our plan was to drive without stopping and get home as soon as possible. This was 1984, remember, and bulky cell phones had only been out for a year. Neither your father nor I owned one at that point. It was nighttime and we were making good time until we got past the West Lorne exit on the 401. What started as a little downpour soon got worse. We slowed down and noticed a lot of cars and trucks had pulled off onto the shoulder. The visibility was terrible. We could barely see more than ten feet in front of us. We were determined to get home and moved slowly and steadily. Your father was at the wheel and I was his extra pair of eyes.

In our earlier years when NADI was travelling on the road, heading home or to a gig, we would sometimes sing a chant your mother taught us: Om Gum Ganapatayei Namah. It invokes Ganesh, the deity who is capable of removing obstacles. Your father and I began chanting Om Gum Ganapatayei Namah but the rainy conditions only got worse. It was getting too dangerous to drive.

Little did we know that as we were pressing forward your mother was also pressing down – her contractions had started. They were coming quick and fast. Simone realized there was no way she could get your mother into a car and drive to the hospital. You were about to be born and the two women agreed to let it happen old school style. Your mother was birthing and Simone was midwife in training.

229

Your father and I reached a sign that signaled an upcoming cut off and overpass, just west of London. We agreed to pull over for a short rest rather than risk driving in zero visibility conditions. As we veered off the highway and into the safety of the overpass, the rain eased a little and the mood became calmer. We took in the serenity for a moment and were suddenly startled by someone opening the back door. A rain soaked stranger got in the car.

Scotty and I looked back to see a First Nations man in the back seat. Maybe he assumed that we had pulled off the road to give him shelter. He introduced himself as Joseph Brant. He was heading back to the Six Nations land on the Grand River – the largest First Nations reserve in Canada and the only reserve in North America that had representatives of all six Iroquois nations living together: the Mohawk, Cayuga, Onondaga, Oneida, Seneca and Tuscarora. Joseph was hitchhiking to the Brantford area when the storm hit. Your father and I didn't have much food in the car but we offered a thermos of coffee and some packed sandwiches. I also had a spare pair of jeans and a sweatshirt in a bag. He put on my dry clothes to warm up.

I don't know what prompted your father to tell Joseph about Tamara's pregnancy and the impending birth. All I know is that Joseph went quiet and then began humming a song. To this day I have no idea what it meant or what it was intended to accomplish. We listened and then tried to join in by singing in unison what we heard.

Eventually the rain started to let up. We planned on venturing out onto the highway and offered to take Joseph as far as Brantford, before heading home. He wouldn't hear of it. We didn't realize it at the time but Joseph, similar to Bamidele, possessed a seer's gift. He had a vision of you being born and insisted that we hurry home as soon as possible.

When we arrived you were already born. Pushed out by one mother and caught by another – Simone."

Scotty paused at this moment and looked up at Sara. Her two mothers had woven arms, legs, and hands around her. It was hard to tell where one body started and another ended. Scotty did a little check in.

"Anybody need a break?" Heads nodded that he should continue. Before continuing, Scotty addressed Sara. "You know, several months after you were born, your uncle and I drove out to the Six Nations community. We brought pouches of tobacco and wanted to thank Joseph for his part in your birth. Here's the weird thing… no one we spoke to knew of a Joseph Brant living there. The only person with that name was a Mohawk leader who had the traditional name of *Thayendanegea* and was also known to Anglos as Joseph Brant. He lived during the time of George Washington."

Simone smiled at Scotty then added another tidbit.

"And the place where the guys stopped, outside of London, is the same overpass where Scotty's dad stopped to pick up Bishnu, on a rainy night when he arrived from India. Nardello and I have passed it dozens of times since you were born, and a few times we pulled over. The overpass, by the way, is near a place called Union Road."

Scotty took a deep breath and let out a long exhale. He continued reading Nardello's document.

"Now there are no more secrets between us, at least that I know of.

Simone and I have discussed estate details and all that will unfold in due course – especially for you, Sara. One matter is left and that is for me to ask a favour of each one of you. Simone and I have set funds aside for this request.

Sal and UB, you two have dedicated so much of your lives to helping marginalized individuals and communities and you rarely take a break. I think the last time you went on a holiday was when you married the four of us in Costa Rica – and that was decades ago.

Simone and I never had a chance to fulfill a dream we had for years. We always wanted to get away and walk the Camino de Santiago in Spain. We ask that you make that journey for us. As you know the Camino is a network of pilgrimages leading to the shrine of

231

the apostle Saint James the Great, in the cathedral of Santiago de Compostela in Galicia. Please take some of my ashes to that holy site in northwestern Spain and set them free. Go when you can arrange the time away and maybe keep a journal of your experiences. When you return, share your account with the others. Meanwhile, I will do what I can on this side to provide decent weather.

I love you both as brothers.

Sara, I want you to also make a pilgrimage with your family. Whenever you can arrange to be away, I ask all of you to travel to Varanasi in India. Bring some of my ashes with you and scatter them on the Mother Ganges. In my studies of meditation, I learned that Buddha is believed to have founded Buddhism in this area around 528 BCE, when he gave his first teaching nearby at Sarnath. Take as much time as you want to spend in India. Sara, both your mother and grandmother hail from this vast region. When you return home, my blonde Telecaster will be waiting for you.

Coyote, I can't think of places in the world that you haven't seen. For decades now, you have been on the road with artists, bands, and festivals. You're the coolest road warrior I know. To honour that fact, a reconditioned 4-stroke Norton motorcycle will be heading your way soon. It's also a way of saying thank you for something you may have helped orchestrate – the arrest and imprisonment of Scarpelli.

On behalf of us all, Coyote, we will always be grateful to you for naming our musical project NADI. We were, and continue to be, a changing river. In this spirit, I offer you a poem I wrote as I sensed my end time coming.

My boyhood was well spent fishing
wishing for perch to break surface
hooked

Rivers are teachers

I sat caught before what is constant
and what is changing constantly

Drones deliver a continuous river

Notes swim around in that surround
Lyrical phrases behave like fish
surfacing
diving
darting

Waves add rhythmic intricacies
settling into subtle cadences

Some enduring part of us
exudes a consistent persistent drone

Some shifting part of us
plays out the tension and stillness
of line reel hook

But how peculiar is this…
just when we shape
the ideal blend of firm
and fluctuating
harmonious and riotous
we hear the swell of a mighty ocean
just around the bend
ready to swallow everything
whole

*Finally, to you Scotty my dearest friend, I have begun my journey
across the blue river into the invisible air, and over to where those
beings continue to express Nada Brahma – sounding the world into
form.*

With all my,\love,

Nardello

CADENZA

The musical term *cadenza* appeared five hundred years ago as a synonym for the Latin *clausula,* meaning conclusion. When I was studying classical trumpet, I understood a cadenza to mean an unaccompanied section where a soloist performs an improvisational segment. Although not exactly a classical reference, I think of a cadenza as a kind of melodic and rhythmic "free-style." The idea is for the soloist to refer back to some of the major elements within the composition. In this spirit, I wanted to create my own cadenza and share some personal insights that informed this novel.

The setting of Sotto Voce is based on a rented, rehearsal space that my band, Blues Train, occupied in the late sixties. The building still stands today at 1340 Tecumseh Road East and serves as the home of Windsor's Scottish Club. The way I described it in the novel is largely how I remembered it. Countless musical events were hosted there. The back wall, by the way, was decorated with a permanent hole where the Detroit rocker, Ted Nugent, threw his guitar into the gyprock.

In the novel, the manager of Sotto Voce appears as Coyote. While this character is fictional, certain qualities were shaped by a real person: Arthur Thomas Woofenden. This colourful figure, known fondly as The Wolf, managed Blues Train. Also, from 1965 onwards, Arthur worked for various talent agencies in Toronto and Detroit. He arranged tours for Ike and Tina Turner, Alice Cooper, Bob Seger, Ted Nugent, Mitch Ryder, Freddy King, Big Mama Thornton, and many others. His love of music and respect for musicians knows no bounds. I met Arthur in my early teens when he mentored me as a young artist. We remain good friends to this day. By the way, the incident where Coyote gets tossed into the creek was based on a real event when Blues Train played for a bikers' gathering in a farmer's field.

Initially, the character of Scotty occupied center stage in my imagination. Bits of Scotty arose from my own lived experience, but larger doses arrived from the creative wellspring of my unconscious. Like Scotty, my high school education was enriched by the music teacher at Herman Collegiate, Mr. Murray Dresser. He supported and deepened my musical understanding in countless ways. The Cleary Auditorium concert with NADI mirrors a similar event that Mr. Dresser and I co-produced called *From Bach to Rock.* In addition, a real-life Mr. Creed cultivated my love of literature and writing. And... if you are wondering if I really did have an affair with a teacher in my senior year at Herman... hmmmm, my lips are sealed on that one.

Scotty embodies a history of complexities, especially the intertwining themes of suffering and addiction. In this connection, I witnessed my brother, a gifted musician, struggle for decades with the twin pulls of alcohol and chemical dependency. He lost that battle in Bangkok, Thailand, where he died alone on the cusp of 2000. My brother, like Scotty, carried an invisible wound that festered beneath his affable personality. I carry the grief of his death every day. It informs my empathy for those who suffer from addictions.

In the early seventies, my brother and I both lived for a period of time at a residential treatment facility called Crossroads in rural Essex County. My brother was getting help from the director, George Bullied. I was exploring community living and pondering whether social work was a path for me. Like Father Ken Jaggs in the story, George Bullied had wrestled with his own addictions and had developed a remarkable capacity to support young people who wanted to get clean and sober. He helped hundreds of addicts and went on to establish a larger facility in Ontario called Twin Valleys.

Referring back to Scotty in the novel, his father (Jake) was modelled after my own dad, Al Diggins. My father did serve in the British Army at the end of World War II and was indeed stationed in India. However, he did not marry a woman from Old Delhi. He came to Windsor and met my mother (who hailed from a Scottish background). Al Diggins, like Jake, picked up a hitchhiker arriving from India and who was making his way to Windsor in the rain. That man later opened the Himalayan Restaurant in Windsor.

From a musical standpoint, the band NADI draws upon the several years I spent composing and performing with Blues Train. As an eight-piece horn band, we combined a spirited mix of arranged music with improvisational freedom. We got to play in stadiums, iconic spaces (especially the Grande Ballroom), and intimate clubs. Of all the people we opened for, Bob Seger was indeed the most supportive.

During my time with Blues Train, we went through four bass players. Sadly, two died, and the longest lasting player was a Brit who eventually returned to the UK. At one point the group was fortunate to hire a Detroit bassist named UB. He was an amazing performer but destined for more of a solo career. Bits of the real UB floated into the characters of Simone and the fictional UB.

As for the fictional UB, and especially his musical prowess in classical, gospel, jazz, improvisational music, and more, I drew upon the Canadian composer, arranger, and musical director Andrew Craig. If you want a sample of how heavy a player Andrew is, imagine the tribute concert in Toronto when Oscar Peterson died. The stage at Roy Thompson Hall was graced by dozens of great jazz musicians influenced by Oscar – including Herbie Hancock. Andrew was given the task of arranging and conducting a choral tribute to Oscar – and also arranged music for 50,000 children singing for Nelson Mandela. I have been fortunate to collaborate with Andrew periodically but even more blessed to enjoy his culinary skills at family gatherings in Guelph, where he and his family live.

The character of Tamara informs the spiritual underpinnings of the story. She is an amalgam of three personal friends who come from a Hindu background. Two are amazing musicians and the third invited me to play at her wedding where I witnessed Supi and her cousins enact an entire dance scene from their favourite Bollywood movie. All three women are deeply spiritual and wickedly funny. Incidentally, I have experienced profound moments of challenge and change while travelling throughout India.

The Yoruban musician and seer, Bamidele, appears toward the end of the novel. He is part Babatunde Olatunji, the great Nigerian musician, and partly composed from my actual friend, Bamidele Bajowa. The latter has returned to Nigeria where he continues to study and conduct traditional Yoruban ceremonies. I have been in ritual processes with Bamidele and can attest to his mystical ability to call in the orishas. On a personal note, I've made three trips to Nigeria and have been swept away by the music and movement I experienced.

Speaking of being swept away, it is my hope that the story engaged your imagination and carried you through the river of time to a significant era of cultural change. There's a quote that has been attributed to Robin Williams (and others) that says, *"if you can remember the '60s, you really weren't there."* Those of us who lived through those times will probably have gaps in our memory banks but, the instant we hear a recording of Santana or Hendrix playing live at the Woodstock Music Festival in 1969, we are transported back to our youth. Those times contained an unforgettable soundtrack. One of my intentions in writing this book was to highlight the communal and spiritual energy of music; that music as an art form can unite a tribe and sometimes give them a voice to cry out for change. May that practice continue in these times.

On a personal note, should you wish to ask me something further or share a reflection from the novel, please email me at:
garyd@garydiggins.com

Wherever you are in life, and in whatever circumstances you are living through, I place my hands together and offer you a prayer for wellbeing.

Blessings, Gary

Made in the USA
Middletown, DE
02 February 2021